# TIDES OF DECEPTION: PAST IMPERFECT

## A Chesapeake Bay Murder

Teresa Crowe

Tides of Deception: Past Imperfect



ISBN: 979-8-9894513-1-9
Library of Congress Control Number: 2024936201

*For those who savor the thrill of every twist, turn, and tale of deception,*
*who embrace the darkness to uncover the light,*
*and who find joy in unraveling a tightly woven plot,*
*this book is dedicated to you.*
*In the labyrinth of life, may we always find the courage*
*to solve our mysteries.*

# Acknowledgments

I am profoundly grateful for the constellation of individuals who guided, supported, and inspired me throughout the creation of this work. My deepest gratitude to my husband, Theodosios Margas, whose unwavering belief in me has been my sanctuary during the long hours of writing and revising. I am grateful to my children, Selina, Diane, and Alec, for always supporting me in my writing and reminding me of the joy of storytelling. To my sister, Kathryn, whose unwavering support has been my backbone through countless times of self-doubt and uncertainty. And to my friends, who have cheered me on from the sidelines, thank you for bolstering my courage to reach for my dreams.

My profound appreciation to my beta readers, Jai and Diane, whose astute feedback honed the raw edges of this story into a polished gem. In navigating the labyrinth of language and narrative, the invaluable help of Alena Orrison—my preliminary editor and wordsmith—has been my compass through multiple projects, including this one.

I extend my sincerest gratitude to All That Matters Press, the publishing house behind this work. Their team's commitment to championing unique, compelling narratives has made this book's journey from manuscript to print a reality. This story has been brought to life through their dedication to storytelling, editorial guidance, and marketing and design efforts. I am forever grateful for their unwavering support in this project.

This tale would not be what it is without each one of you. Your contributions have breathed life into this narrative, transforming it into a tapestry of shared experiences and dreams. Thank you, sincerely.

# CHAPTER 1

My eyes skim across the shimmering surface of the Chesapeake Bay. I inhale the tangy scent of its brackish salty-freshwater mix. Even as a child, I associated the thick smell of the bay with home, safety, and truth. I close my eyes and let the morning sun warm my face. I am the luckiest woman alive. Yes, I've survived many heartaches, but I am not unique in that. The point of all suffering is that it can be overcome, squashed down into nonexistence.

I've moved back to my childhood home. I am living proof that anyone can recreate themselves from a difficult and tumultuous past as long as they keep the dark secrets hidden. To everyone who knew me as a rambunctious, defiant, and troubled girl, I am now an example of success and resurrection, like a piece of jagged broken shard emerging from the sea as a beautiful sand-polished sea glass. The neighborhood expected little from the poor, damaged girl who lost her bearings and her morals. They underestimated me. Look at me now.

I have a successful psychotherapy practice I run out of my home. My mother is well cared for at Sunview Assisted Living. I am financially solvent, thanks to my late husband, George. Seeing and living too much too soon gives someone like me a head start in understanding what it takes to truly succeed in life. You have to possess a strong desire to change your circumstances, take decisive action when needed, and, above all, lock your secrets so deep there is no way for them to escape. Danger lurks when we share the most private of thoughts and deeds. No good can come of it, only terrible, horrible bad. I am a master secret keeper of both my skeletons and the bones of others.

Today, though, is a new day full of possibilities. The morning bay breeze fends off the promise of a sweltering, hot July day. I sip my coffee. In the distance, I see a tower of dark, dense clouds billowing up from the south. A storm is heading our way, a big one. The weather is fickle on our little peninsula. A storm might drench neighborhoods down the road and easily avoid Mystic Beach on its way north. This one looks like it's barreling right for us. I glance at my watch. I have just enough time to take a short walk on the beach before I meet the woman who wants to be my assistant.

I cross the spongy grass of my front yard and walk to the faded, weathered wooden steps leading to the beach. The sun is a brilliant disco ball, causing the water to shimmer and glisten. Rhythmic ripples calm me; they always have. A Chesapeake deadrise glides across the water, perhaps three-quarters of a nautical mile out, its watermen hoisting crab pots onto the deck. A colony of seagulls follows the boat, hoping to grab a piece of discarded bait or fish. One fisherman tosses something off the stern. The shorebirds swoop down in a synchronized motion. The larger gull catches the flesh before it hits the surface and flies away from the hungry group.

The brown sand is coarse between my toes. Warm, small waves cover the tops of my feet. I look under the water's surface at the sandy bottom in search of crabs. Ahead there is a pile of sloughed horseshoe crab shells, probably collected and stacked by a child. With their spiny, hard carapace, they aren't the prettiest artifacts of the bay, but they are interesting. The outer shell is rounded on the front like a horseshoe. A long, sharp spiny tail protrudes out of the back to help the crab right itself if it's flipped over on its back by a wave. This one looks dead, with its shelled spiderlike legs still underneath.

In my high school marine biology class, Mr. Adams told us horseshoe crabs were more spiders than crabs. He said they are in the same subphylum as spiders, Chelicerata. Rather than having mandibles like blue crabs, horseshoe crabs have chelicerae near their mouths on the underside to push food like worms, clams, crustaceans, and algae into their mouths. Mr. Adams explained that a horseshoe crab's blood turns blue when exposed to air. Pharmaceutical companies use part of their blood to help detect toxins that could sicken or kill humans. By unanimous vote, the horseshoe crab is the coolest animal in the Chesapeake Bay.

I continue down the beach. My toe touches a gray and white striped shell, a bay scallop. With its shell closed, the creature inside is likely still alive. I toss it back into the bay, wishing it a long, prosperous life. Open clam and mussel shells litter the shoreline. I bend to pick up a bit of pale green sea glass rubbed smooth by the bay's sandy bottom.

The raucous call of gulls draws my attention further down the beach. I drop the sea glass and shade my eyes to see what's happening. They hover like a swirling white cloud over what looks like a large, beached animal. A rotting odor wafts down to me. I am uncertain if I want to go down and see it. The smell reminds me of when a dead dolphin washed up about a year ago. Clearly, the animal is dead. Maybe I should call the Department of Natural Resources to come haul it away.

I wonder what it is, though. As I get closer, the smell becomes more pungent. I think I might throw up. The stench screams of decay. I push that thought down deep; there's no way I could ever forget the smell of death. The animal is partially submerged in the surf. I can see its body rocking with each push of the waves. I put my coffee cup on a large piece of driftwood and walk down the beach. Wait. This is not an animal. Its appendages flop in rhythm with the waves. A dolphin doesn't have arms and legs. It can only be one thing. A human.

Every part of my body screams at me to run. Yet, I am drawn to see who this is. My feet walk of their own accord. The thing is a male. A light-colored T-shirt clings to the bloated body. The bay has discolored his once-white shorts to brown. A Confederate flag buckle and leather belt cinch them to his waist. I recognize this buckle. His gut is three times its normal size, but as I peer closer, I recognize him.

I kneel, lean closer to look at his face, and repress my gag reflex. I need to be sure, but I don't want to throw up on him. His face and neck look like he has a jellyfish attached. Wait, it's not a jellyfish. His skin is rotting. I catch a whiff of decomposition, lean over, and vomit into the sand.

I wipe my mouth with the back of my hand and turn back to the body. *Bobby Ward, it's you.* His mouth is open; his swollen lips split. His skin shines with an unnatural, glossy sheen. The eyes are missing from their sockets. Seaweed has tangled in his gray hair.

My lips curl up spontaneously. "You filthy, stinking bastard," I whisper to him. "You finally got what you deserved."

Still, I don't want to be caught talking to a dead man. I look up and down the shoreline. It's early. I don't imagine anyone would walk along the beach this morning. I've never run into anyone during my morning walks.

A great gust of wind blows in my face, carrying Bobby's smell up my nostrils. Disgusting. I turn my face to the side and focus on the waves beating upon the shore. Perfect. The tide is going out.

I position myself on the sand next to Bobby's torso, carefully not touching his rotting skin, and shove. The water is creeping up to his belt buckle. I lower my body for leverage so I have more strength. I push, grunting with the exertion. He rotates on his side, closer to the water. I roll him again so his body is now fully submerged. I push back into the water. His distended gut helps him keep afloat.

I walk him out to the protective shoals. The water is up to my shoulders by this time. I brace my feet on one of the submerged rocks on the shoal and push hard. The current is strong here, his body floating out in the bay. The white-capped waves blend in with the color of Bobby's shirt. He's drifting away from the beach.

I feel the wind picking up. This storm will be a nasty one. Good. The nastier, the better. I want Bobby gone far, far away from here. Good riddance and thank God he's gone forever. Now I've got to hurry if I'm going to be showered and ready for my new assistant's first day.

# CHAPTER 2

I'm still dripping as I pass the deserted playground and picnic tables and crest the grassy knoll to my house. I don't see anyone outside. Mystic Beach has a one-way-in/one-way-out road, Shore Drive. If anyone comes into the neighborhood, we all see who it is. Its relative isolation makes for peaceful living, but also wreaks havoc when an ambulance or fire truck needs to come in for an emergency. The roads are narrow and become cramped when parked cars line the edges. Despite its confinement, Mystic Beach is home to me and generations of residents before me.

Just as I walk across my lawn, someone yells out to me, "Clara? Clara, is that you?"

I ignore her and get to the edge of my concrete patio when Barbara rushes up, breathless. "Clara, yes, I thought it was you!" Her breaths pant to a similar rhythm as her Bichon Frise, who seems as winded as she.

Uninvited, she plops down on a patio chair. "Goodness, Clara, why were you walking so fast?" She pauses and looks me up and down. "Hey, why are you sopping wet? You didn't go swimming, did you?" She shakes her head, scolding me like a strict school marm.

I run my hands down the front of my T-shirt and shorts. "Of course not, Barbara," I snip.

Barbara narrows her eyes and waits for me to answer.

"I, uh, I waded out to my shins but dropped my favorite coffee cup. The current pulled it out so fast, I had to jump in and get it," I say.

"Hmmm, I see."

Her mind is spinning the possibilities. While I wait, I notice her dark eyes are too close together. Her eyelids blink open and shut, open and shut. When she scrunches her eyebrows, she resembles a rodent, a disgusting, filthy, rabies-ridden rat. I know the waiting game, though. I'm a master at it.

Barbara runs her fingers through her dried, peroxided blonde hair. In fact, now that I'm laser-focused on her, she and her dog look eerily alike. I shake my head and smile. I have to stop and remind myself I'm not that girl anymore.

Taking a softer tone, I said, "Hey, Barb, nothing to be worried about. Just a dunk in the bay, and my favorite cup is back in my possession."

"You could have drowned, Clara. You know how dangerous those currents can be, especially right before a storm. I don't have to tell you that," she says, staring slightly to the left of my eyes.

I look down at my pink rubber flip-flops. Why does she always have to go there? I turn up the wattage of my smile.

"Of course I know that."

"Weren't you there when that guy from the neighborhood jumped off the boat and got stuck in the mud?" She lets the minute play out.

"Yes, I remember." My heart rate quickens. My stomach churns.

"And you all waited for him to surface, but he never did. You all tried to find him, right?"

Barbara knows the story well. Why is she rehashing this? Does she want to see me squirm and rush to tell her why I was in the bay?

"Yeah, we tried to find him, and—"

"His feet stuck in the thick mud on the bottom. The Coast Guard searched for the better part of four hours. The divers found him only eight feet down, his feet wedged into the thick sludge. I wouldn't want that to happen to you, Clara."

I look down and murmur, "Me either."

"Boy, what a stick in the mud he was!" Barbara tilts her head back and laughs like a horse.

My head snaps up, eyes widening. Her mouth is open so wide that I can see the smooth edges of her $50,000 veneers.

"Come on, Clara." She swishes her hand. "That's all old news. Water under the bridge." She laughs again at her joke.

I look at my imaginary watch. "Really, Barbara. I've got to get going. A new assistant is coming for an interview. I have to get cleaned up before she arrives."

Barbara perches on the edge of the seat but doesn't stand. "A new assistant? Pray tell. Who is she, and where does she come from?"

I am eager to get Barbara off my patio. I'm already nervous about her seeing me walk up from the beach, and now she's asking about my new assistant. Sometimes I wish I had never returned to Mystic Beach. No one can ever escape their past here. The residents know everyone's business, including that of their parents and their parents before them. Owners re-shingle and renovate these 1930s cottages, but the memories remain in the trees, sand, and wind.

I sigh. "I want to hire an assistant to help manage all the appointments for my practice, keep track of client files, and streamline the accounting."

"Oh? You've had quite a few new clients, then?" Barbara fishes.

"Yes, it's growing nicely. I think an assistant will help me organize myself better."

Barbara flips her hair and asks, "Speaking of clients ... do you see anyone I know?"

I snicker. We weren't speaking of clients. Barbara knows better, but she'll keep trying to find out everyone's business as long as she breathes. "I can't tell you anything about that."

She examines her professionally manicured nails. "Hmmm. What about the assistant?"

"Listen, Barbara, I don't want to say anything until I've interviewed her. Maybe she'll work out; maybe she won't. You and I will both find out soon enough." I stand.

Barbara strokes her dog and swipes imaginary sand off her capris. She looks back and forth down the street. No one is around. She steps closer to me and says in a low tone, "You keep secrets better than anyone, Clara. I'm just not sure that's always the best approach. In fact, some secrets can kill you."

Stunned, I freeze. What do I say to that? Did she see what I was doing at the beach? No, impossible. I would have seen her. Nausea rises and threatens to purge. I smile at her, but it's more like a grimace. Heat rises from my neck and onto my scalp. She's bluffing; she's got to be.

Barbara stares at me with those rat eyes. Blink. Blink. Blink. She is only acting like she knows more than she does. The moment stretches. She cackles and flips her hair back, tugs on her dog's leash, and says, "You should see the look on your face. Like you keep any secrets? Right. Anyway, see you later. Come on, Millie. It's time to get back home and check Facebook." She winks at me and walks away.

I hold my hand up and say, "See you, Barbara," but she's already turned her back on me.

# CHAPTER 3

There is no time to waste thinking about Barbara. Addison Marsh will be here soon for her interview. Before hopping in the shower, I reach inside my bedside table to grab a small amber plastic bottle. I dump a couple of my chill pills into my hand and swallow them dry. I've got to get a grip, because I feel on the edge of unraveling.

In the shower, I turn the hot water to full blast. Steam floats to the ceiling. As I scrub my body, flashes of dead Bobby intrude: his decomposing body lying on the shore, the gelatinous look of his skin. Memories of alive Bobby pop up, too: his seawater blue eyes, his raucous laughter after too many libations, his thick, calloused fingers pushing back his Santa-like white hair.

Stop. Stop. Stop. I can't let my brain spiral out of control. Bobby is gone from my life, and that is a good thing, a fitting ending to the type of man he was. Addison will be here shortly. I've got to get myself together. I grab the bottle of lavender-mint shampoo and scrub my scalp hard. The smell of the soap helps me refocus my thoughts and push Bobby far, far away.

I dry myself with a plush periwinkle towel. My heart rate calms, thanks to my favorite little pills. My lungs take a deep breath. Everything will be okay. I slip on my loose gauze capris and push the towel against my wet head. I walk into the living room and startle. A woman is cupping her hands over her eyes and looking through the pane glass of the French doors. When she sees me, she jumps back. I open the door and smile.

"Oh! Hello. I'm Addie, Addie Marsh. I didn't scare you, did I? I'm here for the interview," she stammers.

"Of course, Addie. Yes, I'm expecting you. Please forgive me. I just got out of the shower. Make yourself comfortable." I gesture for her to take a seat in the living room. I throw my towel on the kitchen counter. "Would you like something to drink? Coffee? Tea?"

"No, thank you," Addie replies.

"I hope you don't mind. I'm going to get myself a cup."

I slip a Green Mountain coffee pod into my Keurig and wait while my cup fills up. I pour in some cream and three teaspoons of Starbucks vanilla flavoring. When I walk back into the living room, Addie is looking at my wall of handmade pottery fish.

"These are nice. Did you make them?"

I smile. "Oh, no. There's a potter in North Carolina who makes them. When I visit one of my college friends, I always stop by and pick up one for my collection. I like to call it my 'school of fish.'"

"They're lovely." Addie goes over to the love seat and sits. I perch across from her in my armchair.

"Okay, let's talk about the position. Danny tells me you're the best and I'd be stupid not to hire you."

Addie blushes and looks at the floor. "Yeah, well. Danny is cool, you know? He's always trying to help me out."

"Help you out?" I prompt.

"Yeah, well. He sort of knew my parents. They died in a car crash on Central Avenue about five years ago. I had just started my junior year in undergrad when they died. Danny was the first cop on the scene. He's the one who came to the house to notify me."

"Oh, geez, Addie. I'm sorry. I heard there were fatalities in that wreck, but I didn't know the names of the victims."

"It's okay. It was a while ago." She pauses. "Anyway, Danny was the officer who came to the house to tell me they'd died. When I went to the morgue to identify the bodies, he accompanied me. He explained how the investigation would go, and what I should expect. He even stayed in touch with me afterward to make sure I was doing okay."

"Yeah, Danny is a good guy." A smile forms on my lips. "Tell me about yourself, Addie."

Addie's energy is effervescent. Her smile lights up her face. "I just graduated with my bachelor's degree in social work from the University of Maryland. I'm looking to work in mental health and build a career."

I'm about to introduce myself, but Addie says, "And you're Doctor Clara Elizabeth Starr, LCSW-C. It's an honor to meet you." She continues, "You hold a bachelor's degree in social work from the University of Maryland, a master's degree from Gallaudet University, and a doctorate from the University of Maryland. Dr. Starr, you're a social worker extraordinaire." Addie laughs.

I laugh with her and lean back in my chair. "Well, 'social worker extraordinaire' is going out there on a limb, but I see you've done your homework. And maybe talked with Danny to get the info?"

"Got me! When I graduated from social work school, Danny asked me what I was planning to do next. I told him I wanted to work in mental health, maybe substance abuse, but I hadn't thought more about it than that. He said he was a good friend of yours, and he knew you were looking for an assistant," Addie says. She hands me a manila folder with her resume and college transcript inside.

"Summa cum laude, eh? Brava, Ms. Addie Marsh. Well done." I knew I'd offer her the position even before I saw her academic accolades. She has the education and passion. Her personality pulls people to her. She's simply a lovely young woman who needs a start in life. I can understand why Danny felt drawn to her and connected us.

Addie says, "I've taken additional courses in psychopathology, human behavior, and advanced practice. I have my social work license. I'm ready to roll."

"You're hired. When can you start?"

"Today! Right now! This very minute!" Addie shouts, her smile stretching across her face.

I laugh and welcome her to Mystic Beach Behavioral Health. We both jump when there's a loud bang on the glass doors and turn simultaneously. Danny is on the other side in his navy-blue police uniform, wearing a wide, toothy smile. He doesn't wait for me to get up. He turns the knob and walks right in.

"Hey there, ladies," Danny says, pushing his darkened sunglasses onto his forehead. "I thought I'd stop by to see if Addie needs a character reference. I know of someone with an impeccable character who can give her an outstanding recommendation." He grins and puffs up his chest to look like Superman. "Hey, it looks like there's going to be a severe storm soon. You know the back roads flood when there's a rainstorm. I wanted to send Addie on her way before she gets stuck here in Mystic Beach."

Addie looks at me. I say, "Yes, he's right, Addie. Go ahead home before the roads flood and the power goes out. When God spits a bit of rain out here on the peninsula, the power goes out. By the way, where do you live?"

"Not far, just down the road in Woodland Beach."

"Okay, well, get a move-on before the storm comes. I'll see you tomorrow at nine a.m. Sound good to you?"

"Oh, yes. And thank you, Dr. Starr."

"Call me Clara. Tomorrow, I'll give you an overview of the practice and what's involved."

Addie walks toward the French doors and packs a playful punch into Danny's gut. She pulls her hand back. "Ouch!"

Danny laughs and, with his knuckles, wraps on his chest like King Kong. "Vest, Addie. I always wear my vest."

Addie waves goodbye and walks out. Danny sits on the love seat. He holds his arms open. "Well?"

I smile. "You did good, Danny. She's wonderful. Thanks for sending her my way."

"Always happy to oblige. She's a good kid, Clara. She's had a rough few years, but I think she's going to make it. Thanks for giving her a shot."

"Yeah, she has a good-kid vibe, just like me when I was her age."

Danny bursts into laughter. "Uh, yeeeaaaahhh, just like you."

We both cackle. I redden.

"So, uh, Clara. I don't know if you've heard, but Bobby Ward has gone missing again."

I tighten my facial muscles to prevent them from giving me away. I bring the coffee cup to my mouth and slurp. "Oh, no. Again?"

"Yeah. I just found out when I was asking some of the watermen if they'd seen Bobby around. I wanted to see if I could buy a bushel of crabs off him, you know, before he delivers them to Waterman's Tavern."

"Did Alice report him missing?"

"Nah. She's been through this a million times. Bobby goes on a bender, disappears for a few days, then magically reappears on his boat and brings her and Brian a bunch of crabs. I didn't check with Alice. I just figure he blacked out again somewhere," Danny says.

"Come to think of it, I haven't seen him working his crab pots lately. Those blue buoys are still floating out there now."

Danny looks out the glass doors toward the bay. I follow his eyes. The light casts a strange orange and red glow. Bobby's unattended buoys are bobbing in the roiling waves.

Danny breaks the silence. "Well, wherever he is, I hope he's not out on the water. This storm is a big 'un. Nobody should be out on the bay in this kind of weather. It's much too dangerous."

He stands and stretches, then says he's got to be on his way. This type of weather is a sure signal that there will be plenty of police calls. He extends his fist toward me. My throat muscles are sore from holding back fear. We fist-bump, and he lets himself out the glass doors. A gush of air escapes. I didn't realize I was holding my breath.

# CHAPTER 4

The bulbous, dark clouds float across the sky. Far off thunder rumbles. I love watching storms roll in. When I was a child, I hated thunderstorms. I was terrified of the lightning cracks and the thunder booms. At the same time, I felt a compulsion to go outside to watch. It's hard to explain, but I find thunderstorms to be a form of organized chaos. My mom helped me learn to deal with my fear of storms. Now they bring me comfort in deep places. There's a predictability about a storm blowing through. You can see, hear, and even smell it coming. It will rip branches off the trees, blow osprey nests off their posts, and pelt rain across the patio. When thunder crashes, the earth quakes. The world darkens, waves thrash. Then it passes. Evidence of its power lies scattered on the ground, but even then, when it clears, it leaves behind a purified earth. All is forgiven. That is my favorite part. What was dirty is now cleansed. What was culpable is now made innocent.

This monstrous storm will have a lot of purifying to do today. The tower of dark, ominous clouds looks like it will be relentless. I open the French doors and stand outside on the patio. My hair blows off my shoulders. Whitecaps blanket the bay. In the distance, a group of seagulls rides the bursts of wind. I wonder what they can see from so high above the water.

A ping on my phone alerts me I have a text. My client, Lala, needs to cancel today's appointment. She's afraid to venture out in the storm. I type back that I understand and agree. She should stay home today. I send other texts canceling two other appointments made for today. Everyone who's familiar with this area knows that if you can avoid coming to Mystic Beach during a storm, it's always best. Many of the sewage and well systems are from the early 1930s. Unless you have a cool fifteen grand for a new well, you'll have to make do. We're at sea level. When the storms hit, our entire neighborhood is affected. The power goes out, and the generators turn on.

My phone rings. Mom wants to FaceTime. I press the answer button and her face fills my screen. She backs away and uses sign language to tell me, "There's a terrible storm coming. My room is dark. Are you home? It's important to stay indoors."

I bend my fist forward and bob it up and down, signing, "Yes."

Mom points at me and then, with her wrists facing up and fists closed, taps her index fingers on her thumbs in a way that resembles crab pincers. "What are you doing?"

I form O's with both hands and shake them in front of me. "Nothing. I hired an assistant today." I fingerspell A-d-d-i-e. "Danny stopped by to make sure we were okay. How are you, Mom? Have you seen staff this morning?"

"They came in earlier to give me my meds," she answers.

"Do you need me to bring you anything?" I sign.

Fists closed, wrists down, she taps her index and middle fingers on her thumbs. "No." She looks in the distance as if someone came into her room, then returns to the screen. "I'll be fine. You fine?"

I splay my fingers and tap my thumbnail to my chest bone. "I'm fine."

"There is something you're not telling me, Clara?" Mom signs.

"Nothing. Nothing. I'm fine."

Mom cocks her head and stares at me.

"What? What?" I sign.

"Nothing. I love you, Clara," she signs, holding her thumb, index finger, and pinky finger up, with the other two fingers pressed to her palm.

"I love you too, Mom."

She disconnects the call.

Mom lives in Sunview Assisted Living now. Two years ago, she and two of her deaf friends decided they would all become residents together. That way, they had each other to communicate with while staff helped them manage their medications and activities of daily living. I was skeptical at first. My deaf mother in a facility with all hearing people? The staff surprised me, though. They wholeheartedly welcomed my mother and her friends. They hired someone to come to Sunview every week and offer American Sign Language classes to residents and staff. When someone performs at Sunview, they hire an interpreter for Mom and her friends. They take her on outings almost weekly. Mom loves it. She enjoys making new friends, taking classes, eating meals in their in-house restaurant, and having happy hour cocktails in the cafe downstairs. I think the interaction with people helps to curb her loneliness.

The sky is dark and foreboding. I smell the metallic, sweet smell of ozone. I walk to the edge of the knoll in front of my house to look closely at the bay. The sounds of waves crashing on the rocky shoals intensify. The seagulls have taken refuge in other, safer places. My eyes skirt across the whitecaps. I'm looking for a break in the rhythmic pattern. Is Bobby floating out there?

The first split of lightning lights up the bay. Fat droplets sporadically drop against my hair. A persistent scratch of anxiety irritates my chest. Against my better judgment, I walk down the wooden steps to the shore for one more look. I want to make sure Bobby is long gone. The water levels are rising now that the wind is blowing hard. Water covers the shoreline. I know better than to step down into the water. The current could easily sweep me away in these conditions.

Driftwood that had beached upon the shore earlier now floats back out to sea. Seagrasses contort against the force of the wind. My hair rises off my head. It's a pleasant feeling, but my scalp is tingling with fear.

Unbidden memories of Bobby rise to the surface of my mind. I'm in a dark room, curled under a dark bed. Thunder booms outside. Something terrible has happened, and I don't know what to do. So, I wait. Bobby's voice calls to me. I am paralyzed by fear and relief simultaneously. I am hiding. From what? In my mind's eye, I see the tips of worn black leather boots from my position under the bed. Bobby lowers to his knees and bends down. I see the white scruff of a beard and half of his face, white hair covering the rest.

"There you are, my sweet." His voice echoes in my mind.

A crack of thunder yanks me back to reality. Pounding rain drenches me. I hop up the beach steps and run back to my house. I run as hard as I can. Adrenaline fuels my legs. I feel like I'm running for my life. Maybe I am.

# CHAPTER 5

I burst through the glass doors, the deluge spilling onto the wood floor. I latch the doors, grab the towel from this morning's shower, and sop up the wet spots. On bended knees, I circle the towel over and over, trying to calm myself. I'm breathless from running up the hill. Bobby wasn't there. I scan the surf to make sure he isn't floating out there, planning his return. Nothing, just the sound of crashing waves. Even the gulls knew it was time to take cover.

The storm is directly overhead now. I hear the downpour pounding on my roof and causing the patio wind chime to clang. The boom of the thunder rattles my windows. Distant bolts light up the bay just as my indoor lights flicker and die. The neighbors' lights darken as well. I hear the faint chug of a generator. I don't bother with mine. With today's events, I might as well sit here and watch the storm. It's a reminder to me that we're never really in control of our lives. We like to convince ourselves otherwise, but sometimes forces beyond our reach carve trenches and create hollows. I am a woman filled with underground tunnels, a labyrinth of perilous twists and turns.

Checking the signal on my phone, I see two bars, enough to use in case of an emergency. I walk back to the kitchen to make another cup of coffee, even though it's past my stop-time. I have trouble sleeping as it is, and this cup of java will ensure I have a restless night. Everything feels unsettled, though. Too much is happening, too fast and all at once.

Another crack of lightning lights up the area just outside my patio. I see the faint outline of a figure outside, near the beach steps. I move closer to my window and strain to see who it is. He is standing on the top step, looking out to sea. The male figure seems solid, hands in his pocket under the black slicker. If I didn't know better, I would guess it was Bobby. His beefy shape and the way he's standing look just like him. That's ridiculous. My mind is playing tricks. It can't possibly be him. There's no way he could have emerged from the water, put on a slicker, and come back to life.

I open the doors and feel an immediate blast of wind and rain, and I slam the doors shut as I step onto the patio. I walk just to the edge of the concrete to try to get a better look. The rain is a sheet of water.

"Hey! Hey! Are you okay?" I yell to the figure, hoping he's only a mirage.

The pelting rain stalls my voice. I know the man can't possibly hear me in this storm. I must find out if it's Bobby standing there. As ridiculous as it seems, my life depends on knowing if that's him. The height and shape are about right. His stance looks so familiar. Yet I'm hoping that my brain cells are misfiring. I hope it's only my unconscious playing games with me.

"Hey! Mister!" I try again, hoping he will turn toward me so I can see the shape of his face.

I cuss under my breath. I won't be able to let this go until I know for sure. I turn back and go into the house to get my raincoat. Pulling open the closet by the front door, there it is. Yellow rubber that I haven't touched in a long time. I yank the jacket off the hanger and slide my hands into the sleeves. I press the snaps together as I walk onto the patio. Running from under the patio cover into the pouring rain, I keep my head down so the menacing droplets don't pierce my eyes.

When I make it halfway to the steps, I look up and expect to see the man standing there looking at the waves. No one is there, though. Ignoring the rain and thunder booming around me, I walk a block to look down the side streets. Nothing. I feel sure I would have seen him if he had walked down the street in the other direction. I stand on the top step and look out across the bay. Surely he wouldn't be stupid enough to go onto the flooded beach.

The plinking of the rain on the water's surface draws my attention. The slap on the surface, combined with the crashing waves, is mesmerizing. For a moment, I escape my troubles. I look across the horizon, fascinated by the light show and turmoil. The dark, thick clouds hover low. I realize this vision is exactly how I feel about my life and myself. I am a torrent of darkness sliced open by slashes of electricity. Scars of my tumultuous lifeline cross my soul. Healing fully is probably out of the question. I am like a broken vase. Even if all the pieces are set and bound with gold, my cracks still show.

A gust of wind forces me to grab hold of the railing. For a moment, I wonder what it would feel like to give over to these unrelenting forces. How would I feel just letting go and allowing the current to take me, feeling the water wash over me and take me under? Would I be afraid? Panicked? Would there be some relief, too? I wonder how it would feel to no longer have to battle with myself. God knows I am tired, so very tired. Life can be such a weight.

I sway as a burst of wind catches me. I lift the tips of my fingers, toying with the idea of just letting go, letting go of everything. My tears mix with the rain on my face. I can taste the salt on my lips. There is only so much one person can take. Suddenly, I want my mother. I want to feel her arms holding me like a child, squeezing and reassuring me that all will be okay. When I was a child, afraid of thunderstorms, my mother would take my hand and place it gently at her throat. She'd hum a calming tune for me, my hands feeling the vibrations of her voice. She covered the scariness of a storm with rhythmic flutters of her voice in my ears, on my hands, and through my body. I close my eyes and bring the memory to the point where I can almost feel her touch, her soothing sounds.

The image of my mother feels as solid as it would if she were standing right here with me. I could never break her heart by jumping into the sea. I don't think she could recover, not after my father's death. She never took another full breath after he killed himself. I may have a touch of the same internal darkness that ravaged him, but I can decide to do things differently. I can decide to rise rather than descend.

My fingers tighten around the railing, and I turn to go back home. I tell myself I don't have control here. I can only do the next right thing, and that is to go home and let what will be, be. Walking back to my patio, I decide I probably imagined the man on the steps. Today has been a stressful day. I could have made up the whole thing. I mean, who in their right mind would stand outside in the middle of a lightning storm? Do I actually believe Bobby rose from the dead and decided to hang out at the beach? Yeah, right. I need to take it easy today.

As I lay my soaked raincoat on the outside patio chair, a bolt of lightning strikes again. Only then do I see the faint outline of the man, alone, sitting on one of the swings at the playground. His legs push the swing slowly back and forth, his knuckles peeking from under the slicker's sleeves and grasping the swing's chain. He's facing me, but all I can see is a dark hole in the hood of his jacket.

# CHAPTER 6

The next morning, the sun awakens me with its rays bursting through my bedroom blinds. Today is a new day. I lay on my back with my eyelids closed and let the sunshine warm them. The sadness that crept over me last night is gone. I feel strong, as if I had never considered taking my life down a different path.

Wait. My eyes snap open. I suck in and hold my breath. There was someone standing outside amid the terrible storm. It wasn't my imagination. He had stood there at the top of the steps looking at the Chesapeake Bay. What was he looking for, and why would he just stand there in the middle of a big storm? And just like that, other images swim to the surface of my consciousness.

Bobby Ward is dead. I touched his bloated and decomposing body. I pushed him back out to the current. I'm glad no one saw me doing that. They would have thought me possessed, obsessed, or simply out of my mind. I remember the slippery feel of the silt between my toes and tickling my ankles as I waded out further. His body floated with ease as if he had decided to work with me and not against me any longer. That was a first. When my feet pushed against the rocky shoal and sent him back into the bay he loved so much, I'd felt as though a giant weight lifted from my soul. I don't think I had ever breathed so deeply as I did then. The lightness and the gift of this tragedy only occur to me now. His death is a blessing from God. I just know it.

I slide my feet over the edge of the bed and into my slippers. Muscle memory leads me into the kitchen to make my morning latte: three teaspoons of Starbucks vanilla syrup, one Green Mountain Breakfast Blend pod, and heated and frothed half and half. The kitchen and living room lights are on. I forgot to turn them off before going to bed because the power had not yet come back on. I throw open the French doors and feel the cushions of a patio chair. It's almost dry, but not quite. I return to the kitchen, grab a hand towel, and toss it on the seat. The sun's rays are brilliant as they rise over the horizon. It's my favorite time of the day, when everything is fresh and new beginnings are afoot. The bay is glassy and still. Even the birds overhead are silent in their flight. This feels like a rebirth of sorts. The thrashing and violence of the storm yesterday are now silenced into submission. This new, beautiful life now emerges.

The best thing about living in a small community like Mystic Beach is that we help each other out. I hear distant sounds of chainsaws, no doubt cutting up tree branches fallen in someone's back yard or across the road. Someone will be around to check on me shortly. We all do that for one another.

Barbara walks along the road with her dog in tow and waves. "Clara, how'd you do yesterday? Everything stay put?"

I take a sip of my delicious latte. "Yeah, everything's fine." I look at the branches littered across the front yard. "I don't think anything major got destroyed. How about you?"

"Oh, we have a huge tree branch in the middle of our shed, but the guys are over there cutting it in pieces. No one got hurt, which is the most important part. Hey, did you hear about the accident on Central Avenue last night?"

I shake my head. "I didn't hear anything, but then again, I went to bed early. What happened?"

Barbara walks to the edge of my yard with her dog. "Apparently, a car packed full of teenagers turned the curve too fast. They smacked right into a telephone pole. The air ambulance lifted the driver to Baltimore Shock Trauma. The others went by regular ambulance." Barbara shakes her head. "I wish the county would do something about this. How many people need to be hurt on this road?"

"Well, I hope they're okay," I say. "Anyone who's been around here long knows to take it slow there, especially when it's raining."

Barbara nods. "Yeah, and I think the water is still too high for people to drive through now. So, if you're here, you're here; if you're not, you're not getting in for at least another few hours."

We pause and look out across the bay. Barbara gets ready to continue with her walk, then turns and says, "It's good you came in yesterday morning when you did. I'd hate to think of what could have happened if you stayed in the water during the storm." She smiles, her white veneers forming a grimace. "But who swims during a storm, anyway?"

I fend off the twinge of fear threatening to surface. "That's true." I take another sip while keeping my eyes focused on Barbara's receding backside. She bends down with her poop bag and picks up her dog's leftovers.

My attention draws to someone else walking down the road and across my lawn. He's picking up small branches as he makes his way to me.

"Hey, Brian. How are you doing?" I ask.

"Hey, girl. I'm doing okay, surviving."

"That's right, I heard something about your dad missing. He come home yet?"

Brian drops the pile of sticks along the edge of the patio and sits in a chair, then jumps up. "Geez … look at the back of my pants. I probably looked like I peed myself." He turns around to show me his wet rump.

I laugh. "Oh, come on, Brian. Your butt looks as fabulous as it always does."

He chuckles, turns, and sits down in the chair. "You're right, darlin'. Fabulous is as fabulous does. In fact, a little wet patch on my ass might get more attention than not."

"I love you, Brian. You're one of my most favorite humans."

He blows air kisses to me. "Anyway, Dad … no, he didn't come home. It's not like we're too worried. I mean, come on, he does this all the time. And, frankly, I'd rather him be off like this when he's drinking. You know how he gets. Mom and I have to hide in our rooms behind locked doors until he calms down. Whiskey and Dad make a violent combination."

I nod. I have firsthand experience. Bobby's reputation as a drunken thug is well known in Mystic Beach and, I'm sure, beyond. Still, he's Brian's father. There's always something that makes children cling to their parents, even if the parent doesn't deserve it.

"How's your mom, Brian?" I ask.

He flashes what he calls a fashion model smile and says in a fake French accent, "She's never been better, but of course!"

I stare him down, waiting for a real answer.

Brian straightens his face. "To tell you the truth, Clara, she's doing very well. In fact, she woke up this morning and made us blueberry pancakes from scratch. Pancakes … from scratch. Imagine that?"

"Well, it's truly a day of celebration, then. Hopefully, when he comes home, he'll be sober and manageable," I say, ignoring the tug of the lie in my gut.

"Manageable?" Brian mocks me. He says in a gangster voice, "Someone 'round here must be a social worker all day, every day."

I laugh. "Yeah, but—"

He interrupts and talks in his regular voice. "You're a lovable one, for sure. No, really … I'd be okay if he never came home. I wish he'd just decide to stay with one of his floozies and move on down the road. I think Mom and I would both be the better for it."

"Facts," Brian and I say at the same time. We laugh at our long-time shared quip.

We sit for a moment in our respective headspaces. I watch his handsome face as he stares out toward the bay. He's grinding his jaw. Both Brian and I are familiar with the kind of destructive pain a loved one can cause. It damages the soul and body until you can't discern where the abuse stops and where you begin. What's hard to accept, though, is even when they're hurting you, you still love them. That love makes you weak; it keeps you going back, knowing the cycle will repeat itself.

To lessen his angst, I ask, "How are things at the … where do you work again?"

He rolls his eyes. "I work at the Chesapeake Biological Laboratory. Heller? Must I have to tell you over and over again until you're an old woman?"

I laugh. "That's right, you're the … the …."

He sighs dramatically. "A marine biologist? Marine science? Oceanography? Anything ring a bell?" He chuckles. "No, really, it's all going well. Same ole, same ole."

"Studying anything special?" I smirk.

"Wouldn't you like to know, nosy pants!"

Brian stands and pushes back his hair while flexing one of his biceps then the other.

"Show off."

"Dontcha know it," he says, slapping his wet rear end as he walks back toward the road.

"Tell your mom I send her my love," I yell.

He flings his hand in the air to say he will. I wonder when they'll find out Bobby's not coming home. That will be a cause for celebration.

# CHAPTER 7

The phone rings. "Hey, Dr. Sta—I mean Clara. It's me, Addie. I'm wondering if I should come in to work today, you know, to help get things ready for next week."

"Hi, Addie. Even if you wanted to, I think it would be difficult to get back into the neighborhood with the water levels so high," I explain. "It's okay. We can work on things on Monday. It's Saturday, anyway. You don't want to ruin your weekend."

Addie laughs. "Ha! Saturday, Monday, Friday, Christmas, Easter, it's all the same to me. No, really, I have nothing to do except sit here in my little cottage for yet another day by myself. If I don't get out of here, I'm going to bite all my nails off. And my neighbor has a pickup on one of those hydraulic shock things. He can clear any puddle you've got down there. He's the designated driver in bad weather, floods, snow. You name it, he can do it."

"Are you sure, Addie? You really don't have to venture out."

"Oh, I'm sure, one hundred percent. See you in about an hour."

I'm relieved. The truth is, I could use the company. Even though my neighbors are great and know practically everything I do the minute I do it, it still feels lonely not having a partner to share my experiences. George and I, as dysfunctional as we were, could comfort each other. We weren't always poisonous. In the beginning, we were the perfect couple, he the lawyer, me the social worker. Successful and affluent, we felt like Rose and Jack from the movie *Titanic;* we were on top of the world. Until we weren't.

I am not going down this road right now. I can't do anything except focus my attention in a different direction. I can outrun my past right into my future, and Miss Addison Marsh is going to help me. Addie arrives right on time and stands at the glass doors. I wouldn't have known she was there until I looked right at her as I walked to the kitchen. I wave and gesture for her to come inside.

"Hey there. I'm happy to see you. Make it through the 'puddle,' as you called it?"

Addie smiles. "Ah, yes, John never fails me, or anyone else in the neighborhood, for that matter."

I walk into the living room and point to the love seat. I sit across from her in my usual armchair. Addie looks more at ease today than she did yesterday. I imagine she was nervous. It was a job interview, after all. Addie declines coffee or tea but asks for a glass of water. She follows me into the kitchen and then comes back out again.

"So, I figured we'd spend some time talking about the practice, you know, my philosophy, how I like to work, all that."

"That'd be great," Addie replies.

"I've had this private psychotherapy practice for about five years now. I decided to make the jump when I had reached my limit for bureaucracy and organizational politics. I had already had twenty years of practice and advanced licensure, and once my husband died, I didn't need to rely so much on a biweekly paycheck.

"So, after George died, I sold our Annapolis home and moved back to Mystic Beach, where I grew up. I think my mom had been holding onto this family home for me even though she moved down the road to Sunview. She'd always hoped I'd return to the homeplace. And, well, here I am. That sums me up in a nutshell. How about you? Who are you, Ms. Addison Marsh?"

Addie flushes and looks down. When she raises her head again, her eyes are piercing. *This woman is strong,* I think. *There's much more than what she shows the world on the surface.*

"Well, as you know, I recently finished my Bachelor of Social Work degree at University of Maryland. I've lived in Woodland Beach my whole life. My parents are dead, like I told you. It was Danny who helped me through that. They left me a bit of money, enough to keep me afloat while going to school and working odd jobs. The house is paid off, so I didn't need to worry about the mortgage. As it turns out, I know how to be thrifty when I need to.

"Lots of neighborhood kids called me 'Miss Brainiac' throughout middle and high school, but I never let them get to me. Sure, I loved to read books, but I also loved to play with the other kids on the street. Sometimes I'd prefer to read while they played, which earned me that stupid nickname. I never had trouble in school and, for the most part, never had trouble with friends. As I got older, a few of the girls tried to insinuate I was after their boyfriends, but they couldn't have been more wrong. I definitely did not have my sights on any boys during high school. I had too many friends who got pregnant, got secret abortions, or sometimes were sent somewhere else by their parents. I graduated from high school, then went directly into college for my bachelor's degree in social work. Then, in my junior year ... you know the rest."

I agree. "You're quite the survivor, Addie. As am I. I think we'll get along perfectly."

Addie smiles. I smile back. Then someone raps on the glass door with five consecutive bangs. We jump and look toward the door just as the nob turns. Danny walks in wearing a giant smile and his police uniform.

"Well … hellllloooooo, ladies." He surveys the room like he can hardly believe his luck. "Fancy seeing you two here."

I cough. "Uh, yeah, right. I mean, this is my house and all."

"Right you are. Right you are. Howya doing, Addie? Getting along okay?"

"Oh, yes. I'm doing great. Doctor—I mean, Clara is showing me the ins and outs of being a full-time practitioner."

"Well, that's just great, guys. I thought you two would hit it off once you met each other." Danny looks at me, something passing across his face. "Hmmm … well …."

"Oh, come on, Danny. Spit it out. I can see you're holding something exciting. Out with it," I say.

He coughs into his hand and scratches his chin, a sign of his nervousness. I wait him out. Addie looks back and forth between the two of us but does not interrupt the tense moment. I file this piece of information into the back of my mind. It's a good sign that Addie knows when to keep quiet and wait it out.

"Okay. Well, here's the thing. Remember when I came by yesterday looking for Bobby?"

"Yes. You wanted to buy some blue crabs." My throat constricts. My heart is about to explode. "What about it?"

He looks down and shuffles his feet as if he's trying to figure out how to say what I know is about to come out. "Well, you see, the thing is … well, he turned up finally."

My voice registers an octave higher. "Oh? That's good news, right?"

He scratches his chin. "Well, not really. You see, he wasn't alive when he showed up."

"Oh, my God, Danny!" I stand and walk toward him. "What happened?"

"His body rolled up down the shoreline, around the bend from Camp Walalupe. He was looking pretty bad by then, and to make matters worse, one of the camp kids ran up on him while collecting shells after the storm."

"When did they find him?" I squeak.

"Just this morning. He was lying flat on his back like he was taking a nap, but when the kid took a closer look, he screamed, a little too gleefully, if you ask me, 'Dead body! Dead body!' and went to find the staff person who was walking down further."

I stare at Danny's face to see if he was holding anything back. He seems to be telling me everything. "What do they think happened? Did he fall off his boat and drown?"

Danny's eyes bore into me. "Uh, yeah. It appears that way. The Chief says I need to try to figure out a timeline of events. So, I'm asking around the neighborhood to see when the last time anyone had seen Bobby."

"Okay."

"Well?" Danny asks.

"Well, what?"

He sighs. "When was the last time you saw Bobby Ward?" he asked, using his official police voice.

I stand up as straight as I could and meet his eye with mine. "It's been a while, Officer Cloman. I'd say the last time I saw him was a week ago Friday."

"Where was that?"

"I saw him at the pub. He was with his crabbing buddies like usual. I was there having a drink, too."

Danny's eyes widen. "You were?"

"I was drinking a ginger ale, Officer Cloman." I feel a burn simmering in my gut. He didn't have to do this in front of Addie.

Danny nods and writes a note in his small notebook. "Knock it off with the 'Officer Cloman,' Clara. And you're sure it was last Friday?"

"Of course. I can read a calendar just like the rest of you," I snap.

"Okay. Well, that about takes care of it. I'll be seeing you soon, Clara. Addie, see ya." He turns and walks out the door.

I turn around and try to disguise my shock. I pick a fuzz off the chair cover. When I look up, Addie's eyes shine, and her smile widens.

# CHAPTER 8

I go through the bookkeeping software with Addie and show her how I like to have my notes stored electronically. We discuss billing and the clients who have running balances until their financial situation improves. Addie is quiet throughout and writes notes in her spiral notebook. She practices setting up a fake client electronic record and populates the intake and consent forms to see what they look like. We go over the insurance billing codes that match the diagnoses from the Diagnostic and Statistical Manual of Mental Disorders.

I explain to Addie that I often dictate my notes on my phone and save them as voice files on my computer. Now that I have an assistant, Addie will sit at a desk around the corner and take notes from there. I assure her that all clients will have signed consent forms for Addie's presence in the office and transcribing my notes. She will be held to the same standards of confidentiality as I am.

By the time we finish reviewing the specifics, it's close to lunchtime, and I ask Addie if she'd like to go to lunch. She agrees. We sit in my VW Beetle as I push the button to lower the top.

"Shall we try to navigate the high waters out of Mystic Beach?" I cover one eye with my hand to look like a pirate. "Have you ever been to Pirate's Cove, lass?" I growl.

Addie laughs. "Not for a very long time. I love that place, though. Thanks for suggesting it."

I am happy the water has receded as we drive the back roads to another coastal town. Addie looks at me like she wants to ask me a question. I continue driving while watching her in my peripheral vision. She looks at me, then away, then back at me again. I turn to her.

"Something on your mind, Addie?"

Her cheeks flush red. "Well, it's not really any of my business …."

I let her statement hang in the air, then finally help her out. "The worse that can happen is that I won't answer your question. Fire away."

Addie holds her hair back with one of her hands to keep the strands from looking like Medusa's head. "Well, I was wondering …"

My stomach clenches. I sense she is about to ask me about my husband's death, and I don't think I can bear it. Well, wait. I can bear it. But can I answer her honestly? That is something I really don't know.

Even in difficult situations, my father told me, always tell the truth. It's the only way to come out of hard times, he'd say. I believed that for a long time. Until I stopped. On the other hand, being honest is likely to cause some kind of fallout. It's not always pretty. Either your friend stops being your friend, your employer decides that you're no longer trustworthy after twenty years, or your husband decides that your lie gives him carte blanche to do as he pleases with or without you around.

" … how you felt about it," Addie finishes.

"Wait, what? I missed part of what you said."

"What I mean is, when your father died, I know it was hard. I can relate to it, for sure. But did you ever find out why he did that to himself? How did you feel about all that?" Addie asks.

A deep sigh escapes from my chest. Like a dodo bird, I giggle and cough. Addie looks at me like she's not sure she should be in the car with me at this moment.

"My dad. You're asking about my dad's death? Yeah, that was a hard one. Wait, how do you know how he died?"

Addie opens her mouth but gulps air instead. She raises her hand to offer surrender.

"No, Addie. I don't mean I'm offended by it. It's just that my father died before you were born. How do you know about any of that? Did Danny tell you?"

"No, no. It wasn't Danny. See, my grandparents knew your dad. He was deaf, right?"

"Yeah," I respond.

"So, my granddad and your dad were friends. They knew each other from the neighborhood."

"Wait, is your granddad deaf?"

"Ha, well, he was terribly hard of hearing, but he wasn't deaf, not in the way your dad was, or the way your mom is. My granddad started to learn sign language when he first met your dad. They became fast friends. At least that's what my dad told me, you know, before he died. He used to tell me a lot about your family."

I look to see if she's teasing me, but I see sincerity and curiosity.

"Well, it's really a small world, to be sure. Yeah, it was a terrible time when my dad killed himself. He had depression for a long time. It came in cycles which sometimes left him so debilitated he stayed in the bedroom for weeks. My mom did the best she could, but Dad could be difficult. She'd try to convince him to see someone, but then he'd turn his head or close his eyes so he couldn't see her signs. She'd tap him on the shoulder to get his attention, but he'd just bury himself deeper under the covers. One day, she came home from work at the Maryland School for the Deaf and saw he was still under the bedcovers like he had been when she'd left that morning. When she tapped his shoulder, he didn't move. She tapped him harder, but still he didn't move. When she pulled back the blankets, she could see from the color of his face and the stiffness of his body that he was dead."

We are approaching the restaurant, but Addie remains quiet. Finally, she asks in a low tone, "Did he leave a note or anything?"

I park the car in front of the restaurant door and turn off the engine. "No, he didn't leave a note. Mom found his empty bottle of prescription meds in the bathroom. His death was ruled a suicide, and then, boom, life changed for Mom and me."

"I'm so sorry," Addie says.

"It's okay, Addie. It was a long time ago. Mom and I have done just fine. We're good. I'm good," I say, all the while realizing the hypocrisy in my lie. What am I to do, though? Unzip myself in front of this young woman who has her life together way better than I could ever attempt to do? Expose myself to all the guilt and shame that has plagued me practically my whole life? Reveal myself to yet another person who will judge me and stamp me with a "damaged goods" label? No, thank you, madame. I'm fine as I am.

I look at Addie, who seems more troubled by our conversation than I am. "Hey," I whisper as I touch her arm. "Really, it's okay. Whenever you have a question, always ask me. I'll always tell you the truth. Now, come on. Let's go get some seafood."

# CHAPTER 9

After lunch, I tell Addie to go home and do something fun for the remainder of the day. I drop her off at her house in Woodland Beach and head further down the road to go see Mom. Parking in the lot of the massive facility, I see several residents sitting in rocking chairs along the front of Sunview. I shade my eyes to prevent glare from the sun so I can look at each person. Along the left side, at the end, I see the familiar flurry of hands. Mom and her friends are having an animated conversation about an exercise instructor. They don't see me watching their conversation yet.

Mom's friend Emma signs, "Vallurea! You have got to be kidding. His face looks like he fell out of the ugly tree and hit every limb."

Mom defends herself. "Emma. There's nothing wrong with a person who has their face moved around a bit. It's what's inside that counts."

Jane is laughing so hard that she puts her hand to her mouth to prevent her ill-fitting dentures from falling out. "You two are crazy. He stands in front of the class, asking a bunch of old ladies to raise and lower their arms. Do you think any one of us looks like a crispy little treat?"

I quicken my pace. I want them to see me before I see them say something that can't be unseen. When I'm close, I raise my arm and wave to get her attention. Mom's eyes home in on me; her friends, Emma and Jane, follow her gaze. I wave.

"Hi, Mom." I bend down, and she puts her hand on my cheek.

"Hi, sweetie. I'm happy you came. You can put an end to all of this nonsense with E and J," she signs. "You know the exercise man who teaches class? I think he's handsome. Also, he's sweet and friendly. I think he would make a fine escort to the Annapolis Harbor."

I must look confused because Emma adds, "He's so ugly. What is she thinking? He looks like he ran into a wall."

I shake my head and flick my index finger up near my forehead. "I don't understand."

Jane signs, "Your mom thinks the man would go on a date with her."

Oh. I look at my mother and scrunch my eyebrows.

"What?" Mom asks. "What? You think I'm too old?"

I tilt my head and put my palm on my forehead to show I'm exasperated.

When I look back at the three women, they're glancing back and forth at each other, smiling. That's when I realize they're joking with me. Mom had seen my car pull into the lot.

"You're silly," I sign. Then, "Funny nothing, Mom. Funny nothing."

Mom stands up and hooks her arm in mine then gestures to go inside to her room. She looks scrawny.

"Mom, you feeling all right?"

"Me? Yes, I feel fine."

We're waiting for the elevator when an elderly man wheels up in his wheelchair.

Mom signs and voices, "Edward, hi." She points her finger at me and speaks to him, "Clara. My daughter."

Edward shifts his gaze to me. His eyes look enormous behind red-rimmed thick glasses. He says with a British accent, "Hi, Clara. Nice to see you again." He turns to Mom, raises his thick, calloused hand, and swipes the space in front of his face.

Mom sees my perplexed look and corrects his sign. Her hand waves in front of her face and then closes, all fingers touching her thumb. She voices, "Beautiful. Edward. This is the sign for beautiful."

Accepting his compliment, I speak and sign, "Thank you."

As we're still waiting for the elevator, I sign without speaking, "Mom, you're using your voice? Does he understand your deaf accent?"

Mom's head bobs up and down. "Edward and I have gotten to know each other a little bit." She wiggles her eyebrows. I fake cringe.

The elevator arrives, and we step inside. Edward asks to push number two, but I notice he uses his hand to indicate two as well. This is good, very good. The residents are making an effort to include Mom. I'm glad she's in a community where the members value each other and try to communicate as best they can.

Edward squeezes Mom's wrist and wheels off at level two. Mom and I continue up to the third floor. As we step off into the carpeted hall, I can hear one of the staff members talking with a resident. The staff member's voice is louder than usual. She must be talking to Blossom. As we round the corner, Blossom raises her bony hand to Mom. Mom responds in kind.

I say to the staff member, "Hey, Denise." I sign and speak, "How's Mom doing?"

Denise tries to sign, but she's just gesturing nonsensical movements. I hear Mom stifle a laugh. "Miss Vallurea is doing very well. She has been going to exercise class three times a week. We're so happy to see her involved."

I turn toward Mom and cock my head. Mom swats my shoulder and shakes her head.

"That's wonderful. I'm glad she's keeping up her strength." I emphasize the sign "strength" to look like someone who has massive

The-Rock-like biceps. Mom laughs.

We walk to the end of her hall to her room. Mom turns the handle, and the door opens.

"You don't lock your door, Mom?"

She shakes her head and signs, "No need."

We sit in the wingback chairs. Mom asks, "Do you want anything to drink?"

I shake my head. "How did you handle the storm?"

Mom signs, "Fine. The lights flickered, but the power never goes out here. E, J, and I played cards most of the evening until the med cart came. I slept well." Mom pauses and stares at my face. "What's wrong?" She points at me.

"Nothing. Nothing's wrong. I'm fine," I sign.

She puts her hand on my wrist, brings her head closer to my face, then touches my cheeks under my eyes.

"They're purple. You didn't sleep well?" she asks.

Before I can stop them, my eyes dart to the side. Mom will catch this. It's the way she has always been able to catch me in a lie. I release a deep breath. I can never lie to Mom. For one, she's too astute at reading my body language. Two, she's the only person in my life who makes me feel safe and loved.

I explain to her that Bobby's body washed up on the shore this morning. I sign that Danny stopped by to tell me the news, and that he's trying to establish a timeline because it seems Bobby had been missing a couple days before.

"You know Bobby, Mom."

She bobs her head up and down and mimes someone drinking too much and wobbling.

"Right."

"How's Alice and Brian?" Mom asks.

"I haven't seen them since his body was found."

Mom and I sit, each of us in our individual thoughts. She reaches for my wrist and, with the other hand, asks, "How are you?"

My eyes dart again. "Fine, Mom. I'm fine."

"Tell me," Mom signs.

"Nothing."

Mom cocks her head. I will my eyes to reveal nothing; I am a blank slate. I tell myself to control my breathing because she will pick up on that, too. Before I can stop her, Mom reaches into her basket and pulls out a deck of cards. I shake my head. No, I do not want to pull a card. She fans the deck in front of me and leans forward. Her head gestures to the deck. I shake my head again.

Mom uses her voice. "Pick one."

I sigh dramatically. I know what is going to happen. The cards have a blue background with thirty white stars on the back of each. I reach toward the deck and extract one card near the middle. Great. Seven of Swords. Mom raises her head and focuses on my face. She raises her hand to sign.

I interrupt, "I know, Mom. I know." My eyes meet hers; I've just pulled the deception card.

Mom takes the card and puts it back in the deck. She then takes my hand and puts it against her throat. I close my eyes and feel the vibrations of my mother's hum. A tear escapes, but I let it drop to the floor.

# CHAPTER 10

By the time I arrive home, I'm exhausted. As I walk into my house, I kick off one shoe, then the other. Inside my bedroom, I remove my blue jeans, shirt, and bra and leave them in a heap. I pull on my nightgown even though it's still light outside. It's early, but I've had enough. Time to close up shop for the day. I'm feeling overwhelmed. I have too many balls in the air, trying to juggle them all. All it takes is one mistake, and they all come falling down around me. I'm too old to be dealing with the drama.

I reach my hand to the back of my bedside table drawer. My fingers close around the small amber bottle containing instant calm. A niggling thought crosses my mind, warning me about slipping into old habits. I bat it away. Today was extraordinary, and not in a good way. One or two of these little pills will help me get the sleep I need. Tomorrow, with a fresh mind, I can tackle any problems that drift toward me. I pour one pill into my hand. After a pause, I dump out one more. I want to be sure I'm knocked out tonight. After swallowing the pills dry, I rest my head on my pillow and allow my thoughts to drift.

A downside of living in a small community is that you can never truly escape your past. Generations of families have passed their years here in Mystic Beach. Most have known me since I was a child. There are a few old-timers here who remember my grandparents on my mother's side. My deaf family has always been sort of an anomaly. My mother is from a fifth-generation deaf family, all of whom attended the Maryland School for the Deaf in Frederick. Not only that, but the deaf men in the family follow a long line of watermen, fishing the Chesapeake Bay for blue crabs.

I only faintly recall my grandfather. As a child, I had difficulty grasping his signing. He fingerspelled fast, forming each letter of a word, one right after the other, creating a long train of letters. To a young child who was still learning how to spell, his fingerspelling captivated me. It was like watching a kite fly with tails of letters whipping in the wind. My grandfather had married a deaf woman whom he met at the deaf residential school. They had one child, my mother, who was also deaf. She met my father, John Starr, at the Maryland School as well. He was from a hearing family who couldn't sign. My father often felt left out and spent many weekends with Mom and her parents. They bonded naturally. After their graduations, they married.

Papaw pulled John into the family. He could see the negative effects of John's parents not signing. John became the deaf son he never had. Papaw taught him how to crab. On the weekends my parents were home from school, he took John out on his old and battered Chesapeake deadrise and taught him how to set trotlines with chicken necks as bait and later pull them up to net the crabs. He taught him how to tweak the inboard motor if it should stall out in the bay. John took to crabbing quickly. After he graduated and married Mom, they moved into the family home in Mystic Beach. Papaw and Dad would go out in the early mornings to set the trotlines, check the crab pots, and return in mid-afternoon with bushel baskets of live crabs.

I wanted to go out on the boat with Dad and Papaw when I was younger. I would stomp my feet, sending a vibration through the floor to get their attention. Papaw would look up in the direction of the tremor for a brief moment before returning his attention to the bag of bait. Dad would walk over and cup my face with both of his hands. He'd kiss the top of my head and scruff my hair. They never took me out, though. Dad told me it was too dangerous for a little girl to go crabbing in the bay. One trip, one wayward line, one burst from the engine, and I could fall overboard.

As long as I can remember, my life involved being around the Chesapeake Bay with my family. I learned to pick a crab as a very young child and knew how to avoid the pincers that could lock onto a piece of flesh and not let go. I learned how to use the tongs to pick them up by the shell and put them into the large metal pot on the single burner out in the yard. Mom would let me pour Old Bay seasoning over the top and dump the can of beer into the pot. When the timer rang, I knew a couple dozen delicious blue crabs, now turned red, would be ready for eating.

I didn't understand why Dad was suddenly gone when I was twelve. Mom said he got sick and died, but never more than that. Later, I put two and two together when some particularly mean kids said my "deaf and dumb dad" couldn't handle not hearing in the world. They'd gesture a knife cutting across their necks. When I relayed the stories to Mom, she brushed me off, told me to ignore them.

I remember her particularly abrupt and animated signs. "Don't be silly, Clara. Your father didn't die because he was deaf. If every deaf person did that, you wouldn't have been born. Don't listen to the stupid hearing kids."

It was a confusing time for me, nonetheless. For one, I attended the local schools. I had wanted Mom to send me to the Maryland School like everyone else in my family, but she explained it was only for deaf children. When I'd bring home friends from school, they would gawk and mock my family's use of sign language. I learned to keep my deaf world and hearing world separate. I couldn't tolerate all the questions they had. Why can't your parents hear? Why do they fling their hands like that? Why do they make faces? What's wrong with their voices? All of my play dates became more about my parents being deaf than wanting to play in the back yard or kick the ball down the street. Slowly, I isolated myself.

And I started to lie.

It was easier to make up outlandish stories about how my parents became deaf than explain the truth. My father had tripped and a pencil stabbed him in the ear. My grandparents had yelled so loud at my mother that her eardrums split. Long ago, a voodoo witch from New Orleans cursed my family, and thereafter, everyone was born deaf except me; I broke the curse. The stories became increasingly bizarre the more I told them.

I even started to lie to my parents. They couldn't hear me sneak out of the house at night. My mother would ask me why it was so difficult for me to wake up for school and I'd tell her about being troubled by terrible dreams of the crab boats being swallowed by a violent hurricane. Later, when I started experimenting with drugs and making plans to meet up with the local high school drug dealer, I didn't have to hide my telephone conversations. Mom couldn't hear me anyway. I could pretty much say and do what I wanted.

When Dad died, my grandparents were still living. We continued through our days as if Dad was on vacation. No one had explained to me exactly what had happened to him. The more they pressed me to move on, just get over it, the more I got involved with drugs. My grandparents and mother never confronted me directly about my increasingly erratic behavior. By the time my mother tried to put some real limits on my behavior, I had already learned just to close my eyes and plug my ears, thereby shutting out her scoldings. She had lost her husband and then lost control of her daughter.

It was about that time when Mom told me that tragedy and I would be lifelong lovers. I flipped her the middle finger and stomped off to my room.

One of the sad facts of life I learned as a child is that deaf people are often targets of discrimination, insults, mocking, and disregard. A lot of hearing people think they aren't smart because many of them don't speak. They can be particularly vulnerable to predators who sexually and physically abuse them, assured in the knowledge that their victims' deafness will prevent them from making police reports. Even if they did, how many police officers would really take the effort to do a full report and thorough assessment with someone who doesn't speak or hear? When I'd get in trouble at school, the principal would often let me off with a verbal reprimand because calling a formal team meeting would involve interpreters and the uncomfortable position of being looked in the face very closely by a deaf woman.

There's another side, too. Being the hearing daughter of deaf parents also put a target on my back, especially when I was already walking on the edge of utter chaos. Those same predators find females like me desirable because even if I told my parents about any shenanigans, the likelihood that the police or school officials would take their word for it over the hearing piece of crap is very, very low. I learned that early, too. Bobby Ward taught me that lesson firsthand.

I think about my mother then and my mother now. Her face wears the battle scars of losing her father to the bay, her mother to cancer, and her husband to suicide. She wears grief deep inside her bones, in the way she stoops as she walks and how her eyes take on a faraway look. I wasn't the best daughter then, to be sure. I know I left battle wounds inside her soul, just like the others. I am a good daughter now, though. I became one when I learned how to take back control of my life in those long meetings at Narcotics Anonymous.

As I lay in my bed, reflecting on my family and all the things I had done as a teenager, I am gripped with remorse. I simply won't go back to being that girl anymore. "I will be better, Mom," I say aloud. Everything will be all right. I will take care of everything. Now that Bobby is gone, the world will return to its axis. There's no need for me to hide any longer.

# CHAPTER 11

The sun is hot and bright the next morning on the patio. The extra sleep helped me get myself straight. I feel slightly sluggish from the pills, but my coffee will dissipate that. I am thinking about how Danny is the most irritating person on the planet when he walks up and flops down on my patio chair.

He jumps up and barks, "I need coffee this morning, Clara."

He opens the French doors and, leaving them open, walks into the kitchen. I hear him opening the cupboard to retrieve a coffee mug and inserting a coffee pod into the Keurig. The water swooshes as the cup fills. A spoon clangs against the side of the cup as he stirs the cream. Danny comes out and perches on the chair beside me.

"Hey," he says.

"Hey."

We both look out at the bay. The humidity is thick, and the hot coffee makes my skin slick with sweat. I've known Danny long enough to know he loves the mornings on the bay as much as I do. He also grew up with a father who was a waterman. On the horizon, we see a deadrise skimming along an invisible horizontal line. This one is different. I can tell because of fluorescent pink-colored buoys bobbing near the boat.

"Well, didn't take long for someone to take over Bobby's spot, did it?" I ask.

"Yeah. Can't much blame them. They have to earn a living, too, and with Bobby gone, someone had to call dibs. I guess Shaun got to it first. How much you want to bet he probably anchored there overnight so he'd be the first one there this morning?"

I snort. He's right. There's a code among watermen. You don't encroach on someone else's territory unless you're ready for a vicious fight. The other rule is first come, first get. It doesn't matter if someone is taking over a specific territory or if someone reaches the pier of the local restaurant first. Shaun got there first, apparently.

I don't want to ask about Bobby, but I feel the question picking at my stomach. I put the mug to my lips and take a big gulp of coffee, burning my tongue. That should remind me to keep my mouth shut, I tell myself.

Danny is wearing his street clothes: blue jeans, and a Guy Harvey T-shirt. He props his feet up, clad in worn, leather deck shoes, on the patio table.

"Those shoes look like they've seen better days."

Danny laughs. "Yeah, but they're like my second skin. They haven't failed me yet."

I glance at him, and he smiles, but it doesn't quite reach his eyes.

I sigh. "Okay, Danny, what's going on?"

His eyes widen. "What? I didn't say anything."

"Yeah, but I recognize the look on your face. There's something bothering you. Come on, tell me."

"Clara, it's police business. I'm not supposed to talk to anyone outside the precinct about any of the cases."

I turn my face out to the bay. This will help him feel better about telling me what he's not supposed to tell me but surely will, I am certain. I take another sip of coffee.

"You'll feel better, Danny. You can trust me."

He shifts in the chair so he's squarely facing the bay. "I don't know. There's something about this case with Bobby. The chief wants it to be closed as an accidental drowning, but there's something not sitting right with me."

We watch a flock of sea birds fly low over the bay's surface. I wait, keeping my eyes carefully trained straight ahead.

He continues. "The M.E.'s report hasn't been released yet, but I stopped by to talk to the technician anyway. Do you remember Jacob?"

I turn to face him. "Jacob Masters, who lives down the street from the Woodland Beach Fire Station?"

"Yes, that's the one. He works as a tech in the M.E.'s office. I was there waiting for the M.E. to go over the preliminary findings of Bobby's autopsy. Jacob gestured for me to follow him around the corner in the morgue where the cameras couldn't capture us. He whispered that he thought it wasn't a drowning. He's ridiculous. I mean, we're talking about pothead Jacob, right? But he insists something isn't right. He overheard the M.E. talking into the voice recorder as he was cutting. He says the lungs were not filled with fluid." Danny pauses.

"So what?" I say after a few seconds.

"So," he continues, "if Bobby drowned, there would have been water in his lungs. He would have inhaled water as his last attempt to breathe. Jacob says the M.E. showed him the lungs and where they store air."

I interrupt. "What? Why would the doctor show Jacob Bobby's air sacs?"

"Yeah, I wondered that, too. Apparently, Mr. Pothead is getting his act together and wants to get training to be an autopsy tech."

"Ewwww. I can't imagine doing that," I say.

"Yeah, me either. But anyway, Jacob tells me he doesn't think Bobby drowned."

"Well, did you hear anything from the M.E. himself?"

"No, not yet. He never showed. So I'm not sure what to think now. Yesterday I talked with everyone who knew Bobby."

"And?"

"And witnesses can place Bobby leaving the dock late on Tuesday afternoon. From the sounds of things, Bobby was especially irritable. Apparently, one of the guys had learned that Bobby was stealing crabs from the pots of other watermen. There'd been an argument on the dock. One of the other guys had rushed Bobby and threatened to, and I quote, 'end your life as you know it.' Bobby spat in the guy's face, hopped in his boat, fired up the engine, and gunned out of the slip."

"Who was the guy that argued with Bobby?"

"Sherwood Winters."

I shrug. "Who's that?"

"The guys call him Woody. His home base is in Deale Island, on the shore."

"He's a long way from home, isn't he?"

"Yeah. Apparently, he got into a scuffle with one of the elderly watermen there. The locals told Woody to come over here, do some crabbing, and go back after things settle down. Apparently, the eastern shore watermen don't play nice either."

I loosen my grip on my mug and place it on the table. Although Danny looks troubled, like he did as a kid when he was trying to figure out how to repair a crab pot, I am filled with relief.

"Well, maybe it was still an accidental drowning. I mean, what the hell does Jacob know about autopsies? Half his brain cells are dead from all his pot smoking."

Danny laughs.

"And if the M.E. rules the death as a homicide, then you have a number one suspect. Sounds like Bobby bit off more than he could chew, and this time it was with the wrong person. To me, it sounds like a winner either way."

Danny looks at me and wrinkles his brow. "That's a funny way to put it. I don't see any winners here."

I quickly recover. "What I mean is, from a cop's perspective, you're good to go either way. Of course, Bobby is the real victim here. We should never forget he's the one who lost his life."

Danny watches me. He knows I'm being sarcastic but doesn't want to get into it with me.

"Yeah, well. Maybe you're right. Either way, the case will get solved," he says.

"Damn skippy, Officer Danny," I respond.

Danny stands up and presses his hands down the front of his jeans.

"Okay, Clara. I gotta be going. Nice talking to you." He seems to be waiting for me to stand but then realizes I'm staying put. He leans over to give me an awkward hug, then laughs. "You're always such a good time, Clara."

The edges of my lips attempt to smile, but instead, they hold fast in a straight line. Danny shakes his head and walks off down the road. He waves at Barbara, who is walking in the opposite direction.

I wave to Barbara but stand up as if I'm going inside the house. I don't feel much like conversation today. I feel like I've been knocked off the world. I know who Sherwood "Woody" Winters is; he's sleeping with one of my clients.

# CHAPTER 12

The next morning, I feel like I haven't slept at all when I wake up. The remnants of my anxiety dream make me feel edgy. I dreamed I was in a large hotel packed with people. I pressed the elevator button, but when the doors opened, there were too many people for me to get on. The doors closed, and the next one came, filled. And the next one. And the next. I tried to use my cellphone to dial my mother, but my fingers kept hitting the wrong buttons. I became frantic and asked someone to help me, but the person didn't understand me. My words felt garbled. I desperately needed to contact my mother. I felt sure she would know what to do, but the elevator doors clacked open and shut, open and shut, while all of the riders looked at me with blank faces. I awoke, and as soon as I opened my eyes, tears from dream-crying dripped down my face.

I hate it when days start this way. There's no going back to sleep now to replace it with a nicer dream. Addie will be here soon to start her first official workday; Lala is the first appointment this morning. At least I know I'll get to have a breakfast of sorts.

Addie arrives promptly at 8:30 a.m., plenty of time before the first appointment at nine. I'm at my desk reading notes from my last session with Lala. I ask Addie if she'd like coffee. She says yes, but motions for me to stay seated and goes to the kitchen. She comes back with a steaming cup of coffee.

Addie sits on the love seat and waits for me to finish reading.

"Hey, good morning. Ready for your first workday?" My voice sounds artificially chipper.

"Absolutely. Who's the first appointment?" she asks.

I click out of my notes and bring up the schedule for today. "Up first is Lala Chance. You're going to love her. She is a master dessert-maker. She'll bring something special for us, knowing that she's meeting you."

As if on cue, Lala knocks once on the glass door and walks in, panting. "Hellooooo … hellooooo … and good morning!"

Addie and I stand up and smile.

"I have something for my most favorite therapist in the world." Lala halts when she sees Addie. More subdued, she says, "Oh, hello," and holds out one hand; the other is balancing a big pink cake box.

Addie takes her hand and covers it with her other to give Lala a warm handshake, careful not to disrupt Lala's balance. "Hi. My name is Addie. You must be Lala."

A broad smile erupts on Lala's face. "Why, yes, I am, the one and only. Clara told me she was looking for a new assistant. I guess you're the lucky winner! Welcome!"

I slide across the room to get the cake box, which looks like it's going to topple. I remember how excited Lala gets when she meets someone new. "What have you brought us here?"

Lala swats my arm and opens the lid. Addie and I peer over its edges and are greeted by six colorful rings of homemade donuts. As if mesmerized, both Addie and I murmur sounds of delight. Lala grabs the box from my arm and sets it on the coffee table.

"Go ahead, pick one."

I step back to let Addie pick one first. The six donuts are frosted with pastel-colored icing. Lala had put special toppings on each. Addie reaches for a green-glazed one with purple candies on top and takes a large bite.

"Mmmm, this one is fantastic, Lala. What is it?"

Lala smiles and says, "Mint and lavender. I made the glaze with fresh mint leaves pulverized and mixed with powdered sugar, vanilla bean, and just a little milk. The lavender topping is mottled with blueberries to give it that vibrant color. It's mixed with brown sugar and oats to make a crumble." She looks at me and shrugs. "I've been experimenting with new flavors."

I make a show of closing my eyes and grabbing the first one I touch. I pull out a glazed donut topped with maple icing and bacon pieces. I push it in my mouth. "Oh, Lala, this one is fabulous."

Lala curtsies and pulls out a glazed donut that looks like nine small balls attached to each other formed into a ring. "This one is a mochi donut. I mix fresh strawberries in the dough. Then for the glaze, I incorporate white chocolate pieces. This is my newest creation."

We stand in the living room for a moment while we finish our donuts and lick our fingers. "That was delicious, Lala. Thank you," I say. "Are you ready to start?"

Lala nods and falls on the love seat, causing the undercarriage to strain dangerously. "Addie will be sitting in the alcove right over there." I point to a small area between the kitchen and living room where we're sitting. "She will be in that room working on the paperwork. She'll also monitor the session and take notes for me."

Lala's lips curl downward and begin to tremble. She looks like she's ready to cry.

"Do you remember we talked about this before?"

Lala grabs three tissues from the nearby Kleenex box and wipes her nose. "Of course. I'm totally fine with Addie taking notes and doing work over there. I'm not worried about that at all. It's just …." Her eyes begin to tear up. "It's just that it was a hard week last week."

I cut my eyes to Addie, who moves quietly to her desk in the alcove. I sit down in the armchair. "Okay, let's talk about it."

Tears fall freely down her cheeks. She sniffs and wipes her nose. She looks toward the floor and says, "It feels like everything is crashing down on me. It started when his wife caught us in his shed right before he went missing."

"In his shed?" I ask. I knew Bobby'd been having an extramarital affair with Lala, but I didn't realize Alice had known. It's strange how some secrets are kept hidden away while others become fodder for the neighborhood gossip mill.

"Yeah, Bobby called me down to his house for, you know, a quickie. I told him he was crazy because his wife was still home. He said not to worry about her, that he knew how to take care of things with her. So, I say, 'Okay, I'll walk down now.' When I get to the house, I walk between two houses to the back of his lot. I see the shed door open. So, I walk through, and there he is, with his arm against his tool bench. His drawers are down around his ankles, and I see he's been working himself while waiting on me. I'm nervous about doing this here, and it must've shown on my face. He gets mad and says, 'Get your lard-ass over here and take care of me before you make me do something I don't want to do.'"

"What did he mean by 'don't make me do something I don't want to do,' Lala?"

"I know how his punishments work. A pinch here, a punch there. Bruises, but in places where I can cover them up." Lala covers her face and sobs.

I give her a couple of minutes to vent her pent-up pain. This is the same old pattern. She finds abusive men who exploit her sexually. She's looking for someone to love her, but they're only interested in getting their rocks off. In her guilt and shame, she overeats. A lot. That brings her even more shame and guilt. It's a difficult cycle to break.

"So what happens next?"

"Well, I 'take care of him.'" Her sarcasm thickens, and spittle flies out of her mouth. "Oh, I take care of him. This time when he finishes, he slaps me on my butt and tells me to roll on out of there. Then he stops talking in mid-sentence and looks all wild-eyed. At first, I wonder if he's having a stroke, but then I see he's looking at someone behind me. I spin around, and who should be standing there but his wife. She's holding some sort of meat cleaver and slapping the handle on her palm."

I take in a ragged breath. "Oh, no," I whisper. "What happened then? What did Alice do?"

"She looked at him, then me, then at him again and slapped the flat edge of the knife blade against the side of the shed. She said, 'You'll get yours, Bobby Ward. Just you wait and see.'"

I can't hide the shock on my face. I take a second to regroup and fix my expression so I don't look so stunned. I clear my throat. "And then?"

Lala shrugs. "She just turns around and leaves. Walks right out of the shed and back into the house. Bobby laughs, then coughs that nasty phlegm from smoking so much. He tells me to 'get on outta here,' but I've known Bobby a long time. He's shaken, I can tell. I'm pretty sure something happened between them that I'm not privy to. So, I just leave."

"When was that?" I ask, afraid of what she'll say.

"Tuesday. It was last Tuesday morning."

"Then what happened? Did you see Bobby after that?" I ask.

"No, that's what's got me so upset. Bobby gets what he wants from me that morning, and then, poof! He's gone again. It's like he doesn't really care about me. I know it sounds stupid, but I thought he was going to leave Alice and find a new life with me."

"But how, Lala? How could that happen? What made you think he would to start a new life with you?"

Lala sighs as if I don't understand. "Clara, he told me he was leaving Alice. He says her behavior was getting 'crazier by the day,' is how he described it. But then …"

I sit and wait.

"Then," she resumes, "I go peek in his window on Wednesday morning. He and Alice are hugging each other real tight. Bobby has his eyes closed and his nose buried in her neck. He's swaying with her in the kitchen. But here's the strange thing. When I rip my eyes from Bobby's face, I look at Alice. She's staring right at me. I tear out of there, and that's the last I've heard from him."

Lala looks up at me. "Then, I hear he showed up after all."

"Oh?" I ask.

"Yeah, and you know it darned well, Clara. Everybody knows. Bobby went ahead and drowned himself, getting drunk and falling off that boat of his."

A distant alarm rings from the alcove. It's time to end the session.

"Okay, Lala. We have to stop now, but let's pick up again next time."

Lala stands and folds me into a giant bear hug. She whispers in my hair, "I know you feel it, too. I know you cared for Bobby in your own way."

If she only knew.

She lets go of me and strides across the room. Before she closes the French doors, she yells, "See ya, Addie. See y'all next time."

# CHAPTER 13

After the doors close, Addie comes out of the alcove. Wide-eyed, she crosses the room, opens the glass doors, and gestures for me to sit outside. I stand and follow her, grateful for her direction. I'm not sure what I'm feeling, but I'm sure my face registers shock and puzzlement.

"Hey, that was a wild session, eh?" she asks.

I shake my head. I'm not sure what to feel at the moment. We both look across the bay. The wind carries a slight aroma of decay. It smells like a dead fish or something washed ashore. The birds chirp in the nearby oak trees. A cardinal sits on a bird feeder near the tree in my yard. Its beak plucks at the suet bar. The bird is male, with a bright red rooster-plume and a black mask around its eyes. It sits there looking directly at me. Mom always told me cardinals were messengers from the spirit world. They're supposed to carry messages from those who've died. The bird's calm presence on the feeder makes me think about Bobby. This is a bad path to go down, like a domino effect. Because then I think about George, then my father. Before I realize it, my eyes fill with tears. Addie's hand on my knee brings me back to the present.

"Hey, what's going on?" she asks in a soft voice.

I shrug and exhale. "Oh, I don't know. Life can be so crappy sometimes, so perplexing. One minute a person is here, the next minute, they're not. All of the little, tiny pieces in this puzzle of life. You never know for sure how each connects to the next. It's all overwhelming and mysterious sometimes."

"Yes, it definitely can be. I take it you were not expecting today's session with Lala to go the way it did?"

"Yeah, I guess you could say that."

"Why? What surprised you?"

"For one, I had no idea she was still dreaming about a new life with Bobby. I mean, I knew they had a sexual relationship. Jeez, Bobby's had sex with too many women to count. I thought we'd reached a breakthrough, though. We developed a plan for her to extricate herself from that unhealthy relationship. Apparently, I was under a different assumption."

"I can understand how that might take you off guard. I'd feel the same way. It's easy to see, though, that Lala has low self-esteem. She put up with Bobby's abuse for a long time. And she goes back for more? I wonder if there was a reason she did that. I mean, did something trigger her and make her go back for more abuse?"

I turn toward Addie. I'm surprised, pleasantly so. "Addie, you bring up a good point. I didn't ask about triggers or how she was feeling beforehand. I just kept asking for the play-by-play after the fact. Understanding the motivation underlying her behavior will give me a good measure of where we need to move next in our therapy session."

I'm pleased. Addie's already attuning herself to the nuances of the clients. And me. She is going to be a wonderful addition to the practice. Not only that, but she'll also be a good support for me as well. Maybe I don't need to go through life so alone all the time.

"Addie, thank you. Thank you for being so supportive."

She smiles. "Any time. Hey, I looked at the schedule, and I see this afternoon is blocked out. No more clients today?"

I shake my head. "No. I'm going to a workshop about trauma. It's part of the trauma series workshops offered by the National Association of Social Workers. I registered for it a while ago. Hey, you want to join me? You need the continuing education credits to maintain your license, too."

"Do you think they'd let me in without registering?"

"Yes, I think so. And I'll pay for your registration. Consider it part of the job."

"Aw, thanks. I appreciate that." Her eyes spot something in the distance.

I turn and see Barbara walking her dog. I groan. Addie cocks her head and looks at me.

"It's Barbara, my nosy neighbor. She'll stop by, don't you worry."

As if on cue, Barbara and her dog shuffle across the lawn and up to the patio.

"Clara," she says.

"Barbara."

"Who's this?" She sounds like an owl as she extends her hand.

"This is my new assistant, Ms. Addison Marsh."

Addie reaches out to shake her hand.

"Oh, what a pleasure to meet you, dear," Barbara croons. It takes all I can muster to not roll my eyes. "Tell me, who is Miss Addison Marsh?"

Addie smiles. "Call me, Addie. I live in Woodland Beach and have my whole life. I just graduated from social work school. I'm working with Clara as her assistant. Not much to tell, really."

Am I seeing things, or did Addie just bat her eyelashes at Barbara? I want to bust out laughing but know it would not bode well for me if Barbara thought we were making fun of her.

"Oh, I see. Woodland Beach, huh? Are you related to Julie and Jason Marsh?" she bats her own eyelashes.

Addie looks at the ground. "Um, yes. They were my parents."

Barbara says, "I remember them well." She lets the sentence linger, so she can sink in the hook. "It seems to me your father had a bit of a drinking problem, didn't he?"

Addie's face flushes, but she raises her head and looks directly into Barbara's eyes. "Oh? Did he? And how would you know that?"

"Well, I wouldn't know specifically, of course, but I know quite a few of the old-timers who go to the pub. It seems your dad spent a lot of time there, huh?"

"That could be. It was right down the street, but I'm sure you know that already," Addie says.

"Indeed, I did. It was such a tragedy, your parents dying while you were so young. Well, you weren't a child, I know, but still. It's a harsh world to navigate on your own, wouldn't you say?"

When Addie doesn't respond, Barbara continues, "I'm wondering, did the police ever find that the crash was related to alcohol? Of course, nothing was printed in the *Capital Gazette,* but I often wondered, seeing as how your dad did enjoy his libations."

To Addie's credit, she holds her poker face. "He did indeed. The police and medical examiner released the autopsy report only to the family. I asked the editor not to print any additional information, good or bad, because of its potential effects on me, the orphan." Addie throws a dart right back and then holds a fierce stare.

Barbara isn't finished. "Yes, this small community can be so incestuous, can't it?" she says, emphasizing the 'cesssss' to make it sound like she was a poisonous snake. There is something in the way Barbara holds her body. She stands more upright and raises her chin as if she were a queen looking down upon her subjects. "But still, I am curious. Was your father drunk when he crashed the car into the telephone pole on Central Avenue?" She lets down her mask of benevolence.

Addie stands and looks her square in the face. "Now that you mention it, the answer to your question is, yes, he was impaired."

Barbara puffs up with pride at her acuity.

Addie continues, "You see, as he was driving home after an oncology appointment with my mother. Oh, she had stage four uterine cancer, but I'm sure you know. They were upset and surprised, as you can imagine. The stress of the diagnosis and the uncertainty of all of our lives caused him to take his eyes off the road momentarily. When he looked back, there was a car coming head-on in his lane, a teenage driver. Dad swerved to miss the kid, but he hit the pole instead. Head-on collision with the pole; they died instantly. At least, that's what the police told me."

Barbara looks like a fish, opening and closing her mouth without words.

Addie keeps going. "And just to satiate your curiosity, I asked the *Gazette* not to publish anything, not only because of the poor orphan left behind," Addie makes an exaggerated sad face, "but also to protect the kid's name. He was a new driver, learning how to use a stick shift. He had trouble with the one-handed steering and one-handed gear shifting. What's done was done. Mom and Dad weren't coming back."

Barbara has the good grace to look down, ashamed. I didn't even know the whole story, and Addie just laid it out there, the bad and the ugly. After what seems an eternity, Barbara gathers her wits and prepares to leave.

"Oh, well, so nice to finally meet you, Addie. I know you will learn so many new things about the people around here." Barbara winks and walks off with her dog.

Addie sits back down, and we sit silently for a good five minutes. Then I look at her and say, "Wow, Addie."

Addie looks back at me and wipes a tear off her cheek.

"I didn't know all of that, and apparently Barbara didn't, either. That must have been terrible for you. Why did you tell her all of your personal stuff?"

"Because," her voice is strong, "there's only one way to deal with difficult truths. You deal with them head-on. Otherwise, the lies take on a life of their own and drown you. Just snuff every last good thing out of you."

I nod, well aware she'll think I'm agreeing with her. That's not what I'm thinking, though. I think Addie Marsh will either be my savior or at the crux of my implosion. Her strength both terrifies and awes me. This woman, who is half my age, is standing on her own two feet and fighting as if today will be her last. I hope when the time comes, she'll stand by me, too.

I stand and smile. "Lunch? Then the workshop?"

She grins. "But of course, Madame. Adam's Ribs would be divine."

## CHAPTER 14

After the workshop, Addie and I head back to my house for a glass of wine and to watch the colors dance across the bay's surface. It feels good to have her here. She will be a great help with my therapy practice, yes, but there's more there. I can't remember the last time I had a friend, much less a female one. I take a sip of wine as a faint smile plays on my lips.

Addie asks, "What are you thinking? You're smiling. I want in on the secret."

I turn to her and hesitate. I'm not sure I want to reveal my vulnerability, the excitement I feel at the prospect of having a real and true friend. "Oh, I'm just thinking about how we make a good team."

Addie sips her wine. "Yeah, I think so, too. It's so hard to find good people you can trust. Like your neighbor, Barbara, it seems like a lot of people have these underlying agendas. They want to know your business or have you reveal some deep, dark secret. There are so many things I like about growing up, living, and working in a small community. The one thing I definitely don't care for is how personal and public information gets intermingled. There's always someone with a secret, always someone wanting to find it out."

I chuckle. "I understand what you mean, Addie. It's hard to heal from deep wounds when you're surrounded by people who know exactly when and where those wounds occurred in the first place."

"But you moved away for a time, right? When you got married?"

Oh, no. Is she going down this path? "Yeah. George got a job as a lawyer in a high-profile Annapolis law firm. We moved into a beautiful home overlooking the Severn River. I worked for a mental health agency, which obviously didn't pay enough to afford that standard of living. George's salary did, though. It was my one experience of living the lifestyle of the rich and famous," I say, imitating Robin Leach.

"Then he died?"

"Yep, and I moved back here to my mother's house. Hey, you want a refill on the wine?" I stand and head into the house.

"Sure," Addie says.

I return with the rest of the bottle and fill our glasses. Just as Addie opens her mouth to continue the conversation, Danny hoots from the road. He strolls toward us.

Both Addie and I smile at the same time. "Hey, there, Danny," says Addie.

"Hey, ladies," Danny smiles, bounces down then up from a chair. "I'm going to get myself a wine glass, too." He returns a minute later with a glass in his hand. He reaches for the bottle and pours.

"What's up, Danny? Are you off tonight?" I ask, peering at his casual clothing.

"Yeah, I'm off tonight, but really, how 'off' can a police officer be when we're investigating a case?"

I stiffen. "Oh? What kind of case?" I ask, not convinced I want to know the answer.

"Well, here's the thing. The M.E. called the chief early this morning. You do know that the M.E. and Chief are childhood friends, right?"

"Of course, isn't that always the case?" I say, sarcasm permeating my tone.

"Yeah, well, it seems Jacob was right about Bobby's death. It doesn't seem like it was a drowning. The M.E. told the chief he's going to rule it a homicide."

I gulp some wine before speaking. "A homicide? Oh, come on, you know it was probably a drowning-while-drunk accident. There's a lot of them out on the Chesapeake Bay."

"I know, I know. I thought so, too, but the M.E. says his lungs weren't filled with the amount of water you'd expect in a drowning. He said it appears the body had been in the water since Wednesday, but when he died, he's not so sure. He guesses maybe Tuesday afternoon or evening or possibly right before he took his deep dive in the bay."

I don't know what to say next, so I sit quietly, willing the trembling in my legs to stop. My hands are shaking, so I put my wine glass back on the table. I glance at Addie, who is staring right at me.

Addie says, "Well, it's good the M.E. is putting the story together. How do you fit in with the case? Are you investigating it yourself?"

Danny rakes his fingers through his hair. "Yeah, I'm working the case. Chief says I know more about the dynamics of players than just about anyone."

"What does that mean?" I ask.

"It just means that if there was anyone who wanted to do Bobby harm, I'd likely know who had a grudge, that's all."

"You mean, you'd know the long list of people who had grudges," I say.

"Right, meaning just about everyone in Mystic Beach."

Addie says, "Tough job, Danny. Good luck with your investigation."

"Yeah, thanks, Addie. The preliminary autopsy report will be sent out soon. So, as of today, it's an open homicide case."

Danny sips his wine. I get the feeling he wants to say more, but he's procrastinating. I am definitely not going to be the one to prod the sleeping bear. If he has something to impart, he can say it or not; I don't care. The three of us look out over the water.

After a few minutes, Danny says, "It's so beautiful, the bay. On evenings like this, the water is still and calm. On days like Friday, it thrashes like it's possessed by a demon. It's hard to understand a thing that can be so polar opposite on any given day. With the volatile temperament and underlying, unpredictable danger, I'd say we have our very own Scylla and Charybdis, Chesapeake Bay style."

Addie's forehead crinkles, and I laugh. "Way to show off your Greek mythology class from high school, Danny."

All three of us laugh. It feels good to be with my oldest and newest friends, like we're a trio, like we'll always have each other's back. It feels natural to be myself with these two. Well, mostly myself. There are things Danny knows that I don't ever want Addie to know. I'd hate to do anything that might make her question our budding friendship.

Danny sighs. My little friendship bubble is straining to burst. I don't think I will like whatever he's going to say next. Danny has two tells. One is when he rakes his fingers through his hair. The other is when he huffs a deep sigh. When they both come at the same time, watch out; something big is about to emerge.

"So, eh, Clara. I have to get down to business and come up with a firm timeline now that we can estimate when he died and when he was dumped in the bay. So, a few days ago, you told me the last time you had seen Bobby was a week from last Friday at the pub. You were drinking ginger ale. Are you sure that was the last time you'd seen him?"

My heart rate vibrates the walls of my chest. I wonder if anyone can tell that I'm ready to explode. My palms are starting to sweat. I fix my face so I appear to be thinking. Danny knows something, but he's not going to tell me. He takes his job seriously, and he knows me well.

"Now, let me think. Yes, I was at the pub on that Friday. Yes, Bobby was there with his drinking buddies. But I think I ran into him again that following Tuesday morning, though, now that I think about it. I was going into the Royal Farms to get a cup of coffee. He was in there waiting for his breakfast sandwich. Yes, that's right."

Danny stares at me. "What did you talk about in the Royal Farms?"

I scratch my nose. "Nothing much, really. He said hello. I said hello back. He asked me what I had been up to. I told him not much. That was about it."

Danny lets the moment stretch. I hold my breath. Addie looks from me to Danny, then back at me again.

"So, for the record, the last time you saw Bobby Ward was at the

Royal Farms at the breakfast counter. What time was that?"

"I, uh … uh … let me think. It was about ten a.m."

"Kinda late for Bobby to have breakfast. Wouldn't he have already been out on his boat?" Danny asks.

"Well, yeah, I guess. I never really thought about it. I don't know, Danny. What do you want from me?" I snap.

After a few awkward minutes, Danny stands up and tries to act nonchalant, but I know him too well.

"Okey dokey, then. That about does it. I've got a Netflix movie I want to watch before I go to bed. I have to get the most out of my night off. G'night, you two."

He reaches over to give my shoulder a squeeze. Addie's eyes widen, but she does a good job of covering it up. Just as Danny's feet touch Shore Drive, he turns and calls to me.

"Oh, by the way, I'll be by tomorrow morning to talk about this more."

# CHAPTER 15

I lay in bed watching the digital numbers on my alarm clock make their rounds. By 6:00 a.m., I'm tired of laying here. Although Addie won't be here for another couple of hours, I can't go back to sleep. I sit up and see half my blankets pooled on the floor. My bed looks like a tornado blew in. The beginnings of dawn bleed through my blinds. I get out of bed wander towards the kitchen for my vanilla latte, the one sure thing I can control.

By 6:15 a.m., I'm sitting on the patio, watching the beautiful colors across the horizon. There's no better place in the world than Mystic Beach. Propping my feet on the outdoor patio table, I take a deep breath. I know my sleepless night was because of Danny's late visit yesterday. I didn't like his tone and the looks he gave me, in front of Addie no less. I'm going to have to deal with him. There's no way around him, and he knows me better than anyone, even my own mother.

At 6:45 a.m., when I'm on my second cup of coffee, here comes the devil.

"Now, why did I have a feeling you'd be here early, Danny? Is it my irresistible nature?"

Danny laughs and sits down. I look at his clothing; apparently, he's not on duty at the moment.

"So, to what do I owe the pleasure of this visit?"

Danny's frowns as he drags his fingers through his thick, dark hair. "Okay, Clara, here's the deal. We know Bobby didn't drown. His lungs weren't filled with water. The M.E. puts the time frame of death probably sometime on Wednesday, most likely early Wednesday morning following the tides."

I interject. "But the question is, how do you know he was murdered? Okay, maybe he didn't drown, but that doesn't mean he was murdered."

"Okay, so what are you thinking?"

"Maybe he was out on the boat and decided he'd had enough. I mean, you know, he wasn't in the best health. For one, he drank way too much. He was overweight. He had a long list of people who hated his guts. Maybe he just wanted it to end."

Danny shakes his head. "Come on, Clara. You know Bobby as well as I do. He was meaner than a rabid dog, but he was also arrogant as all get out. He'd never kill himself. Think about it. Did Bobby ever give you any indication he was fed up, even when he had gotten himself in a pickle?"

Danny leans forward and stares right into my eyes. As much as I know him, he knows me even better. He knows very well that I know Bobby has been in some horrible situations before and never showed one ounce of ending his own life. If anything, he'd threatened all manner of people to take their lives. Danny's right, and he knows I know it.

"You're right. Okay, then tell me. What do you think?"

He leans back. "I think someone killed him. He wasn't shot or strangled or even beaten."

"What about the discoloration on his skin?"

Danny pauses, his eyes snap towards me. "Umm, how do you know what his skin looked like?"

A nervous laugh escapes me. "Oh, well, come on. There was news around the neighborhood. Plus, we've had all sorts of dead things wash up on the shore. Remember the dead dolphin that washed up not too long ago? The dolphin's coloring had changed from a sleek gray and white body to a reddish-orange blotchy discoloring. I'm assuming Bobby's body looked the same way."

"Okay, yeah. He was discolored, but according to the M.E., it's not unusual for bodies to have abrasions and cuts when they roll along the bottom or up against the rocks. The M.E. ruled out strangulation, gunshot, and drowning. He's running some tissue tests to see if there were drugs in his system. So, an overdose or a poisoning. That's what I'm thinking."

I'm considering all of the plausible possibilities. I could see an overdose. Everyone knows Bobby liked to do drugs, mostly prescription pills, and even some amphetamines to keep him awake during the heavy crabbing season.

"What about any of his drug-dealing associates?" I ask. "It's not out of the realm of possibilities that someone in his crew did him in, right?"

Danny turns the idea over in his mind. "True, true. That's a good point." He pulls a small notebook and pen from his back pocket and jots down a note.

Another thought pops into my mind. "And what about that guy? What's his name? The one who fought with Bobby about stealing his crabs?"

"Oh yeah, right. Sherman? Sher—"

"Sheriff ... wood? Woody."

"Yes, yes. That's right. Sherwood Woody Winters. Yeah, he was a mean mongrel from Deale Island, right?"

He finishes writing his note and looks at me. "And, uh, Clara, I'll need to know about your clients."

"My clients?"

"Yeah, I hear around the neighborhood that you see a few people who are also ... how should I put this ... 'known associates' of Bobby Ward."

I shake my head. "Oh, no, no, no, Danny. No way in hell I'm going to have even one minute of conversation with you about my clients."

"Come on, Clara. This is important. I'd rather not have to subpoena you to court or get the judge to sign a warrant to seize your records."

I can't believe Danny is going this route. He knows I can't say anything about my clients, not even their names.

"Uh, Danny, have you ever heard of therapist-client privilege? Like, it's a Maryland law? Ring any bells?" Now I'm just taunting him.

Frustration fills his face. "Suit yourself, Clara, but one way or another, I'll have to rule out your clients. It could be very embarrassing for them if I have to get a court order for their notes. Then everything will be opened up, and all their secrets will come out." He fixes a smug look on his face.

I respond with my own smug look. "We'll see if the judge will grant you those orders."

We're at a stalemate. I don't want to get something stuck in his craw and then he goes ahead and bulldozes my clients because he got into his feelings. Danny's inquiry isn't malicious. Unlike Bobby, he's not the revenge-seeking type, but I know not to underestimate him. When Danny gets something fixed in his mind, he's like a starving dog with a bone. He will not let go until his jaw is ripped right from his mouth.

I soften my tone. "Look, Danny. We're not at odds here. I want the murder to be solved as much as anyone around. I'll talk to my clients and suggest they contact you if they have any information. I'll ask them to sign a release of information form to share their details with you."

Danny's body loses its tension. "Okay, good. Thank you, Clara. I really appreciate any help you can give me."

I smile. "I've got you. You'll figure this out."

"Okay, gotta run. My shift starts soon."

As soon as Danny turns his back to me, the smile on my face drops into a grimace. This is not going to be easy, that's for sure. What Danny doesn't know is that each one of my clients has a motive for murdering Bobby. There's no way around it: Bobby Ward deserved to die a horrible death.

# CHAPTER 16

Addie arrives about a half hour after Danny left. I must have a scowl on my face because she asks me if I'm feeling okay. I tell her I am but don't want to talk about it. She nods and heads to the kitchen to get herself a cup of coffee. When she comes back, she tells me she's already organized the office files and cataloged spending accounts onto one spreadsheet. This is only her second day officially working, and she's already proven herself to be invaluable. I can't imagine how I actually got by without her.

Right on time, Alice Ward walks in for her first appointment. Addie had told me Alice had called to make an appointment yesterday. In truth, Alice had long wanted to get into therapy, but her life with Bobby at home was so chaotic that she kept putting it off. Now, with Bobby's absence in her life, I guess she's found the time. I am really happy to see her.

When she walks through the door, Alice steps into my open arms. We hug. When I pull back, I say, "I'm so glad you're here, finally." She smiles, and her eyes begin to tear.

I introduce her to Addie, who welcomes her with an embrace as warmly as I did. "I'm glad to meet you, Alice. I'm so sorry to hear about your husband."

Alice thanks Addie, who moves into the alcove with her computer set-up. Alice perches on the edge of the love seat.

"Oh, I don't know what I'm supposed to do, Clara." Her voice sounds strained.

"I know, I know. It's so hard to lose someone," I respond.

Alice chuckles and says, "I wasn't talking about Bobby. I meant I don't know what I'm supposed to do in a therapist's office. I've never seen one before. What do I do?"

We both laugh, and I explain she just needs to make herself comfortable and talk about whatever she wants. Alice settles into the love seat and looks out the glass doors toward the bay.

"Well, I guess it always does go back around to Bobby, doesn't it?" she starts. "I don't need to tell you much because you already know what kind of a jerk he was."

I wait for her to continue.

"I don't suspect that people know the most of it, though. Oh, I know some people thought I was weak for not leaving him the first time he bruised me up. But the ones who've lived here for generations, well, they'll have a different view of things. Our families had known one another for a great many years. Two long family lines of Chesapeake watermen. It was bound to happen that families married off their children as a way to merge the two enterprises. Bobby's father didn't gain much from me being a female and all, but he did increase his value because now the two families would work together catching blue crabs. That merger helped our families unite and, combined with both boat crews, we had ourselves a little fleet of crabbing deadrises.

"It didn't take long for Bobby to take a swing at me. I could never have left, though. First, it would have brought terrible shame on the family. Second, it would have left my family impoverished. Bobby's father wasn't obligated to split his share of the earnings. My father would have been shamed in the community. Wouldn't have been anybody who would have hired him. No, I had to figure out a different way."

Alice and I sit in silence to let her words sink in. "Bobby didn't know any better, anyway," she continues. "He was only acting like his own father behaved towards his mother. It was a different way during that time."

"How did you make it through all these years of marriage?" I ask, curious not only for her own experience but also for selfish reasons. I wanted to discover how to make a successful marriage work because I had clearly failed.

Alice smiles. "Oh, you kind of just figure it out as you go along. Things are different now. Women have choices and make their own money. If I were a young woman now, I would have surely left him. When you're trapped as I am—as I was—you just find ways of handling things yourself. This year would have been our fiftieth anniversary."

After a moment, she lets out a deep sigh. "I guess that's all over with now."

"How are you feeling, Alice? I mean, about Bobby's death?"

Alice's face shows her ambivalence. "Well ... I'm not sure I know exactly how I feel. I know part of me is happy that living with an angry, drunken, cruel man is now over. When Bobby disappeared, it wasn't like he hadn't done that many times before. Every time he'd go on a bender for a few days, it meant I also had a few days to myself. I had invited Brian over and made my special blueberry pancakes for him. We sat on the back porch and drank coffee. We talked like we used to, back when he was a teenager in high school. That boy ... oh, how I love that boy."

I nod. "Yes, he's pretty special, that's for sure."

Alice smiles at me, her face taking on a glow. She knows how much I love Brian, how much I understand him.

"But when Bobby was around, I'd never see Brian. You know, ever since he was in high school and his father caught him with another boy on the pier." She pauses, angry red rising to her cheeks. "I understand Bobby was probably shocked about it, but he didn't have to beat Brian so badly. And that poor boy, he got hit, too.

"It was after that I knew I'd have to protect Brian until he was old enough to move out on his own. I would do anything in my power to keep that boy safe. He's my world; you know that, Clara."

"Yes, I do. I feel protective of him as well."

"I know you do, sweetie. It takes a village and all that. Anyway, if I am going to be completely honest with you, I have to tell you I'm more relieved than anything now that Bobby is gone. I don't have to worry about me or Brian getting hurt. We can just go on and live our lives without having to watch our backs."

I know exactly what Alice is saying because I feel the same way. I no longer have to wonder when Bobby is going to expose my secrets if I didn't do what he wanted me to do. I am finally free, and I imagine both Alice and Brian feel the same way as I do.

As the session ends, Alice stands and embraces me. "You were always a good girl, Clara. I know that."

I pull back and laugh. "Oh, come on. I wasn't really a good girl. Everybody knows that."

She takes my face in her hands. "Oh, Clara, my girl. There's a big difference between a good girl who's had to live with bad experiences and a girl who hurts others intentionally, without remorse or concern. I stand by my word. You're a good girl."

Before I can stop myself, I feel tears drip down my cheeks. I flush with embarrassment. Alice turns toward the door, allowing me to save face. I walk her out to the patio and close the French doors behind me.

Alice glances back. "I didn't want to say anything with your new assistant and all, but I just want to assure you that whatever Bobby had on you, it's all laid to rest."

I know better than to deny this. I've always thought that Alice knows more than she lets on. She walks back towards her house. After she turns the corner, I realize I didn't ask her if she wanted to make another appointment.

# CHAPTER 17

After Alice leaves, I make myself a glass of iced tea and tell Addie I'm going out to the patio to reflect a little before the next appointment. I walk across my yard to the stairs overlooking the bay. I have long known of Alice's marital troubles with Bobby. Shoot, the whole neighborhood has followed their saga throughout the years. Alice never talked about her abuse directly, like she did today, but it was easy to infer when I'd see bruises around her collarbone or wrists when we chatted at the grocery store. Alice is close to Mom's age. I don't think my mother would have tolerated that kind of abuse, but you never know. One person's story is different from another's. There's a whole cycle to abuse which determines whether a person stays in a violent relationship or leaves it. It's complex and difficult and traumatic.

Alice's comment about a secret Bobby had on me has unnerved me, though. What does she think she knows about Bobby and me? I think it's highly unlikely he would have divulged information about our connection, but one can never tell with Bobby. He was a master of manipulation. If I shift to my clinical social work brain, I'd say he met all of the characteristics of a psychopath. He had no remorse for what he did to people. He disregarded people's privacy and would threaten to expose you if you didn't pay up or didn't do what he wanted. He lacked compassion and a true connection with anyone, including his own wife. That's what makes me feel so bad for Lala. I believe she genuinely had feelings for him, but, as she found out time and time again, he only wanted what he wanted and then had no use for her.

Then there's this whole homicide investigation with Danny. He wants me to disclose my client information, but I'm just not going to do that. Besides the fact it's illegal, I don't want him or any other officer to jump to conclusions. Sure, Alice had a reason to want Bobby dead, but so did a lot of people. Many in this neighborhood won't care a hoot that he's gone. Did Alice have the gumption to actually kill him, though?

For that matter, last week's session with Lala is equally disturbing. After all, he had used her up like an old paper towel and tossed her in the trash. Maybe Bobby had taken one too many jabs at her. Plus, the humiliation of finding Alice in his embrace after their rendezvous in the shed might have been enough to tip her over the edge. With Bobby gone, Lala would have a real opportunity for a better life. She was getting so much stronger. I could see that in her sessions with me. How many times had she told me she wanted just to get him out of the picture but didn't know how? Maybe she had come up with a plan of action.

The French doors open, and Addie steps out on the patio with her own glass of iced tea. I look at my watch and see it won't be long before the next appointment. I gesture for Addie to join me at the beach steps.

"So," Addie starts, "a tough session with Alice, huh?"

"Yeah. I don't know how she could put up with him all these years. You know, one time Bobby beat Alice so severely that she blacked out and awoke to find herself lying on the kitchen floor in a puddle of blood. Alice texted Mom and asked if she would take her to the Anne Arundel Medical Center emergency room. Of course, Mom took her to the hospital. She never told me what they discussed, if they discussed anything." I shake my head in disbelief.

"That sounds like a horrible way to live," Addie says.

"When I was a child, we could hear yelling and banging almost every week at our house."

"Jeez, that would have to have been loud to travel the length of a couple of blocks."

"Right? When Alice would finally come outside, she held her chin high. We knew just by how she looked that an inquiry into what happened would not fare well. Even Barbara, if you can imagine, wouldn't dare ask Alice about anything. We all just pretended it wasn't our business and left it alone. Today was the first time Alice has actually said anything to me about it. Somehow, her disclosure made the magnitude of her suffering real."

Addie pauses for a few moments, then whispers, "Are you okay?"

"Yeah." I sigh. "I'm okay. I just needed a few minutes to decompress." I decide I'm going to make myself vulnerable with Addie, to make an attempt at a real friendship. "Danny stopped by this morning."

"Ooooohhh, a morning date?" Addie teases.

I chuckle. "Uh, no. In fact, it was the opposite. He's investigating Bobby's case as a homicide."

Addie's eyes widen. "Oh really? Why do they think he was murdered?"

"Well, the M.E. ruled out a drowning because his lungs weren't filled with water. There were no gunshot or stab wounds. I guess they think he was poisoned or something, but they're awaiting the lab work for confirmation."

"Could he have killed himself, like an overdose or something?" Addie asks.

"Yeah, that's possible, though we all know Bobby was so arrogant, he'd kill someone else before he killed himself."

I watch as Addie's mind turns over the possibilities. "What about someone strangling him? Or maybe someone smothered him and then dumped him into the bay. It sounds so mafia-like, doesn't it? But then again, he was dealing drugs, right?"

"Yeah, he was the neighborhood drug dealer. He dealt with all sorts of unsavory characters. Maybe one of them did him in."

"How did you learn about Bobby's drug dealing?" she asks innocently enough.

Poor girl, there is so much she doesn't know about me. I decide to give her some personal information. I want to build a real friendship. I'm tired of putting on a false face and only letting conversations about myself go only so deep.

"Well, when I was in high school, I used to buy drugs off Bobby."

"Get out! Seriously?"

I feel the beginnings of embarrassment creep up my neck. "Yeah. I was struggling with my dad's suicide. I was so angry. I started to fail my classes. I hated my mother and blamed her for his death. I became unmanageable and unruly. I guess Bobby could see that. Hell, everyone could see it. And one day after school, Bobby approached me and opened his palm. There was a little white pill in the center. He told me it would calm me down and give me some control."

"And did it?"

"Did it what? Give me control? Oh yeah. I didn't know it at the time, but he was dealing in some heavy-duty benzos. He came along at the right time with the right drug, and wham! I ate them like peppermints."

"Oh, no. Is that what Alice meant by your secret being laid to rest?"

I make a gesture of a gun shooting. "Bull's eye. Things got pretty bad. Everyone knew I was addicted. Before I graduated from high school, Mom sent me to an inpatient rehab to recover."

"And did it work?"

"Yeah." I smile. "It really did work. The therapy groups helped me to express my anger and not keep it bottled up. I had a nice psychiatrist who helped me understand I was reacting to a trauma. A natural reaction to an abnormal situation."

Addie smiles. "That's so great, Clara. I'm glad you got things worked out, and look at you now. You're a healer yourself and such a role model to so many. You succeeded when you could have just drifted deeper and deeper into the hole. Brava!" She claps her hands.

I give her a lopsided grin. Yeah, I was the epitome of successful rehabilitation. Until I wasn't. Addie and I walk back to the house for the next appointment.

# CHAPTER 18

"Shelby Cross, so happy to see you today," I say.

Shelby is, by nature, a quiet and passive man. He's well-dressed in gray slacks and a pressed white dress shirt. His smile reveals brilliant, white teeth that contrast with his dark skin.

"How's Marshall?"

He walks into the room and lowers himself gently onto the love seat. "He's great. We just had our pool resurfaced and ordered new patio furniture. So, pool parties are back in session."

Shelby puts his left hand on his knee, and I notice a polished gold band on his ring finger. I look up at him and raise my eyebrows. Shelby's smile emerges as he lifts his hands to give me a better look. The gold band has a round sapphire inlaid in it. The ring is stunning. My lips curl into a smile.

"What's this?" I ask in a cheeky tone.

"This little old thing?" Shelby teases. "We did it, finally. Marshall proposed and presented me with this beautiful ring. How could I refuse?"

"Did all this happen while you were in Honolulu last month?"

Shelby Says, still smiling, "Yes. It was the perfect place for the perfect union. We got married on the beach as the sun set on the horizon. I couldn't have asked for a better setting to marry the love of my life. We had to come home early, though. We had some unfinished business to handle. We got back about a week ago."

"Oh, Shelby, I'm so happy for you both. Please tell him congratulations from me."

I look at Shelby. He seems so happy, but it isn't as if he and Marshall were the type of newlyweds who don't know one another. Marshall was already quite a bit older when he and Shelby got involved when Shelby was only seventeen. They've been together for over thirty years. I guess Marshall finally decided to marry Shelby now that he was about to enter his seventies. Despite the age difference, I knew Marshall took good care of Shelby and was rewarded with Shelby's loyalty and companionship.

"Is there more, Shelby?" I ask, curious about the look on his face.

"Well, yes, there is another reason to be happy."

I cock my head and wait for him to continue.

"I'll give you a hint. Ding dong, the king is dead! The king is dead! The king is dead!" he sings to the tune from *The Wizard of Oz*.

Oh, no. Another client with a motive and opportunity?

"Bobby Ward, dead-dang-dong!" Shelby shouts.

"Ehhh …yes, he's gone. You seem ecstatic about this, though."

Shelby's face becomes animated. "Well, yes, I'm happy. It couldn't have happened to a better guy."

I discern a strong sense of vindication is at the root of his elation. "I know Bobby caused you a lot of pain when you were younger—"

"Pain? Oh, sweetie, that's an understatement. He caused me irreparable and traumatic harm. It wasn't that he beat me to a pulp when he discovered his son and me on the pier while we were in high school. And it wasn't that he then turned his fists against Brian, his own son. The physical abuse of all that was the easiest part to heal from. Bruises and broken bones heal. It was the persistent taunting and scapegoating that made my teenage years a living hell," Shelby says as if he's winded.

"Yes, Bobby did terrible things to you, Shelby," I say softly.

Shelby starts to cry. I move over to the love seat and set my hand on his back as he expels years of anger, embarrassment, and torment through his tears. He grabs a tissue and blows his nose. He sobs heavily for a few minutes. I sit by him with my hand on his back, but otherwise motionless and silent. I hadn't realized Shelby was holding all of these memories after so many years. I knew Marshall had fulfilled some need inside him, almost a fatherly need. Now that I think about it, Shelby found Marshall shortly after that incident. Shelby didn't need to worry about his own parents; they were liberals who embraced their son's love for men. After they met Marshall, they weren't concerned about the age difference, either. Marshall is as gentle as Shelby is. They made a perfect match then, despite their liaisons while he was still technically a minor, and they make a perfect couple now. Their relationship makes me hopeful that true and authentic love is still possible, even for damaged people like me.

Shelby takes another tissue and wipes his eyes. "Sorry, my feelings just erupted. I feel so stupid crying over something that happened so long ago."

I move back to my chair. "No, no. Shelby, it's okay. Sometimes we don't realize how much we repress in order to function and act like normal human beings. It's a necessary coping mechanism. You're just feeling the release of something you've held onto for a long, long time. It's okay."

"But, you see, Bobby never stopped taunting me. It never ended. It's just that he was such a terrible person. He gave no thought at all about how his behavior hurt other people, even his own son. Bobby thought himself so self-important and felt he could do whatever he wanted without regard to anyone else. I despise that man. No, wait. I despised him. The asshole is now gone, gone, gone. No wonder the world seems like a new place.

"And his body rolling up onto the shore?" Shelby laughs with a touch of hysteria. "Imagine rolling that big body of his off his stupid crabbing boat? Imagine his bobbing for a minute or so and then glug-glug-glug down to the deep, dark bay? Imagine his fat, rubbery face dragging along the sandy bottom, rubbing across the sand and rocks and probably his own crab pots? It's a perfect ending to an imperfect man."

Am I really going to ask him this next question? I blink my eyes and open my mouth, but nothing comes out. Shelby looks at me with an amused expression.

"Uh, Shelby. Wow. That's a vivid picture you paint there."

He shrugs.

"So, uh … do you know all of that, like, from firsthand experience?'

"Clara, are you asking me if I killed him?" A smile plays on his face.

I feel like a deer caught in the headlights. Maybe I should just let it lie. Maybe I don't need to discover more about this. What if he says something I can't unhear? I'm not sure I'm required to report a homicide once it's been committed. I mean, I have a duty to warn if someone expresses homicidal thoughts toward another person, but in this case, the victim is already dead. Law or no law, there's no way I could report Shelby, anyway. He was as much a victim, if not more, than many other people around here.

Shelby watches my face as my mind performs mental gymnastics. He grins at me, and I know he'll wait me out. He learns my techniques quick; he learned this one a long time ago.

"Okay, so, Shelby, no," I stammer. "I am not asking you if you killed him. I'm not going to ask you, either. I'm under no obligation to inquire or report or even know. I am definitely not asking you if you killed him."

Shelby examines his fingers and appears to scrape something from underneath his nails. His eyes meet mine, and although there is a faint smile on his lips, his eyes show great sadness. I understand that kind of sadness, I absolutely do.

"Well, I'm glad you're not asking, Clara. I'm glad you don't feel the need to know, because whoever did this to Bobby, Clara, whoever did this did many people a great favor. You know that as well as I."

There was never a truer sentence than that one. I'm glad I didn't ask him. I'm glad he didn't offer an answer. Some things are better left unknown, and some things can't be unknown once you know them.

# CHAPTER 19

Addie and I sit on the patio at the end of the day. Tonight, we're sharing a pitcher of red sangria with oranges and apples floating on the surface. I feel over-exhausted, as if I spent the day running a treadmill without stopping for water. We're silent as we watch the seabirds riding the evening breeze.

I loll my head to the right and say, "Tomorrow morning, I'm going to go visit my mother at Sunview." Before I can stop myself, I add, "Do you want to come with me?"

Addie looks over and smiles. It feels good to have a friend.

The following day, Addie meets me at my house so we can ride to the assisted living place together. I push the button on my VW Beetle so the top goes down. The sunshine is strong, and, for a pleasant change, the humidity is low. I drive us off the peninsula on the narrow two-lane road that leads out of the community. The trees are flush with deep green leaves, the color of July. Ten minutes later, we're parking in front of Sunview.

Addie and I enter the front doors and I punch in my phone number to identify myself as a visitor. The young woman at the front desk wishes us a nice visit. At the elevator, Edward rolls past, heading to the dining area. He fist-bumps me and continues without speaking.

The elevator doors open on the third floor. Immediately, we hear loud yelling.

"Get your hands off me. I don't know who you are. Somebody, call the police!" the resident shouts.

We hear the soft, reassuring voice of a staff member helping to calm down Mrs. Rodriquez. As Addie and I pass the room, we see an upturned food tray on the carpet. The staff member isn't at all fazed. She sits in a chair next to Mrs. Rodriquez and talks quietly to her.

As we approach my mother's room, we see the door is open. I wave Addie to follow me in. My mom, Emma, and Jane are sitting around a table playing cards. No, wait. They're not playing cards; Mom is giving a tarot reading to her friends. As I walk into the room, my mother flips over the card representing the future. It's an Ace of Cups. Mom and I sign at the same time, "There's a new love in the near future." Mom sees me sign and starts to laugh. Jane turns around to see who she's smiling at and shines one of her own.

"Hi, Emma. Hi, Jane," I sign.

"Hi, sweet girl," Emma signs. "Who's that with you?"

Before I can respond, Addie lifts her hand and fingerspells, "A-d-d-i-e, my name," as she points to herself. Her signs are not as fluent as my mother's and her friends, but I can see by their expressions they're impressed.

My mother stands and puts her hands on Addie's shoulders. "I know you," she signs. "You look like your parents."

Of course, Mom knows her. I forgot that our families have known each other for a long time. My mother's eyes tear as she hugs Addie in a tight embrace.

"I'm so glad to see you. Are you and Clara friends?"

Addie bobs her fist up and down. "Yes, we're friends. I work for her, too. I'm her a-s-s-i-s-t-a-n-t."

Mom shows her the sign for assistant, and Addie repeats it.

"Good, good." Mom shoos away Emma and Jane, telling them she will catch up with them at lunch. The two women smile and walk across the hall to Jane's room. Addie and I take a seat on Mom's love seat.

"What's all this?" I ask as Mom scoops up the tarot deck.

"Oh, Jane keeps wondering if there will be a new lover in her life."

"And she picked the Ace of Cups," I sign. Mom and I nod knowingly. "Well, good for her. She needs something to keep life exciting."

Mom looks from me to Addie. "What's up with you two?"

I sign "nothing," at the same time Addie signs the word, "killed."

Oh, boy. Mom is not going to let this slide, even though Addie slaps her hands down on her knees.

Mom raises her eyebrows in mock exaggeration. "Murder?" She looks at me.

I sigh. "Yes, Danny stopped by and told me they're investigating Bobby's death as a murder," I sign. "They say he didn't have water in his lungs. So, the M.E. ruled out a drowning." I shrug, hoping that will nip the conversation in the bud. I should know better.

Mom rubs the palms of her hands together as if she's trying to get warm. "Ooooooooooh, I love a murder mystery. Who do you think killed him?"

The glint in her eyes is creeping me out. I wave her off. Then she signs to Addie, "Who do you think?"

Addie rubs her chin like some sort of detective. She fingerspells, "W-o-o-d-y?"

I can see Mom trying to figure out who Woody is. Addie signs slowly, "His name is Sherwood Winters from Deale Island. He and Bobby got into a fight at the pub. Bobby threatened to hurt Woody. So, that's where I'll place my money."

Mom bobs her head like she's putting that file into her memory. She points at me. "Who do you think?"

"Mom, I don't know. This isn't right, just picking out people randomly, wondering if they are killers."

Mom swats at me. She pulls out her tarot deck and shoves them at me. She gestures to pick one. I shake my head. She pushes them farther toward me. I sigh and shake my head again, this time with an eye roll. She pivots and turns to Addie. I try to interrupt, but Addie has her hand positioned and is deciding which one to pick.

I whisper, "Don't, Addie, don't."

My mom uses her voice and yells. She flicks her fingers at me angrily. "Sign! Don't talk. Sign!"

I feel bad. I know I shouldn't ever speak without signing in her presence. I learned that lesson as a young child. It's disrespectful, but I'm so darn afraid Addie will get caught up in something she doesn't understand. And I can't hardly just blurt it out, especially not here.

Addie's finger rests on a card near the middle. Mom pulls it out, flips it over, and lays it on the table, then indicates for her to draw two more.

Three cards: the Ten of Swords, the Knight of Swords, and the Wheel of Fortune. Mom looks at us, her eyes intense. She hums to herself and closes her eyes. Addie looks over at me, wondering what she's doing. I just tip my head in Mom's direction. Addie will find out soon enough.

Mom lifts her hands and signs slowly so Addie can follow. "The Ten of Swords shows us a finality, an ending of something. You can see from the picture of the person lying face down and the ten swords stabbed into the back, and blood pooling around. This represents a tragic loss, yes, but more importantly, a closure to a situation."

Addie tries to interrupt, but Mom points to the cards and continues. "The Knight of Swords is a restless, anxious young man. He is the restless mind that storms and searches for a target. He feels slighted and is hostile, but he's on the move. He may be on a path of taking care of an offender himself. He doesn't think things through but rather exacts punishment swiftly.

"And now, the Wheel of Fortune. What a roller coaster ride those two are on," Mom signs and points to the man and woman behind the large sailing wheel. "This card means change, a series of events going up and down endlessly. These changes, though, free us from the past. This is Life's lesson: fundamental change is imminent. We cannot avoid change. Embrace the lesson, and you can receive many benefits."

Mom grins at us as we sit there, stunned. Addie's mouth hangs open. I cock my head and look at my mother with utter love. My mother, who is a little on the odd side, but has good intentions, is the safety I will always go to. I can see Addie trying to process whether this is all a big game or whether there was something to it. If only she knew. My mother, her mother, and her grandmother, as far back as I can remember, always had some sort of mystical abilities. I never talk about it with anyone because, let's face it, who would believe me? There are those who have been long-time friends of Mom's. They came to the house, and now they come to Sunview just for one of her readings.

Addie signs, "But what does it mean? What?"

Mom looks at me and smiles. I turn to Addie and sign and speak, "It means that Bobby was murdered by someone who has long held a grudge against him. It could be a man or a woman, but the person had reason. It's hard to say whether this is an up event, like the ending of a long struggle or the culmination of a series of lessons, or a down event, like something more tumultuous is ahead. Likely it means both simultaneously. Whatever happens next is going to be a wild ride."

Mom leans over and puts her hand on mine. We both look at Addie, who is staring at us. What Addie and Mom don't realize is that there are a ton of knights roaming around who would have sliced Bobby's throat in a minute. Even me.

# CHAPTER 20

When Addie and I return to my house, she pulls up the schedule on her computer. She comes out of her alcove and says, "You have a—"

"Johnston Burr," I snap.

"Uh, right. Johnston Burr, but you received an email from the jail on Jennifer Road, someone named Greg Overly, a parole officer or something? Here, I printed out the paperwork."

I glance through the court order and the form I am to complete for Mr. Overly after each session. I'm familiar with the process, unfortunately. Johnston Burr was freed early from his five-year drug trafficking sentence in exchange for substance abuse treatment. If he misses even one of our appointments, he could go right back into the Jennifer Road facility.

There's a knock on the door, but it's not coming from the glass patio doors. Instead, the person is knocking on the door that faces the driveway around the other side of the house. I wiggle my eyebrows at Addie and walk to the front door. I pull open the heavy door as my eyes drift down to a very small man. If he not for the shaggy beard, I might have thought he was a child. He is slight, and, combined with his red hair, red beard, and piercing blue eyes, I find myself fascinated by this caricature of a person. Johnston stands still, watching my face as I take in his physical features. I gather myself, smile, and open the door to allow him inside.

"Hi, Johnston. My name is Clara Starr. Please come in."

Johnston walks through the foyer and stops at the entrance to the living room when he sees Addie. I brush past him and stand beside her. His nostrils flare, and his eyes seem to ignite, but he says nothing. He shoves his hands in his front pockets.

"This is Addie Marsh, my assistant. She helps with scheduling and keeping the electronic files up to date. She will also be completing the paperwork you need for Mr. Overly. Of course, she is legally obligated to keep confidential anything you say while in session, except if you express an intent to harm yourself or someone else. Otherwise, we will keep most of what we discuss confidential. I will write minimal notes on your court form to let them know if you're keeping appointments and making progress."

Johnston looks unconvinced but continues to stand. I gesture for him to sit on the love seat. Addie moves off into her space, and Johnston lowers himself.

"What is it that you want me to tell you?" Johnston asks.

He's playing a game. Sorry, Johnston Burr. This is not my first rodeo. I start, "Let's begin with some easy stuff. Tell me about yourself and how you came to be here in my office."

"Well, ummmm, I … I just came out of Jennifer Road, but you already know that." He snickers. "I spent two years in jail before I got early release. Overly says I need to meet with you for help with drugs, but I'll tell you right now, I don't have a problem with drugs."

"Oh? I see in your court papers that you were convicted of drug trafficking and possession of a controlled substance. Is that not a problem with drugs?"

I can see Johnston sizing me up. I meet his stare and maintain eye contact. He needs to know I can handle him. He looks past me at my desk and leans back with one arm on the back of the love seat.

"Okay. I know what the papers say, but I was set up."

Skepticism is written on my face. I've heard this excuse many times and even used it myself in a past life. No. He doesn't get to blame anyone for his own choices and mistakes.

He must be able to read my mind. He raises both hands in surrender. "No, really. Hear me out. I know guys like me have one-liners all day long to convince people we're not as bad as what society or the judge says. And, truth be told, I have ingested my share of substances. And, yes, I was under the influence when I was arrested. That is, under the influence of marijuana, which is technically a controlled substance, at least at the time, but …" He reaches into his back pocket and extracts his wallet. He pulls out a card. "Here's my medical marijuana card. So, the situation wasn't exactly how the cops said it was. I was a minnow who could lead them to bigger fish."

"Okay, then tell me about the trafficking charge. What's up with that?"

"I'll tell you what's up with that." His neck and face are turning red, his eyes a brilliant blue. He seems to be struggling to maintain control of his temper.

I stand and ask him if he would like some water. When I return, he seems to have regained his composure. He takes a sip, then continues. "Bobby Ward. That's what's up with that."

Wow. I didn't expect that. "Okay, tell me more."

"Bobby Ward set me up, the bastard. He had asked me to hold on to a bag of pills while we were at the Royal Farms store. I figured they were oxys, since that was Bobby's specialty. It was a lot, maybe five hundred or more. So, Bobby asks me to hold on to them while he goes around the corner to collect his money. Not more than two minutes after Bobby rounds the corner, five cop cars screech into the parking lot. They jump out of their cars with guns drawn. I'm looking around like, 'What? Where's the shooter?' when one of the big cops, the mean one who has a reputation in the neighborhood, slams me down on the pavement, grinding my chin into the ground. It doesn't take them long to find the damn bag in my pocket. And the rest," he sweeps wide his arms, "is history."

My mind flicks back to the Knight of Swords card that my mother flipped over. This guy certainly has the energy of an angry knight set on revenge. Hell, if I were him, I would, too.

"So, when were you sprung from jail?" I ask.

"About a couple of weeks ago. I think it was on a Monday."

"So, like, " I do the mental calculations, "you mean like last week Monday?" I don't like the feeling I'm getting with this discussion.

Johnston belts out a loud bout of laughter. I see Addie roll her chair and peek around the wall to see if things are okay. Johnston is laughing so hard that his eyes are leaking tears.

"Um … is there something funny here, Johnston?"

He can barely catch his breath. "Uh, yeah," he says as spittle flies from his mouth.

I wonder if he has a serious mental illness when he calms and says, "I'll tell you what's so funny, Dr. Starr. It's hella funny that Bobby Ward's body became food for the crabs. It's funny that after all of Bobby's conniving, stealing, lying, cheating, beating, and *setting people up*, he's now fallen victim to die by his own sword."

Goosebumps pill on my arms. His own sword, huh?

"And I'll tell you something else," he continues. "Ain't no one going to mourn the death of old Bobby Ward. He got what was a long time coming."

Johnston stands and asks for the bathroom. He knows how this system works. I point to the bathroom and yell as he walks away, "The pee cups are in a basket on the sink." He'll have to leave a urine sample to test for drugs.

He turns and smiles in a way that makes me think he must have been an adorable child at one time. "I'm sure they are, Dr. Starr. I'm sure they are."

# CHAPTER 21

Well, that's just great. Every one of my clients seems to have a motive to want Bobby dead. I am among them as well. The simple truth was Bobby was an abusive, arrogant, drug-peddling, mean person. He hurt people any way you look at it. Danny has his work cut for him, that's for sure.

Addie finishes up the notes from today's sessions. She'll join me on the patio soon. For now, it's nice to be alone with my thoughts. I'm not sure how to approach this whole situation. There's still a lot of missing information about the person who killed Bobby and why. It's good you can't be convicted of murder just on the why alone. If that were the case, this whole neighborhood would share an entire wing in jail.

Addie opens the door while balancing two glasses of iced tea. I stand to help her when I hear a "hello" in the distance. It's Alice and Brian. They walk up to the patio and sit. Alice introduces Addie to Brian. They are not far apart in age. Addie enters the house and returns with two more glasses of iced tea with lemon wedges perched on the rims. For several minutes, we're quiet, looking out across the bay, watching Shaun make his final pass on his pink crab pots for the afternoon. He'll chug back to the dock soon to hand over his bushels to the restaurant liaison. Then he'll wash down the boat, wind the lines, and prepare things for tomorrow morning.

Alice breaks the silence. "Thank you for meeting with me the other day, Clara. I enjoy spending time with you, but I don't think I'll need to come back for therapy. Brian and I have things handled just fine." She smiles.

I take a sip of my tea. I suspected as much. Alice is of the old-school generation; one never airs out dirty laundry in public. "It's okay, Alice," I say. "I just want you to know I'm here if you need support."

"Well, I appreciate that, Clara. I really do. You're my favorite girl."

I look at Brian. "How's it going?"

He looks off in the distance, his facial expressions hard to read. "Oh, it's going. There's a lot to settle with Dad's things, like his boat, all those crab pots. I have half a mind to keep them and work the water when I have some free time."

Alice snorts. "Free time? You?" She chuckles, but her hands slide over to his arm. "Brian is a hard worker, you know. He barely has enough time to get some sleep."

Brian looks at his mother. "Well, you know, I've been working on some exciting stuff in the marine lab."

"Really? What are you working on?" Addie asks.

"We're trying to duplicate some of the healthy bacteria using all kinds of marine life. We're working on oysters, crabs, and—if you can imagine—pufferfish."

"Hmm, what do you mean 'working on'?" Addie asks.

"Well, some of the bacteria is very healthy for the bay, but it's in short supply with the rising temperatures. The bad bacteria seem to be taking over and are messing up the delicate ecosystem. I've been putting in a lot of hours trying to isolate particular elements of the bacteria."

"Sounds fascinating," Addie says in a monotone voice.

Alice and I laugh. After a minute, Brian laughs, too. "Yeah, I guess it sounds kind of boring, doesn't it?" He shrugs.

Addie, Alice, and I all nod in unison. "So, how are you two getting along?" I ask.

Alice and Bobby look at each other and smile. "We're doing great, Clara. I know I don't have to put on airs for you," Alice says. "You know how Bobby was. The truth is that things are quite the way I like it."

"And I'm moving back in with Mom at the house," Brian adds. "It'll be just us this time. No need to fend off Dad and his liquor."

"I'm glad the two of you will be together at the house. If there's anything I can do to help, please, let me know," I say.

"Of course, and I know you mean it," says Alice.

Alice and Brian empty their tea glasses and stand to leave. I stand and give them both big bear hugs. Alice opens her arms to Addie, who walks into them as if she's known her all along. We say our goodbyes, and they go on their way. Addie and I watch them and only speak after they've walked around the corner.

"They're really nice," Addie says. "Brian seems to be super smart."

"Yeah. Marine microbiology has always fascinated him. When we were in middle school, he built an entire marine ecosystem in a big aquarium. His project topic was about how the aquatic ecosystem maintains homeostasis when certain marine life is eliminated. It was kind of a big deal. I think he won first place."

"Wow. I don't even think I knew what the word 'ecosystem' meant in middle school," Addie says. "Is it a good thing Brian is moving back home to be with his mother?"

"Oh, yes. Alice and Brian have always been so close. It was Bobby who stood between them. If you looked up the word 'homophobe' in the dictionary, Bobby's ugly mug would be there."

We both laugh. Then Addie says, "I'm glad I never had any run-ins with Bobby. He sounds like a real asshole."

"That he was. Addie, why don't you go on home? One of the things about having a private practice is that I can stop working whenever I want."

Addie stays seated. "Sounds good to me. Can I ask you about the tarot reading yesterday?"

My face flushes. Some people don't believe in mystical forces. Growing up, I interacted with two groups of people: those who believed in the gift and those who thought it was part of the dark arts. As I got older and other kids began to tease me, I learned to keep Mom's readings private. I'm not sure what prompts Addie's question.

"Sure, what's on your mind?"

Addie appears hesitant. "What do you think about your mom's reading?"

I shrug. "She's read tarot cards for as long as I can remember. It's kind of a family thing."

"Yeah, I know. I have some vague childhood memories about my grandparents and your parents. Like they'd have these get-togethers with the cards."

Of course. I guess her grandparents were believers.

"Oh, right, right. So, if you're asking me if I believed Mom's reading? Well, all I can say is that my mother is almost always on point with her readings."

"Okay, so then the killer would have been on some type of revenge-seeking mission, right?"

I'm not sure where she's going, but my stomach clenches. "Okay ...."

"So, then, maybe we can learn more about who had reasons to benefit from his death. I mean, there's got to be only so many people who have a grudge, right? It's not like either one of us would have reason to want Bobby dead. It can be a process of elimination." Addie rubs her hands together. "Dr. Starr, I think we have a murder mystery on our hands."

I feel the goosebumps prickle on my skin.

# CHAPTER 22

My relationship with Bobby was complicated. Of course, it was always unhealthy. I mean, the guy got me involved in using drugs as a kid. There's more, though, that I don't want to think about. It makes my gut hurt. I punch my bed pillow to fluff it up and flip it to the cool side. My mind skips across memories, especially ones I'd rather forget. I don't think sleep is coming anytime soon. All of this stuff going on with Bobby, his murder, the investigation, Alice and Brian—they all dredge up my past. I wish I could tamp it down, close the door, and seal it up. My life is on a much better path now. I can't afford to have it messed up by someone stumbling upon my secrets.

I fling the blankets off and shift onto my left side. I stretch my arm and reach to the other side of the bed, thinking of George. Although this is the same bed we shared in downtown Annapolis, it's now in what used to be my mother and father's bedroom. I run my hands down the smooth cotton sheets. *Oh, George, how did we get things so wrong?*

Knowing full well my mind will torment me if I go down this path, I still close my eyes and remember the smell of George's cologne, his well-trimmed hair, and hazel eyes. I remember our first date when he took me for a midnight boat ride on the South River. We were pleasantly surprised that we lived not so far apart. I remember the cool air blowing my hair back as I sat in the seat on the bow. He stood behind me with one hand on the wheel and the other on the throttle. Up and down, we glided on top of the water, watching the lit homes that lined the river's shores. It was that first night when he gently kissed me goodnight and asked when we could meet again. A few months later, George asked me if we could be exclusive, to see if we could make a relationship of this.

On the pier one night, he placed his hands on my shoulders and said, "Clara, I would like us to be a dinner reservation for the rest of my life."

I wrapped my arms around his neck. "Yes, let's do it."

We were older, both of us in our late forties. For me, being so heavily involved with drugs and then getting straightened out took lots of therapy time. When my non-addicted friends were coupling and planning families, I was still in the throes of grief and sobriety. It was no surprise to my counselors that I hadn't properly grieved my father's suicide. I first laid my eyes on George during an outpatient recovery meeting. He had been saying something about pulling oneself up by the bootstraps or some other such craziness. I tuned him out. Everybody thinks they have the answer for everybody else.

After weeks of meetings, I got acquainted with the group members, even George. He had a face that penetrated the iciest of glares. Eventually, we went out for coffee. The more I got to know him, the more I realized he wasn't such a bad person. He had been through some rough times, too. It didn't take long before we fell in love. A few months later, we went to the courthouse and got married. We were getting older by the minute and didn't want to waste a minute more.

I learned quickly that George was a high achiever, the proverbial Type A personality. His ambition and drive never waned. He had graduated from the University of Maryland Law School in the top two percent of his class. He started his career as an attorney for Baltimore City nonprofit organizations. By the time I met him, he had plans to move up into a higher financial bracket. He applied for positions at several high-profile firms. One night after a particularly grueling interview, George came home feeling defeated. However, later that night, he received a call from one of the partners offering him a job. After he hung up, we jumped up and down in our tiny apartment living room. It was the best moment of my life. I had finally turned things around.

Money flowed like a river when he got that job. We moved to a big waterfront home in downtown Annapolis. Large floor-to-ceiling windows overlooked the Severn River and all the sailboats. I had worked in a small, nonprofit mental health agency. George's income blew mine out of the water. We had what we needed and then some.

We decided we no longer needed our NA meetings. We were finally able to reap our rewards. George ramped up his work hours. His billable hours by the firm surpassed every other attorney. His bosses were happy. We were happy. Looking back, I should have known that working those types of hours and being under so much stress would take exact a price somewhere. I am a woman who can see only what I want to see. I can turn away from anything that causes me discomfort or insecurity. I blame myself for what happened next.

One evening, as I was hanging George's jacket in the hall, I found a small plastic baggie with white powder inside in his coat pocket. The shock of it made my heart flutter and hands tremble. I tried to convince myself that maybe it was some type of protein powder that George loved to drink. I had seen baggies of what I thought were vanilla powder and thought nothing of it.

I needed to be sure. I opened the bag and dipped my finger. I rubbed the residue on my gums. They zinged. A long-asleep demon awoke. The truth is that I didn't have the willpower to throw the baggie away. I was faced with a choice: confront George or put it back where I found it.

I didn't want to argue with George. We'd been doing so well all this time. Maybe all of this was temporary to help him crest the work for a large case. Like I said, I can convince myself of just about anything. I remember that night so clearly. I put the baggie back in the pocket where I found it. I thought George and I would figure this out, just like we had done long ago in those meetings.

Later, I would learn I had made the wrong choice.

# CHAPTER 23

The next morning, the ping of a text message pivots my attention to my phone charging on my headboard. I reach back and grab the phone.

```
Danny: Hey, you awake?
Me: Yeah
Danny: Me too. I couldn't sleep. My mind is in the weeds about Bobby's murder.
Me: Any luck?
Danny: Not much. You?
Me: Me what?
Danny: Any luck with your clients?
Me: Ugh
Danny: Well?
Me: No. Nothing yet.
Danny: ok. Have a good day.
Me: You too.
```

I didn't expect him to check in with me quite so quickly. Truthfully, it makes me feel a little paranoid. Is he watching my clients come and go? Does he know which clients I'm seeing and when? I shake the thoughts from my mind. I am letting this get the best of me.

Because I have nothing better to do, I search "how quickly can toxicology reports take for an autopsy." A list of results populates my phone. I click on the first couple.

Apparently, toxicology reports can take up to several months. *Perfect, that gives me plenty of time,* I think. Wait. What? Plenty of time to find out who killed him? I'm not guilty here. I don't have to worry about when the report will come out and what it will show. As I think more about it, I realize that no matter what the report says, everyone knows Bobby had a dirty hand in whatever made him end up in the bay. I haven't met a single person who was authentically mourning his death.

It says on my phone that toxicology testing is routine for autopsies. They run tests for the presence of prescription medications and illegal drugs, like opiates, amphetamines, marijuana, alcohol, and barbiturates, then interpret the findings. I'm sure Bobby's results will light up like fireworks. The article says the M.E. will extract samples from blood and urine as well as tissues from the liver, brain, kidney, and—ew!—the eyeball. He'll look at the contents of the stomach. Disgusting. If any of the first round of tests are positive, they will send out the specimens to more specialized labs. Four to six weeks is standard, the website indicates.

Another ping. It looks like it's officially time to wake up. Everyone is trying to communicate with me. It's Mom.

```
Mom: Have you found the knight yet?
```

Ugh. Mom, can't you stop? That's not what I type in my phone, though.

```
Me: No sign of the knight
Mom: He's coming. Prepare yourself.
Me: Okay Mom. Love you
Mom: Love you
```

Mom's intentions are good, but sometimes her "gift" makes her obsess. Eventually, it will all calm down once something else distracts her attention. I wish it were as simple as her pulling a card with the name of the murderer on it. I know it doesn't happen that way. She gets these feelings, like little clues that float around her mind like fairy dust. I don't have time for that today.

Addie comes in a little early, fixes herself a cup of coffee, and sits with me on the patio. She wipes the sweat from her forehead. "It feels like it's going to be a hot one today."

I feel the prickle of sweat already on my neck. "And here we sit, drinking hot coffee." I glance over and smile at her.

We're quiet and relaxed when a patrol car stops in front of my house. Oh, no. It's never good when Danny drives the patrol car. He sits there for a few minutes, appearing to read something on the police computer screen. He opens his door and slams it a little harder than I expected. His poker face is on as he proceeds to the patio. I watch his lean form in his navy-blue police uniform. Danny has gotten more handsome as he's aged. I still can't understand why he never married. Wait. What? No, no, no. I know better than to let this idea settle into my mind. Danny walks over and stands facing Addie and me. I gesture for him to sit in one of the chairs.

"Addie. Clara."

Addie and I say hi simultaneously. We look at each other and grin. Danny stares at us, not finding this funny. I feel the pinch of anxiety.

"Hey, Danny," I say lightheartedly. "Want a cup of coffee?"

He shakes his head, but I stand. Whatever is coming next, I need a moment to gather myself. I raise my eyebrows to Addie, who declines my offer.

"I'll be right back," I say and walk into the kitchen. I root inside one of the kitchen drawers behind a stack of dish towels. My fingers wrap around an old prescription bottle in my nightstand. I unscrew the lid and dip in a finger to fish out a Xanax. I know I shouldn't do this, and I normally don't, except when I'm feeling out of sorts and on the edge of panic. Popping the pill in my mouth, I turn on the faucet and use my hand to cup some water. I slurp down the water and the pill, then wipe my mouth with the back of my hand and fill up my coffee cup.

When I step back onto the patio, Danny and Addie are talking about her job. I come in at the end of the conversation.

Addie says, "Oh, I love it. I couldn't have a better job with a better boss." She turns to me and smiles.

Danny's eyes connect with mine. "Clara, I need to talk to you. Do you want to go inside where it's more private?"

I consider this; I really do. I've spent a whole lifetime keeping secrets. It's never gotten me anywhere. It's never saved a marriage or a life. It's never brought me a close friend. It's never shielded me from the consequences of my own actions. Now I don't keep secrets. Well, for the most part. There are still some things I can't reveal, no matter how much I want my life to go in a different direction. Still. I want Addie to be my friend.

"It's okay. We can talk in front of Addie."

At first, I think Danny is going to refuse. He pushes his hair back with his hands and rubs his chin, which I now notice has a shadow of unshaved whiskers.

"Okay, I guess it's better if she's here, anyway."

I feel a surge of anxiety and the warming edges of the Xanax. If he's willing to talk in front of Addie, then it can't be all that bad.

"Clara, I really need to see your clients' files."

"No, Danny. I said no. I already told you," I say, but Danny persists.

"Come on, we need to catch a killer, Clara. Do you want me to go to the judge for a warrant?"

The warming edges are now crisp with flames. "There's no way, Danny. Look, I know none of my clients have anything to do with Bobby's murder. I told you I'd talk to them, and I did. There's nothing there."

Danny's eyes simmer. "Oh, there's something there. I know it."

"Oh, really? And how would you know this?" I hear my voice take on a childlike tone.

"Because I've grown up in this community, just as you have. I know that you see some … well, people with issues." He emphasizes the word "issues" with something that sounds like sarcasm.

"Oh, *issues*, huh? That sounds ominous, Danny. In fact, *issues* could be a synonym for murder, right? You sound like you yourself have never had *issues*." I let the word snake out of my mouth.

"Clara, watch it. I'm here on official business. You're talking to a police officer who has asked for information. Are you saying you refuse to provide it?"

I look at Addie. Her eyes are like saucers. She can't see him push me around like this. I want her to see how a grown woman handles her business.

"That's exactly what I'm saying, *Officer.*"

"I see. Well, in that case ...." Danny reaches into his uniform pocket and extracts a white sheet of paper. He reaches toward me with the paper, but I don't dare touch it.

"What's this?" I say, hating how my voice is registering at a higher pitch. The bastard had already seen the judge and gotten the warrant.

"It's what I told you would happen if you refused to cooperate."

I shake my head in disbelief. I figured that no judge, especially a local one, would issue a subpoena for my records, and yet here it is. I take the paper from Danny and scan its contents.

"You're making me do this?"

Danny crosses his arms against his chest. He can be so arrogant.

"So, what do you want?" I ask, toning down my voice.

"I want your records, Clara. I want to talk with you, but I can see you're in no mood for that right now. So, for the moment, your records will suffice."

"Look, a client is coming soon, and I'll need some time to get them."

Danny cocks his head. He doesn't believe me.

"I will. I just need some time, especially if you want all of my records. That could take quite a long time."

"Don't worry. I don't want all of them."

"Oh? Well, whose do you want, then? And for what time frame?" I feel the tendrils of fear slink around my heart. I don't want to do this, and Danny is fully aware. How can my clients feel safe with me if I hand over their most private records to the police?

"I want the last month of records for Lala Chance, Alice Ward, Shelby Cross, and Johnston Burr. I also want any of the records for this week, and next as well."

I take a big sip of my coffee and swallow hard. "Wait. How do you know I see those people?" I ask.

"Come on, Clara. I know who you see."

I shake my head. "No. How do you know?"

His neck turns red, and he breaks eye contact.

He doesn't have to tell me. I already know. "You've been watching my house, haven't you?"

Danny has the good graces not to respond. What a jerk. He's been sitting outside spying on me and my clients.

On a whim, I ask, "Was that you on the steps during the storm?" Now it's my turn to cross my arms.

Confusion clouds Danny's face. "What?"

"You heard me. Was it you?"

Danny shakes his head. "I don't know what you're talking about. Why would I sit in a thunderstorm across from your house and watch you? Do you have something to hide, Clara Starr?"

I sneer. "That's a low blow, even for you, Danny."

He stands and looks out at the bay. The wind has picked up, and clouds are rolling in. When Danny turns back to look at me, the hardness in his eyes prompts me to take a deep breath. It's a little scary, that look.

"Clara, I'll be back tomorrow. Have the records ready," Danny says as he turns to walk to the car. He slams his door even harder as he gets back into his patrol car.

I wait for him to turn the corner before I look at Addie. I stand and say, "Addie, cancel all the regular sessions scheduled for today. Then call Lala, Shelby, Alice, and Johnston to schedule individual meetings today. Tell them it's urgent. Explain I will give them more details when I see them." I turn and walk through the French glass doors. I hear Addie fall in step behind me.

This is going to be a terrible day. Addie walks to her computer to set up the files for the notes she plans to take today. I say, "Uh, no, Addie. We will not bill today's meetings as sessions. They'll be just informal visits. No clinical notes taken today."

Addie looks perplexed. "No notes? Are you sure?"

"I'm one hundred percent sure. No notes from today's meetings."

# CHAPTER 24

Lala bounces into the room an hour later, breathing hard. Her hands are empty of her signature pink cake box. Of course, she had no time to make anything special.

"What's going on, Clara? Why the emergency meeting?" she pants.

I gesture her to the love seat. She stands a moment longer and wipes at the sweat dripping a path from her forehead onto her cheek. Addie goes to the kitchen to get her a glass of water. Lala grabs a tissue and plants herself on the sofa. "Okay, I'm sitting. Can you tell me what's going on?"

I rub my hands down the front of my pants, still deciding how to begin this. My tongue swipes across my front teeth, and I realize, to my utter horror, I forgot to brush them.

"Uh. Well. The thing is ...," I stammer.

Lala is impatient; it's one of the issues she works on with me. My mind momentarily snags on the word "issues." I try again. "Okay, here's the thing. Danny came by to see me." I can see Lala's mind grinding as she tries to figure out the secret message. I continue, "This morning, he presented me with a judge's order for my client records."

Lala's eyes widen; fear now occupies the space where her curiosity was just a moment ago. I try to address it before it becomes unmanageable. "I know, I know. It's surprising and awful and stupid—"

"And totally uncalled for! Clara!" She's yelling now. "When you asked if it was okay to have Addie within earshot, I said, 'Sure.' I know she's a social worker, and so are you. I trusted you, and if you trusted her, I would, too. And now you're telling me that Danny—no, strike that, that a *judge* wants to see my personal therapy files. The therapy files where I told you *everything.*" Her voice reaches a screech.

"Wait, Lala. Wait. Let's just calm down for a minute."

Lala jumps out of her seat and begins pacing around the room. "And I suppose you wrote everything down in those notes. Every. Thing. So, now a judge, and Danny, and, *oh, my god, everyon*e—" She's starting to teeter like she's hyperventilating.

I yell to Addie to get a cool washcloth and more water. I can hear the legs of Addie's chair scrape against the wood floor. For a millisecond, I wonder whether the scrapes put scratches into the floor. Lala is propping herself up against my desk. Sweat is running down her face. Addie rushes in and puts the cool cloth on Lala's forehead. Addie and I lead Lala back to the love seat.

"Sit," I instruct her. "Take a sip."

I offer a glass of water, but Lala's mind is elsewhere. Addie reaches down and lifts Lala's hands. I put the glass in her hands and lay my hands over hers. I guide the glass to her lips. She takes a sip and swallows. Her fingers tighten. She brings the glass to her lips and chugs the water all at once.

When she's finished, I hand Addie the glass and say, "Another."

After twenty minutes, Lala seems to have regained her senses. The three of us I sit quietly in the living room.

Lala looks at me, resignation filling her eyes. "Then he'll know," she says. "Then they'll all know."

I see Addie's head turning towards me out of my peripheral vision. I wish I knew what to do, but I don't. I don't want to ask too much because I don't want to know too much. At the same time, I am protective of Lala, and of all my clients. I reach over and squeeze Lala's hand.

"Whatever it is, whatever happens, I will always be here for you, Lala. You know that, right?"

Tears drop from Lala's eyes. She looks up at me. "But there are some things that I didn't want anyone to know. There are things that even you, Clara, don't know."

"Tell me, Lala. You can tell me."

I see Addie subtly shaking her head no. She's probably right, but I want to help Lala. I don't want her to go through all of this alone. I can be there for her. I know what it feels like to have no one on your side. You feel like the earth is about to crack open and swallow you. It's the loneliest feeling in the world. I am not going to let my clients flounder through life like I had to. No. It's not going to happen. I move to the sofa to sit beside Lala. I put my palm on her back.

"No notes?" Lala asks.

I shake my head. "No notes."

Lala begins. She goes back to the beginning of her and Bobby's relationship. He had started having sexual relations with her when she was in high school. This, I knew. Lala said that Bobby had promised that he would leave Alice once she was legal, and they'd leave Mystic Beach and go somewhere where no one would know them. She had wanted to quit high school, but Bobby told her no. He said the law would come after them if she left without finishing high school. They'd arrest him, and she'd never see him again. No, she had to be patient and wait.

Lala had waited, and then waited some more. She graduated from high school. She kept asking Bobby when they'd be leaving. At first, he put her off, told her he was working on the plans. The more time passed, the more Lala kept bothering him.

"Until one day, he punched me in the cheek," she says. Addie and I gasp at the same time. Lala bobs her head in affirmation. "Yeah, he punched me full force right in the cheek. It didn't break any bones that time, but it took a long while for the swelling and the bruise to go down."

"Did you tell anyone?" I asked.

Lala shakes her head. Tears drip down her cheeks. "I was so in love, or I thought I was so in love. I had just been hounding him too much. I needed to trust him and let him get things figured."

"It never got figured, did it?" I asked.

"No. It was like he knew he had hooked me. I was so in love with him. Yeah, I was hurting because I had imagined a whole future with him. I didn't care that he was so much older than me. I figured that if he loved me, then I was worth something. Gradually, I learned to accept what he offered, even if it came with some physical pain. I mean, look at me, Clara." Lala opens her arms as if to present herself. "Who would want to be with me, anyway?" She grabs a handful of flesh and stretches her skin out. "Look. Look!"

Lala's tears cascade down her face. Addie offers the Kleenex box. Lala takes two and blows her nose. For a minute, we sit and listen to the sounds of Lala's sobs.

"What else, Lala?" I whisper.

"I couldn't," she says.

After a minute, I ask, "Couldn't what?" My heart is beating against my chest. I'm sure Addie and Lala can hear it through my shirt.

"I couldn't take it anymore. I just couldn't. Something had to be done."

"It's okay," I whisper. "It's okay. Don't say anything more."

Lala tries to speak, but I interrupt. "No, Lala. Don't say anything."

"You know more than most, Clara. After what Bobby did to you, you know what I mean."

# CHJAPTER 25

When Lala leaves, Addie brings me a glass of iced tea out on the patio. The thick, humid air feels like I'm inhaling soup. I have a headache, but I have to see three more. Lala's reference to Bobby's impact on my life upends my emotions. I mean, it is no surprise that Bobby was the catalyst for the crash-and-burn period of my life. No one could shield me, not even Mom, from the judgmental eyes of everyone in the neighborhood. My drunken and drugged craziness was out there for all to see. But I had dealt with that. I crashed and burned right in front of everyone as my marriage came to an abrupt end. George's death set me straight, but that's a story for another time. I don't have time to take a trip down memory lane just because Lala reminded me of my shortcomings. She's right, though. I am no better than her—or anyone else, for that matter.

Shelby Cross walks to the patio, waving hello, but without his beautiful smile. He knows it's unusual for me to call for an urgent meeting. He sits beside me on a patio chair. I ask him if he wants to come in, but he says if it's okay, he'd rather just chat outside. The breeze envelopes us and, as strange as it might sound, gives a feeling of comfort and protection. I feel it, too, which is why I agree to just have the sit-down out here. Addie joins us with a glass of tea for Shelby and one for herself.

"So, what's this all about?"

"Well, Shelby, I hate to say it, but it looks like my client records are about to be turned over to the court."

Shelby glances down at his fresh-pressed white denim pants. He picks an imaginary piece of lint and brushes imaginary dirt from his shiny shoes. When he looks up, there is a hardness behind his eyes. "Okay, and?"

I am unaccustomed to his abrupt tone. I much prefer the flamboyant, loving, and energetic young man who is dazzlingly in love with his new husband. "Well, I just thought I should tell you so you're prepared if the police come to talk to you."

He stares at me. "Let the police come. I'll tell them a thing or two about that asswipe, Bobby Ward."

"You mean you're okay with them knowing that Bobby had caught you with Brian back in the day? You're prepared for that?" I ask.

He waves his hand to shoosh me. "Girl, everyone already knows that I am openly gay. I mean, look." He flashes his diamond wedding band. "Now, with Brian, it might be a different thing. I don't know if he's out yet. I'm not worried in the least about people knowing that Bobby caught us, then beat us to a pulp. I mean, really, we couldn't hide it from neighbors then. What do I care now?"

Shelby has a point. The incident was several years ago, and since then, Shelby and Bobby have rarely crossed paths. Despite the prejudices Shelby endured from growing up in a conservative area like Mystic Beach, he has always been true and authentic. It's one of the things I love most about him.

"Now, there is one thing that I'm sure the police don't know. This might bring some angst, but I've always been open about my life. Life is easier to deal with that way."

A leaden ball drops in my stomach. I'm not prepared to hear what Shelby has to say. Even though I've been his therapist for several months now, I know he had been working up to tell me one of the secrets that had leveled him flat on his face. I can see a kaleidoscope of emotions skitter across Shelby's face. Addie mistakenly thinks Shelby is reluctant to talk in front of her, and she asks him if he'd prefer her to leave. He reaches over and places his hand on her knee.

"See, Clara, the thing I have been wanting to tell you is now at the forefront because of this situation with the police. It's like having the Band-Aid ripped off, and I think it's a good thing."

I brace myself. "Okay. What happened?"

Shelby adjusts himself in the chair and looks at Addie, then me. "So, the time with Brian when we were in high school, it wasn't just getting caught and enduring Bobby's beating. Bobby wasn't content with leaving it at that," Shelby said. "It would never have been cleaned up so simply, not where Bobby was concerned. Bobby was always into making money, and that made him open to doing some sick shit."

I feel like I might throw up, but I wait for Shelby to tell me. Something about his story is triggering something buried deep inside, so deep that I had nearly forgotten it was there.

"About a week after the incident," Shelby continues, "Bobby approached me when he saw me hanging out at the harbor downtown. I hardly recognized him because he was showered and shaved. I tried to walk away, but he reached out, put his hand on my arm, and told me to wait, to give him a chance to say what he's got to say.

"So, I waited. Bobby told me he had a little proposition for me, one that would prove lucrative for us both. I hadn't met Marshall at that point. So, Bobby tells me that he knows someone who knows someone … you know how that goes." Shelby rolls his eyes. "So, he said that this person would pay big money to have a video of gay sex."

Addie's eyes widen. "'*A video of gay sex?*' What the hell?"

"Yeah. He said that if I let him film me a couple of times, I'd make a thousand dollars each for about thirty minutes of sex. I'll never forget it. He said, 'Seeing as you're already having gay sex, why not earn something for your trouble?' The only exception, he warned me, was to leave his son out of it. He said, 'Brian isn't gay, and I don't want you changing him into something he ain't.'"

Shelby pauses so long, I ask, "And? Did you do it?"

"Hell, yeah, I did it! Two thousand dollars for an hour doing something I was already doing? But then, I should have known. Bobby can never leave anything alone. He kept asking me to do more and more. After I met Marshall, I told him no. I told him I'd found someone I liked and wanted to be with."

I can feel another earthquake on the way.

"Bobby couldn't pass up a deal. So, he blackmailed me. He told me if I didn't make more videos, he would share the ones he had with Marshall. I was young, you know. I believed him. So, for a while, I went along with it. I let him make the movies and came up with excuses to Marshall why I was leaving for an hour here and there. Ultimately, years later, he showed Marshall the movies anyway."

"What?" Addie shouts.

"Yeah, by then, he had accumulated a nice little library of porn films where I was the star. Then one day, when I wasn't home, Bobby came by the house to share his collection of films with Marshall."

I cover my face with the palm of my hand. Bobby is unbelievable. *Was.*

"Marshall, my beloved, acted like he knew it all along and asked if he could get copies of his own. Imagine?" Shelby's laugh tinkles in the breeze. "Yep, my love bought the set from Bobby and told him he better never talk to either of us again."

"And did he lay off you from then on?" I ask.

"For a long time, yes. But then, not too long ago, in fact, he paid me a visit. This time, Marshall was out on an errand. I didn't want to let him in the house, but Bobby raised his voice, 'Well, I wanted to talk to you about the gay porn.' So, I rushed him inside. You know where we live, Clara, in that upscale part of Annapolis. You lived in the same neighborhood with George."

Yes, I remembered.

"So, Bobby told me he wanted to show me something. He was talking about the amazing world of technology. I ignored him, but when Bobby positioned his phone so I could see the screen, I saw what he was talking about. He had created a deepfake."

Addie and I looked at each other, puzzled. "A what?" Addie asks.

"A deepfake. Artificial intelligence technology can manipulate visual images and audio to put a person's face on someone else's body. They can put a voice skin on the video so the viewer hears my voice and watches my face on someone else's body. In this case, Bobby had created a deepfake of me with hundreds of men, having sex. He, or whomever, made it look like I'd been making these videos all along. Bobby blackmailed me with his deepfake videos. He said that if I paid him ten thousand right then, Marshall would be none the wiser.

"I tried to talk my way out of it, you know, reason with Bobby. Totally stupid, I know. Except this time, I wasn't sure that Marshall would believe it was a fake. Marshall and I have been dealing with some incidents involving minor infidelity. I thought that if Bobby told Marshall about this, that would be the end of it and he'd kick me out, even if those videos were fake. I was trapped, and Bobby knew it. So, I went into our safe and pulled out ten grand in cash."

"In cash?" I ask in amazement.

"Yes, Marshall and I have what we call runaway funds. If ever we need fast cash for any reason at all, we have a safe with, oh, about fifty thousand inside. I had planned to replace the money that afternoon before Marshall arrived home from his trip."

I am afraid to ask but know I must. "Uh, Shelby … when was this? When did Bobby try to blackmail you?"

Shelby looks down at his lap. "This is the bad part. A couple of weeks ago, Bobby had come to me to make another attempt at blackmail. I told him to go get lost, and he threatened me with releasing the videos."

"What did you say?" whispers Addie.

"I told him this was the last time, and if he came by again, I'd kill him dead with my own bare hands." Shelby pauses. "And I never did see him again. Nor did anyone else."

# CHAPTER 26

This day keeps getting worse. Shelby leaves, and Addie goes into the kitchen to refill our iced teas. While she's inside, Johnston Burr calls my cell phone and tells me he can't leave work to come for a meeting today. I understand. If his boss reports him as MIA, there will be issues with his parole officer and more scrutiny into this situation. I tell Johnston that the police are asking for records in the investigation of Bobby Ward's death. Johnston seems unbothered.

"So? What do I care if they ask for your records about me? We only had one session. And believe me, the police are well aware of Bobby's and my drug empire." Johnston laughs, his lungs wheezing from smoking too much.

"True. I just wanted to make sure you're aware I'll be turning over my records," I say. I try to have a positive regard for my clients, but Johnston tries my patience.

"Yeah, fine, fine. Makes no difference to me. I know whatever I tell you in those sessions and whatever you write down in your notes is public information."

"Well, not public," I say as I try to defend myself, but Johnston interrupts.

"Public information. Nothing is private, not with a felon on parole. So, you don't have to worry about that. Now, if they decide to follow me around," his laughter is deep and raspy, "well, that might be a different thing."

"Oh?" I ask.

"Let's just say you can lock a man up for a crime, and most times, the man will have done the crime. There is a certain sort of revenge that happens to someone who gets convicted for a crime he never committed in the first place."

Oh. He's referring to Bobby's set up. Yeah, I guess that would make me want to seek revenge if someone framed me to take the fall for someone else's mistake.

"Johnston, look, I know I don't have to remind you of this, but you know whatever you tell me isn't really private anyway. I'd have to report anything you do that seems … well, illegal. I'm just saying, don't tell me anything that you want to be kept private."

Johnston belts out a laugh. "Oh, you don't need to remind me of anything, Dr. Starr. I am well aware of how things work. But I thank you for reaching out to give me fair warning."

As we disconnect the call, I have a budding anxiety yet again today. I didn't like the ease of Johnston's tone, as if we were talking about whether he'd prefer a piece of peach pie over apple. I know prison is the prime place for teaching everyone, even those who were never hard criminals to begin with, how to be a better, stronger, and more violent criminal. Something about Johnston's demeanor when I saw him yesterday and the underlying controlled rage in his voice now makes me certain that if anyone could harm another human being, it would be him.

Addie comes outside and asks me who called me. I tell her about the exchange with Johnston.

"There's something about that man that gives me the willies," Addie says.

"I know, me, too. I'd hate to run across him in a dark alley."

"Right? He radiates anger and distrust. It's like he wears it like it's a cologne."

I laugh. "Now, just one more. Alice."

Addie glances toward the front yard. "Ayup. And here she is," Addie says in a singsong voice.

"Well, hello there," I call to Alice and Brian. "Come join us for some iced tea?"

Alice shakes her head. "No, thank you. We're on our way to Homestead Gardens. Brian and I are planting a vegetable garden in the back yard." She looks at Brian, who reaches an arm around his mother's shoulders.

"Yeah, we're going to plant some fall vegetables, like snap beans, carrots, and cucumbers, maybe a little kale," he says. "They'll be ready to harvest September or October."

Both Alice and Brian seem happier. Alice no longer has her face pinched. Brian looks freer than I've ever seen him. Even though the tragedy of someone getting murdered is usually seen as horrible, in this case, I think it worked out for the best. Of everyone I know, me included, Alice and Bobby suffered the most and for the longest time. They deserve a reprieve, both of them. At least they can rebuild a happy, loving, and nurturing life. It's better late than never.

I smile. "That sounds like a marvelous project for the two of you. Listen, Alice, I wanted to give you a heads-up that Danny stopped by earlier, in an official capacity, that is. He presented me with a subpoena for my clients' records. I wanted you to know I have to turn over the notes from our session last Tuesday."

Alice's smile reaches her eyes, and she steps forward to give me a hug. I stand and allow the older woman's embrace to blanket me.

She pulls back and looks into my eyes. "Oh, Clara. That's just fine.

There's nothing I need to hide from you. Danny can look at whatever he needs to. There's nothing to bring back Bobby, and, dare I say, we're all to benefit from that."

Brian is watching his mother with an intense look on his face. I wonder what he's thinking, but he recovers quickly. "Yeah, Clara. Don't be worried about anything. We're an open book, right, Ma?"

"That's right, son. Nothing we need to be ashamed of."

What an odd thing to say to each other. Maybe they're sincerely relieved that Bobby is gone. Brian can return home; Alice doesn't have to worry anymore. It seems everyone I've talked to is truly and utterly happy that Bobby doesn't walk this earth any longer. I can't say I blame them; I feel the same way.

Sensing they will soon leave, I say, "Well, this was the easiest meeting of the day. Thank you for understanding. Go look around Homestead Gardens and find the perfect seeds."

We say our goodbyes, and I sink into the patio chair.

"Whew, this has been a long day," Addie says.

"Yeah, it sure has."

"You don't think any of them have anything to do with Bobby's murder, do you?"

"Nah. I really don't. Johnston is a wildcard, though. The truth is, I'd be perfectly fine with never finding the killer."

"It sounds like Bobby was a horrible, horrible individual. Everyone he came across ended up hurt in some fashion."

"Ain't that the truth."

Addie gathers her belongings. We agree that tomorrow will be an easier day for paperwork and case coordination. After she leaves, I stay on the patio until the sunset colors pink and purple and orange. I am so very thankful that everyone is understanding about Danny receiving their therapy notes. I am also relieved that my own story with Bobby is not written down; it's all locked up securely deep inside me. It may occasionally arise from my unconscious and give me nightmares, but that I can handle. It's the other stuff that needs to stay put wherever it is.

# CHAPTER 27

This morning Danny parks in front of my house and strides to the patio where I sit with an apple turnover and a cup of coffee. He's smiling as he reaches for the second turnover on the plate and returns to his chair.

"Well, you're looking happy today," I say with a hint of sarcasm.

"Yeah? And why shouldn't I be? For one, it's Friday. I love Fridays. And second," he pauses for effect.

I sip my coffee and do my best to look unimpressed. "Okay. What else?"

He smirks. "The M.E. released the preliminary autopsy report to the chief."

I choke on my coffee and some dribbles on the front of my T-shirt.

"Yes. The M.E. confirmed that Bobby did not drown because there was no water in the lungs or the stomach. He found moderate amounts of alcohol and amphetamines, the combination of which could have killed him."

I'm confused. "Wait, how did they get the results so fast? I thought it took weeks to months to get the results."

Danny claps his hands as if he's just solved a complicated puzzle. "Under ordinary circumstances, that's true."

"Uh … aren't these extraordinary circumstances?" I ask.

Danny laughs. "Indeed they are. Apparently, the medical examiner's office is partnering with a private forensic lab to process analyses faster. The feds issued a grant fund a while back for private labs to work with M.E. offices because there's a backlog all across the country. Maryland apparently wants to streamline court proceedings. We are to become a national demonstration project for equitable and efficient court processing. The program is specifically for homicides. And Bobby Ward, of all people, is one of the first to be tested in this pilot program."

I rub my hand over my face. What are the chances that this new program would come to Anne Arundel County at precisely the time that Bobby Ward washes up on the shore? My mother's words about my "love affair" with tragedy sing through my mind.

"So, you know what killed Bobby, but does it lead you any closer to finding the killer?" I ask.

"Speaking of which," Danny reaches for the stack of paper on the coffee table, "I presume these are those files I asked about yesterday?"

I drink more coffee. Danny rubs his sticky fingers on a nearby napkin and picks up the stack. He flips through the pages.

"Thank you, Clara. I know this wasn't easy for you. I'm sorry I had to pull out the big guns to court order their release."

I sigh. "I know. I just feel so protective over them. If I thought that any of them could have murdered Bobby, I would have told you." Then a thought occurs to me. "Hey, wait. You said that the autopsy findings were only preliminary. What do you mean? Why isn't there an official report?"

Danny resumes his original thought. "Yes, yes. Well, though the drugs and alcohol combo may have caused his death, there was some kind of strange pathogen, a bacteria, I think, found in Bobby's liver. The forensic lab couldn't identify it specifically. They don't want to mess up the pilot program, so they're calling in a specialized forensic toxicologist connected to the Centers for Disease Control to examine some tissue samples."

"Huh. Interesting. Well, I hope you catch your perp, Danny."

Danny glances at the smug look on my face and, for a moment, appears bewildered. I can't imagine what he's thinking, and I'm not going to go down that road with him. The sooner he buttons up this case, the better for everyone involved.

Danny stands and stretches. He reminds me of the boy he used to be. I can't believe he became a cop, but I guess there have been stranger things. My mom reads tarot cards. I became a social worker. Bobby became a dead, drug-dealing, no-good SOB. Go figure how people find their paths.

"I'll talk with you later. Is it okay if I stop by later today? Maybe bring a pizza?"

I smile. "Pepperoni and green pepper?"

He winks. "See you later."

I finish the last dregs of my coffee and prop my feet on the table. I hadn't planned on seeing any clients today. I am going to relax and read a book. Barbara walks down the street. For the first time in a long time, I don't feel dread at seeing her face. I don't think anyone knows about my interaction with the … err … body.

I call out first, "Hi, Barbara. It's the beginning of a beautiful day."

Barbara says, "It sure is," then rushes over to me like the neighborhood gossip will burst from her lungs. "Hey," she starts and looks over her shoulder, "have you heard anything about the," she lowers her voice to a whisper, "*murder*?"

I don't know why she's whispering. No one else is around. I can't help myself, but I say a little too loudly, "Murder? There was a murder?"

Barbara shushes me. "Come on, Clara. I know you're friends with Danny. Did he give you a hint about how the investigation is going?"

I shake my head. "No, my guess is as good as yours. I don't know a thing."

Barbara leans in, pulling the leash so her dog also seems to lean in. "Well, I heard a rumor that Woody Winters was called in for questioning yesterday."

"Oh, really?" This was news to me. Why didn't Danny tell me about that?

"Yes. Apparently, one of the high school teenagers was caught with a bag of small blue pills. The kid was so scared that he started crying and peed his pants. He told the police that Woody had told him to hold the bag for him."

I swear, some things never change around here. "And so what happened then?"

"Well, the police asked Woody to come down to the station. I'll bet he denied it all."

I'm missing something. "And?"

"Well, Woody was there quite a while. My old flame, remember Ricky?"

"Oh, yes, I remember him well."

"Ricky told me Woody went to the pub and started drinking last night, like really drinking hard. Woody was good and drunk when he started cussing and yelling that the kids around this neighborhood can't be trusted. Their lies slip from their mouths the moment they get in trouble. And on and on." She opens and closes her hand like a puppet.

"Well, I'm not surprised. Are you? No one wants to take responsibility for their own actions." My face pinches in disgust.

Barbara stares at me until I feel uncomfortable. The familiar feeling of embarrassment starts to rise up my neck. Then, to my surprise, Barbara moves to sit beside me.

"I know what people think of me," she says.

"No, I didn't mean—"

She cocks her head and cuts me off. "Wait. I know that I get over-involved in other people's business. I can't seem to keep a man in my life for anything. I've had too many marriages, too many failed relationships, too many ups and downs with too many people. I know I can be difficult." She sucks in a deep breath. "But the thing is, Clara, I am a good person. Really. I don't like seeing so much trouble among residents in our small community. I know who Bobby was. I know who you were. Geez, I know that everyone knows who I was, too. That's both the beauty and the curse of being born, raised, and living in the same place with the same people. But when it came down to it, if anybody needed my help, I'd be there at a moment's notice. I wouldn't leave anyone hanging if they truly needed my assistance." She puts her hand on my knee. "And that includes you, Miz Clara Starr. I know I can be overbearing, but I am here if you ever need me."

For a moment, I can't speak. I've never seen this side of Barbara before, but, then again, I've never really allowed it. She's calmed the inner turbulence in me that had worsened over the last few days. I put my hand atop hers.

"Barbara, that's the nicest thing to say. Thank you. I appreciate you," I say.

She stands to go and gives me a side-eye. "Let me know if you find any dirt about the murderer." She winks and tugs on the leash of her dog.

People amaze me. Here I was, sitting down and wondering how all of this would end up, and poof! I learn something about Barbara that I've never known my entire life. She has a heart there, I think.

My phone rings; it's Alice.

"Hey, there, Alice. How are things?"

I hear a loud sniffle followed by a sob. Immediately, I am on high alert.

"What, Alice? What's going on?"

Alice mumbles words that have no meaning. She spits out a garbled stream interspersed with loud sniffs.

"Wait, wait. Slow down, Alice. I can't understand you. What's happened?"

I hear her labored breathing. She covers the phone and speaks to someone, but I can't understand what she's saying. Then she uncovers the receiver. "Clara?"

"Yes? What's happened, Alice?"

"Oh, Clara, they think I did it."

"What? Why? Who?"

"Danny. He came to my house and said I had to go to the station."

"Oh, that's ridiculous. Why would he do that? What's wrong with him?"

"Clara, he said they want to ask me about Bobby. They think I had something to do with my own husband's murder."

# CHAPTER 28

I burst into the police station with my anger building. When I get to the front desk, a female police officer with her hair tied tight in a bun asks how she can help me. I try to control the tone of my voice, but it trembles anyway. I'm frightened and angry.

"I'm here to pick up Alice Ward."

The officer types something into her computer. She shakes her head and says, "Sorry, we can't let her out her yet."

My fists clench. "What? Why? I'd like to speak to your supervisor."

The officer holds my stare for a few seconds, then abruptly turns and marches into a back room. I can hear her voice but can't make out what she's saying. I hear another low voice, then a loud sigh as someone stands up from the desk. A burly man comes out from the back room. He has a paunch and grey hair.

"Clara, nice to see you," the officer says.

"Yeah, Dennis. Listen, I'm here to pick up Alice. She said something about being questioned about Bobby's murder. It's ridiculous, you know. Come on, we're talking about Alice here. You know her as well as I do." I can't stop my mouth from spitting out the words at a dizzying pace. "So, I've come to get her, take her home. Unless, of course, you're going to be an ass—I mean a jerk—about it. So, what's it going to be, Dennis?"

I know I'm crossing a line, but I tend to go overboard when I'm frightened. To make matters worse, I'm on display for everyone to see. I look behind Dennis and see some other officers gathering to see what the commotion is about. They all look familiar, but we don't socialize in the same circles. The Londontowne and Mystic Beach police officers are a cliquish bunch.

Dennis leans closer to me and lowers his voice. "Clara, look, I can't give you all the details, but Alice is going to be here for a little while. We asked if she'd come to the station to talk with us, and she agreed. We'll let her call you to pick her up, but we're not quite finished."

I start to speak, but Dennis holds his hand up. "Come on now, no, no. This is going to be done by the books. For chrissake, Clara, we're investigating a murder. This is how it's going to be. You'll just have to accept it for now."

I look at Dennis like he's growing two horns on his head. Officers gather in a cluster, staring at me, some smirking. I flash back to being hauled here as a high school student when I was caught with pot. My mother thought spending some time in the holding cell would scare me into being a good girl. She was afraid of losing me, but it was a humiliating experience. I felt like a caged animal in a zoo with onlookers gawking at me. I feel that way now.

"Okay, Dennis. Okay. When can I get her?"

"It should take a few hours, then we'll let her go. Unless she confesses to a crime," he responds. "In that case, I can't promise she'll be going home." He pauses and looks behind him. "There's a lot going on here, if you know what I mean. I promise you, Clara, when we're finished questioning her, we'll let her call you to pick her up."

I know Dennis is trying not to be a jerk, but I feel enraged. There is nothing more I can do right now. I nod my assent, then go out to my car in the parking lot. Before I leave, I text Danny and ask him what time he's coming by with pizza. I have to get to him first, before anyone at the precinct tells him I busted into the station and made an ass of myself.

Danny replies that he'll be over shortly. He needs to go home and change, then pick up the pizza. I get back in my car and drive home to wait for him. I can't believe this day has already come to this. I know there were a lot of issues between her and Bobby. She has plenty of reasons to off him, but so does everyone else. Everyone in this town knows Bobby was a thieving, mean, abusive jerk. Why would they put so much energy into finding the person who did us all a favor, and I mean *us all*.

When I get home, I wash my face with cold water in the kitchen sink. I'm drying my face when Danny walks in.

"Hey," he says.

He puts the pizza box on the table and comes to the kitchen with his arms open. I walk into them because there's nothing else I can think of doing. His arms wrap around me, and he places his chin on the top of my head. I can't help it, but I start to cry.

"Hey, now, hey," he whispers. "It's going to be okay. You'll see. It's all going to be okay."

I feel my tears soak into Danny's T-shirt. We embrace in my kitchen for several minutes. We sway slightly, like rocking a baby. Danny has always been the steady one in my life. I've never felt judged or afraid or uncertain when Danny's around me. Throughout my tumultuous childhood, he was my go-to person. He'd listen to me rage and cry and scream. When my father died, I'd oscillate from one extreme to the next. He'd listen when I needed to talk. He'd hold me like he's doing now when I felt broken. I push away from him and turn towards the refrigerator.

"Iced tea?" I ask.

"Sure." Danny pulls several paper towels off the roller, grabs the pizza box, and heads outside.

After I fill two glasses with ice and pour the tea, I follow behind. As I sit, Danny hands me a slice of the pepperoni and green pepper pizza. I take a bite and let the flavors coat my mouth.

"Mmmm. Angelina sure knows how to make a good pizza, doesn't she?" I start.

Danny murmurs his agreement. We watch a flock of seabirds soar in a gust of wind over the bay. The salted air is thick. There's a gaggle of geese floating worriless on the water's surface. The caw of the seagulls and the sounds of the waves brushing the shore help my nerves settle. I can hardly believe what's happened over the last weeks. It seems as though my world has turned upside down. Alice wouldn't hurt anyone. I know she wouldn't, yet she's being interviewed now with no one there to talk to or hug. Maybe I should have called Brian. He's sure to be devastated, if he even knows.

"What are you thinking?" Danny asks.

"I'm thinking about Alice being locked up. She's alone there. I just don't get it, Danny."

He swallows the bite of food in his mouth. "She's not 'locked up,' Addie. She's being questioned, is all. But, I know; I can't believe it, either."

I turn to stare at him, the beginnings of a thought causing me distress. "Danny, did you bring in Alice yourself?"

He looks at me. Is that guilt in his eyes, or am I imagining it?

"No, Clara. I wasn't the one who pulled her in."

"Well, then, what happened?"

"I can't go into details. The papers that you gave me this morning? I handed them over to the chief. I think he knew better than to send me over to get Alice. I love Alice, just like you."

"Why did they have to put her in the car at all, Danny?"

"She doesn't drive. You know that, Clara. Chief wanted her down at the station. He knew he could get her there by flustering her and then offering a ride."

"What a jerk," I say. "But how did it go down like this? What made the chief think that Alice is the one who killed Bobby?"

He shakes his head back and forth. "Good question. I mean, I know what you know about Bobby and Alice's relationship. It was terrible."

"He hit her!"

"I know, I know. Maybe that will be a part of her defense."

"Wait, what? Her defense? You make it sound like she's already guilty, Danny. What the hell?"

He puts his hands up. "No, that's not what I'm saying. If Chief decides to arrest Alice, it means he was already checking up on leads."

"What about Woody? He's positioned himself in the seat of distinction after threatening Bobby in public."

"Look, Alice isn't the only one we're questioning. But one thing I do know. Whoever did this will spend the rest of their life in prison."

# CHAPTER 29

Alice hasn't called yet. So, I decide to stop by Sunview to visit Mom. Even more than just visiting, I need her to do a spread for me. I feel as though my world is in shambles. I tossed and turned in bed last night. I had another one of my recurring dreams about being lost in a big city and unable to find my way home. I hate having dreams where I'm lost and can't get back home. I wake up frazzled and tired.

As I walk into Sunview's double doors, Edward is on his way out to sit on the porch. I punch the automatic door button, and both doors swing wide.

"Hey, young lady. You're looking lovely as usual," Edward says.

"Thanks, Edward. How are you doing?" I ask, but authenticity doesn't ooze from my voice. I'm in a hurry but I don't want to be rude.

Edward keeps rolling. "All's well, my dear. All will be well," he says.

I turn. "What? What did you say, Edward?"

Either he hears me, or he doesn't. He continues outside as the automatic doors close.

I take the elevator upstairs to the third floor. As I walk onto the floor, I hear a distant conversation between staff and a resident. They're laughing about something. I race to Mom's room and walk in. Mom's sitting on her sofa, watching a video on her iPad. She senses my presence and looks up. She starts to smile but then readjusts her facial features into concern.

She holds open her hands, palms facing upward and moves them side to side. "What? What?"

My eyes well up, and tears drip down my cheeks. I rush to sit beside her and allow her arms to encircle me. I start to sob. Mom holds me like she did when I was a child. When I finally gain control over myself, I pull back. She reaches over and wipes away my tears.

"Tell me," she signs.

I tell her. I explain how Danny presented me with a court order for my notes. That although I had to provide them, I didn't know they'd be used to suspect Alice.

Mom interrupts, "Alice?" she signs with the letter A on the side of her face.

"Yes, Alice. They pulled her in for questioning. They think she might have murdered Bobby. I tried to get her, but Dennis said I had to wait until they finished questioning her. Hopefully, she'll call any minute, and I can pick her up. They're making a mistake. I know it."

Mom asks, "Do you think your notes made Dennis suspect she killed him?"

I shrug. "I don't know. But it seems unusual that I would hand over my notes to the police in the morning, and by the afternoon, Alice is at the station being questioned. I feel terrible."

Mom notices my trembling. "Is there something else going on, Clara? You look very upset."

I shake my head forcefully. "No, Mom. No. But could you do a reading? You know, the timeline spread?"

Mom reaches into her basket for her cards. She spreads out the full deck on the coffee table and asks me to pick five cards. One by one, she flips them and puts them in a line. When all five cards are laid out, she pauses for a minute, then begins.

"Card one is the history card. Judgment is a major arcana card. There has been a lot of self-evaluation and snap decisions. You have been faced with a lot of questions, and renewal is afoot.

"Card two is about recent events. The Moon. There is a lot of fear and anxiety, possibly about unveiling secrets. Deception, insecurity, and misconception are surrounding recent events.

"Card three is the present. Two of Swords indicates that you're at a crossroads, but you're not sure what to do. There is a difficult decision to be made. Something is dividing your loyalty, making you choose between two things or people."

Mom looks puzzled. I cast my eyes down to the cards, indicating I want her to continue.

She sighs. "Card four is the near future. Major arcana card, The Tower. There is sudden upheaval, change, or disaster. Ah, Clara, there is much pain and destruction on its way.

"Card five is the far future." Mom smiles. "Oh, this is good, the Ace of Swords. Despite the upcoming chaos and disorder, there will be a breakthrough. Truth will become known and bring new plans and victory."

Mom gathers the cards and shuffles them into the deck. She puts the cards away and looks at me. She wants to know what's going on. I just can't even begin to explain what's happening. My mother is many things. She's kind and understanding and open. She's also firm in her beliefs and thinks she knows what to do better than me. I don't want to start a conflict right now. Mom doesn't know. She can't possibly know everything, no matter how strong her gifts of intuition and foresight are.

"I can't explain now," I sign to Mom. "I'm going to see if I can pick up Alice. Maybe they'll let me in to visit her."

Mom opens her arms. I give her one of my bear squeezes. Despite her frail and bony stature, Mom is a lot stronger than people believe. Mom responds with a bear squeeze of her own.

I jump into my car and drive the five miles to the southern district precinct. The sun is still glaring down on the black asphalt parking lot, causing heat waves to ripple. I slam my car door and rush to the air-conditioned vestibule. The same officer is sitting behind the desk.

"Hey, there. Look, I'm sorry about my earlier behavior," I say. "I was upset that my friend was here. Her name is Alice Ward. I shouldn't have come barreling in like that, but I was distraught. I've come to pick her up."

The officer holds up a finger, signaling me to wait. She goes back to the office and emerges seconds later. She walks around the desk behind a closed and locked door. I hear the lock being opened, and the door swings open.

"Come on through. I'll take you back to see Ms. Ward."

I follow the officer through a series of hallways and locked doors. She escorts me down a hallway where there are three interview rooms. Alice is in the last one.

"Alice," I whisper.

Alice looks up from the metal chair on which she's sitting. Her face hangs in despair. She looks like she's aged twenty years since yesterday. Her gray, curly hair puffs up on one side. As if self-conscious, Alice reaches up to flatten her hair.

"Oh, Clara. I must look terrible," she says as her eyes fill. "I don't know what happened. I was in the back yard working on the garden. You know, the one that Brian and I are working on? I was getting ready to pull some weeds when an officer came into the yard. He said he had some information about Bobby's murder that he wanted to discuss, but he preferred to do it at the station. I was afraid because the officer kept staring at me as if he knew something about me. I didn't feel like I had a choice. So, I got into his car, and we came here."

"I know. I know. It's going to be okay, Alice. I'll take you home."

Alice says, "They said … they said …."

"Don't worry, Alice. We don't need to talk about it now. Not here with everyone listening in and watching. Let's talk later, okay?"

Alice nods, and the officer leads us back to the lobby. I sneer, and the officer turns to look at me.

"I mean, really? Alice is an old lady. What were you all thinking?"

The officer turns back around and ignores me. There has to be some misunderstanding. My mind flits to the memory of Mom's reading about revealing secrets and having to make a choice. I know a little bit about secrets, that's true. But making a choice? Well, I know Alice is innocent. Despite all the harm Bobby inflicted upon her, she doesn't have a violent bone in her body. I'll do whatever I have to in order to help her. Hopefully, I won't destroy both our lives in the process.

# CHAPTER 30

While we're driving, I reach over and squeeze Alice's arm. "I'm going to help you get this sorted out. Danny, Brian, and I will help figure this out."

Alice shakes her head in disbelief. "Danny? Right. He's the one who started this."

"What do you mean?"

"Wasn't it Danny who gave you the court order for your notes? And wasn't that how they decided I'm a murderess?"

"Wait, Alice. Let's not get ahead of ourselves. No one thinks you're a murderer."

"You weren't in that interrogation room with that officer. He kept saying he knew 'there was more to the story' than I was telling. He looked at me like I was already tried and convicted." Alice's lips tremble.

"Don't worry, Alice. We'll figure this out. I called Brian and left a message for him."

Alice murmurs, "Brian?"

"Yes, Brian," I assure her.

"Does he know what happened?"

I shake my head. "I don't know. I called when I realized you were at the station. Maybe he'll be at the house when we arrive. Alice, I know this is a lot to handle," I say. She doesn't respond.

"Somehow, we'll solve this. And, anyway, I know you didn't kill him."

Alice turns toward me, and, in a meek voice, says, "What makes you so sure, Clara?"

I don't know how to respond. I mutter something unintelligible.

"Let me tell you something, Clara. There are a great many things about me that you don't know. Oh, I may appear to be some loose-brained old woman who can barely handle her life. Maybe that's how I *want* to appear to some folks. But there's one thing that you and anyone else should never do."

"What's that, Alice?"

Red anger climbs up her neck. Her voice strengthens, "Never, ever underestimate me. I am capable of many things that would send a shudder through your bones. 'Is she capable of murder?'" She laughs.

"That's not even the proper question, now that I think about it.

"'Oh, not Alice, poor, sweet, oblivious Alice,'" she imitates Barney Fife. "Ha! People forget I was married to that abomination of a husband for almost my whole life. It may have looked like Bobby had beaten me into submission, and, yes, maybe he did in some ways. But there is nothing like a woman who's found her teeth. And believe me, Clara Elizabeth Starr, I have found my damn teeth."

I am shocked. I don't even try to utter a single response because the energy behind her rage is freaking scary. I have never seen Alice act anything other than sweet and slightly uncomprehending. This woman sitting in my passenger seat is nothing like that. I wonder if I've ever known her at all. I swing my car into her driveway.

Brian must have heard because the front door opens, and he rushes out. He goes to the passenger side and opens the door for his mother. Alice grabs him in a fierce hug. I turn my gaze to give them privacy but then turn back when I hear her voice. She's whispering something into his ear. He leans toward her almost imperceptibly, and she continues to speak. Her grip on his shoulders tightens, and she shakes him a little. His eyes raise to mine, but his face is unreadable. When she unlocks her arms from around Brian, he steps back as if he's lost his balance. Alice stomps toward the house and up the steps. The door slams.

"What was that all about, Brian?"

"Uh, well, you know, she's pretty upset and all. I mean, who wouldn't be? She's been accused of murdering my dad. I think the reality of it all hit her pretty hard."

"Yeah, but—"

"And anyway, I'm sure she's tired." He blows out a half-hearted chuckle. "So, I should be going," he says, turning away.

"Wait. Brian, wait." He seems reluctant. "Listen, I don't know what's going on. I don't have to know. I want to help Alice. I don't think she did this, Brian. I don't think she could kill him."

I have Brian's attention now. "Oh?"

My face reddens. I'm giving too much away. This is not going like I thought it would. "No. I mean, how could she? Brian, she's old. She's a softie. She could never, ever hurt someone. Even I know that."

Brian looks amused. "Oh, really? Are you sure about that, Clara?"

All at once, I'm not. In fact, I am not sure at all that Alice isn't involved in this somehow. I know she didn't do this, but for the first time, I wonder how many other things I don't know. Brian sees my facial expression change and walks toward me.

"Look," he whispers. "I know that you know how things have been with my dad. His violence, his drinking and drugging, his crazy mistresses all over the place."

I'm shocked. I didn't realize that Brian knew the extent of his father's extracurricular activities. I mean, I know Brian knows firsthand about his dad's violence and drinking. He knows about the drug dealing and sexual liaisons, too? That's news to me.

"Dad got what was coming to him, no matter the who or the how of it, all right? Let's not get too deep in the whodunit part. Instead, let's figure out a way to get Mom settled and back to a new chapter in her life. Okay?"

Brian's right. Even I know how terrible Bobby was in life. Everyone, and I mean *everyone*, is much better off with his body in the morgue. Now, I just need to figure out how to keep Alice out of the police's crosshairs. First, I need a Xanax to get my nerves calmed down. Then, I can figure out what to do next.

# CHAPTER 31

When Addie arrives on Monday morning, I'm still in bed. I can't shake this awful sense of foreboding. It feels like every cell in my body is screaming something in a language I can't understand. If only I could put all the pieces together, maybe things would surprise me and turn out okay.

Addie walks into the bedroom and opens the curtains. I shield my eyes from the unforgiving sunlight. I can smell the coffee in her hand before I open my eyes and see it. She puts the cup on the nightstand and picks up my prescription bottle and overturned wine glass. Her foot kicks the empty wine bottle on the floor. She bends down to retrieve it from under the bed.

As she goes out the door, she chirps, "Time to get up, Clara. Lala will be here soon, and you have work to do. Oh, wait." She goes into the bathroom and sets the bottle, wineglass, and prescription bottle on the bathroom vanity. I hear the squeal of the shower faucet turning on and then the beating water against the tub. She gathers the items again and says, "Let's go, Clara. Now. The shower is ready for you."

I sit up and take a deep, cleansing breath. I plant my feet on the hardwood floor and wrap my hands around the scalding cup of coffee. The burn of hot coffee singes my tongue. After several test sips, I stand up and shed my pajamas on the floor. A hot shower might help me scrub the feeling of desperation from my soul.

A little before nine, a police car pulls off to the side of the road in front of my house. I already know who it will be, and he does not disappoint. Danny opens the door and stands outside his cruiser. His smile lights up his face. I can't help it; I smile back. He walks over and pulls me into an embrace. His broad shoulders steady my anxiety. I gesture for him to sit beside me, but he shakes his head.

"Thanks, but I've got to be going in a minute or so. I just wanted to stop by and see how you're doing today. I tried texting you several times last night but didn't get a response. How are you?"

I sigh. "I know. I'm sorry, Danny. This whole thing with Alice has me bothered. I want to help her, but I'm not exactly sure how to do that." I look up. His face softens, and he puts his hand on my shoulder.

"Yeah, I can hardly believe it myself. She looked pitiful sitting in the station. You're a good friend, Clara."

"I know, but I just feel like I should be doing more."

Addie opens the French door and steps onto the patio. "Danny! It's good to see you," she says.

He smiles. "Hey, there. How's things?"

Addie's eyes briefly catch mine. "Things are all good. We're just getting ready to start the workday. Do you want a coffee? Maybe one to go?"

Danny's features fall back into police mode. "Nah, but thanks. I have to start my day as well. I'll see y'all later." He strides to his car.

"What was that about?" Addie asks.

I take a sip of my coffee. "Oh, he was checking on me. Just the idea that the police think Alice is implicated in Bobby's death ... I feel terrible about it."

Addie sits beside me. "I know. It's terrible. Do you think Alice killed her husband? I mean, I wouldn't blame her if she did. He was a real tool. He used up people and threw them out like trash. I mean, look at what he did to Lala."

Addie's remark stuns me. "What do you mean?" I ask.

Addie looks out at the bay as if gathering her thoughts. Does she know something that I don't? If so, why doesn't she just come out and say it? Maybe there's more to Addie than meets the eye. I wait her out.

"Well, remember her last session? I mean, Lala expected him to leave Alice. He'd promised her."

I'm not following her line of thought. "Yeah, but then Alice walked in on them in the shed."

"Right. Lala probably thought that would seal the deal. I mean, their liaison had been discovered. There was no need for secrecy. So, what if … what if …."

"Lala killed Bobby when he didn't leave Alice? Is that what you're inferring?" I'm not only shocked but indignant. I'm surprised that Addie would talk about a client like that. She only started working here recently.

"For that matter, Addie, Alice could have knocked him off because she found out what was really going on. I don't see how your line of thinking takes the blame off Alice and puts it on Lala."

Addie pushes her hair back behind her ear and looks at me. Her eyes are intense. "Or … or …" I dread what's coming. "… maybe they're in it together." Addie sits up taller.

"Uhhh, I don't know, Addie. Lala and Alice working in cahoots to kill off Bobby? I mean, they didn't have much in common, aside from Bobby and the fact that he was a lousy person and treated them both badly. I just can't see them teaming up on this one."

Addie sighs. She knows I'm right. I secretly wonder if she's read too many true crime books. She has a skill for imagination; I'll give her that. A part of me wonders if there's something more to Alice's story. The rage she dumped on me yesterday surprised me. I mean, I suppose it's possible Alice could have killed Bobby. Then again, it could have just as easily been me. I mean, really, everyone around here is holding onto a grudge.

Addie has been staring at me. A flash of emotion crosses her face. Is it anger? Frustration? "What? Why are you looking at me like that?" She looks like she suspects even me.

The strange expression quickly morphs into her regular, day-to-day face, friendly and open. "Nothing. I'm thinking about everything that's happened. Everyone around here has secrets."

Her eyes bore into me. I'm not taking the bait. She's probably right, anyway. Everyone has secrets. Yes, even me, but that doesn't mean I'm going to open up and spill my guts. Not to her. Not to anyone.

"Yeah, well," I start. "You're probably right about that. I've never met a person who didn't have a bone or two tucked inside their closet." I laugh, but it sounds false even to my own ears. "Anyway, how about we think about the next client. After all, they pay us to listen to their secrets, don't they? To help them make sense of all that they've endured?"

Addie grins. "That's true. We're professional secret keepers, aren't we? But…" She hesitates.

"But what?" I ask.

"Well, it couldn't hurt to poke around and gather more information about people's relationships with Bobby. I mean, if you're certain that Alice didn't kill him, then we have to see what other evidence we can find. Right?"

She has a point. The whole thing borders on the unethical, but we don't have much time. Although Alice was only questioned, the police might decide to charge her.

I shake my head. "I don't know, Addie. My clients aren't paying me to investigate Bobby's death. They've got other stuff to be concerned about."

"Well, look at it this way," Addie says. "If you can find out who the real killer is, then you're doing them a favor by taking any suspicion off them. You're actually helping them by ruling them out, one by one, so they don't have to undergo scrutiny from the police. Know what I mean?"

Yes, I know what she means. If I can find out more information, then I can control the narrative. I can decide what is revealed and what is kept secret. I know Addie isn't thinking about it that way, but there's a lot that Addie doesn't know. There's a lot at stake here. For them and for me.

# CHAPTER 32

Just as Addie and I stand up, Lala walks across the front lawn.

"Hey, hey, hey, girls. How's it going?" she sings.

I forced a smile onto my lips. "It's going good, Lala. How are things with you?"

Lala shoves a pink cake box toward us. Addie cradles the box as Lala tells her to open it. "It's a very special treat this week."

Addie opens the box, and a look of horror skims across her face. I bend over the box to see what was inside. Lala had made cookies this time. The sugar cookies are cut in the shape of dismembered body parts. Chunks are missing, as if bitten away. The body parts are gory, covered in frosting that looks like blood and something green that resembles slime. Deep in the box is a cookie formed in the shape of a head. Gray icing it. One eye is colored a brilliant blue, while the other appears to have been ejected from its socket, with blood seeping out. I can't keep the astonishment from my face.

Lala bends over laughing. She laughs so hard that her lungs start to wheeze. Tears slip from her eyes, and she wipes them with the back of her hand. Every time she starts to speak, a fresh bubble of laughter bursts. After a moment, she realizes that Addie and I are not laughing with her.

Gathering herself, Lala says, "Oh, come on, girls. This is funny, right? I mean, what? Are we supposed to walk around all morose and crap? Crying crocodile tears? Going through the motions of saying, 'How horrible it was that Bobby was murdered!' Or 'Oh, what a heinous crime'? Clara, if there's one thing I learned well in therapy with you, it is never to lie to yourself about your feelings. It's one thing to keep them private, away from the eyes of others. But lying to oneself contributes to a deeper problem, more suffering, more self-sabotage."

What Lala is saying is true. Maybe these cookies are Lala's way of coping with the loss of Bobby. Maybe she's trying to do the best she can. There's a whole body of literature about jokes, often inappropriate, that doctors make about their patients. It's a way to cope with the stress of their jobs and to bond with others who are undergoing the same types of stressors. The cookies, while grotesque-looking, certainly get their message across. Maybe this is Lala's way of expressing her emotions. The cookies do look crazy, but, hey, I'm feeling crazy myself. I start to laugh.

"See? See there?" Lala says. "Think about it for a second. Body parts

… bashed up, butchered, balls of dough—Bobby parts." She snorts.

I see the edges of Addie's lips start to curl up. Her shoulders shake, which causes me to honk. For a second, I put my hand to my mouth in astonishment before belting out a burst of raw laughter. I put my arm around Lala's shoulders and guide her inside.

Lala finds a comfortable spot and settles on the sofa. She dips her hand into the bakery box and pulls out a foot. She wiggles her eyebrows as she pops it whole into her mouth.

"So, tell me how you're doing," I prompt.

Lala's eyes sparkle. "Actually, Clara, I've been doing fantastic."

"Oh?"

"Yeah. Something about Bobby being gone for good has set me free from feeling so—I don't know—burdened. All these years I waited for him to leave Alice, for him to come to me. But you know what? He never did. I can see how he strung me along like I was some kind of puppy. I mean, who the hell does that but a bad person?"

Something about Lala's demeanor makes me pause. I should have her focus on healing from the years of abuse, low self-esteem, and compulsive eating. That's where our focus has been all along, but something stops me from going in that direction. For one, I'm curious how much Lala knows or is involved with Bobby's murder. If Lala is responsible somehow, that will get Alice off the hook, but could I really turn in Lala to the police? Her history of extensive child abuse by her parents, then later sexual abuse by sundry malcontents throughout her life, made her vulnerable to being exploited. As Lala started to heal, anger replaced self-hate, which is a good sign. She has a lot to be angry about. The goal should be for her to express her anger, cleanse herself of it, and blame it on the perpetrators instead of herself. That's the proverbial ground zero, the starting point to rebuild a strong sense of self. So why am I thinking about asking more about the Bobby situation?

"Uhhh … hello? Anybody home?" Lala sings.

I snap back to reality. "Sorry, Lala. I was just thinking about where we will go from here."

"Where we'll go?"

"Yes, I mean, what path to take towards getting you back on track, making you feel better, and strengthening yourself to feel confident in the world."

Lala laughs. "Bobby's death was a good push in that direction. I wish I had realized sooner how good it would feel to have him gone."

First Addie, then Lala bringing up Bobby's death. I feel like the universe is pushing me to solve Bobby's murder. I know enough from living with my mother that unseen energies will continue to push someone toward a lesson until it is finally learned. My shoulders relax as my own path becomes clear. I shift my position in the chair.

"So, let's talk more about Bobby."

"Bobby? Why would we want to talk about him? He's gone, gone, gone."

"And?" I ask.

"And he's now a part of my past, not my future."

"Is there a part of you that misses him? Misses what you had together?"

Lala looks out of the glass French doors. "You know, it's like the changing of a season."

"How do you mean?"

"Well, take the Chesapeake Bay, for example. In the summer, the sunshine glimmers off the bay. The seagulls dance on the sea breezes. Boaters of all types float up and down the bay, crab boats, sailboats, cargo ships, and cruise ships, right? Marylanders eat blue crabs on outside picnic tables; their fingers turn red from the Old Bay seasoning. They use their mallets and pop-pop-pop the shells until they can reach the delicate white meat inside. It's all a part of the summer season. Beer and crabs. Boating, beaching, swimming.

"By the time winter arrives, all the recreational boaters are gone. Their boats are shrink-wrapped in tight white plastic. By December, even the crabbers are finished harvesting their crabs. Do we miss the summer? Do we miss being out on the water? Sometimes, but if you've lived near the bay all your life, you can see the beauty of the winter bay. Do you know what I mean?"

I did. The water becomes cold and looks clearer. Tides change. Low tides are lower. Most people stay indoors, but not me. I like to walk along the shore when the air is crisp. Winter quiets life around the bay. There are no shouts and screams of delight because the playground is empty of children. There are no picnickers with their plastic tablecloths and food spreads. During the cold months, I can easily spot deer walking through the clusters of trees that line the shore. The lack of leaves lets me see farther than I would in spring, summer, or even fall. There is a desolate beauty along the bay. Next to summer, when I gorge on blue crabs and corn on the cob, winter is my favorite time. I know exactly what Lala means about the seasons of the bay, but I don't understand the analogy and how it applies to her relationship with Bobby.

Lala continues. "So, the season of Bobby and me was over. I just didn't know it. What I thought was for real was only a delusion, a season, nothing more. He was never going to leave Alice. I know that now. Something had to be done. I couldn't take it anymore."

I realize I'm holding my breath, waiting for her to reveal something.

My breath whooshes out of me. "Okay…."

Lala reaches into the box for another cookie. She considers the red icing that flows out of the hand cookie. She seems to have finished what she wants to say.

How do I ask this? Do I want to know the answer? I think of Alice sitting at the police station alone in the room, appearing to be a hundred years old. I think about how Brian is Alice's only lifeline now that Bobby is gone. Maybe Bobby himself was only part of a season of Alice's life. I think about how many people Bobby hurt, even me. Why could no one stop him from inflicting pain on everyone around him? The only intervention that could bring any semblance of relief was for Bobby to disappear without the fear of ever returning. If Alice can be brave, so can I.

"So, Lala. Look, you know how much I believe in you, right? You know that whatever you tell me doesn't leave this room. Even if … even if it's something terrible. Your secrets have always been safe with me. You know that, right?"

Lala watches my facial expressions. After a moment, she nods. "Yes, I know that, Clara. You've always watched out for me, even when I couldn't watch out for myself."

"So, Lala …." I take a deep breath.

"Yes?"

"So … do you know anything more about what happened to Bobby?"

"Like what? Like how he looked when he rolled on the shore half-eaten by crabs?"

Whoa, what? There is a tone that rings of sarcasm. What is she implying? Does she know something about me and that morning? Is she trying to tell me something other than what I'm asking?

"No, of course not," I say, gathering myself. "What I mean is, are you somehow involved in Bobby's disappearance?"

Lala's face is impassive. I can't tell what she's thinking about or whether she's going to lie or tell the truth. From the corner of my eye, I see the top of Addie's head appear around the wall separating her workspace from the therapy session. It feels like we're in a time warp, and I'm starting to get hot. I can feel sweat form above my lip, my heart pounding a thousand beats a minute.

Lala shifts on the sofa. "Are you asking me if I killed Bobby? Is that what you're after, Clara?"

I answer by staring into her eyes.

"No. I did not kill Bobby. But it's only because someone else got to him first."

There is more answer to the question than she's telling me. I know her well, her body posture and facial expressions. I can tell when she's lied and when she hasn't.

"Do you know anything more about it?"

Lala shakes her head. "The thing is, Clara, I know you asked the question, but I get the feeling that you don't want to know the answer. It's like you're fishing for information from me, information I can't offer you."

"I'm sorry, Lala. I really am. I don't mean to pressure you."

Lala lowers her voice. "Look, I firmly believe that if a gift arrives in your life, one that brings your happiness back, you don't try to send it back. You accept it with grace. You learn to accept these life blessings and not question too deeply. You know?"

Relieved, I smile. Yes, I know.

Lala continues. "You remember how Mr. Rogers used to say that when you're in trouble, there are always helpers? You go find a helper whenever you feel afraid or lost or unsafe. Do you remember?"

Yes, I loved watching Mr. Rogers. He was always full of life lessons broken down into small chunks so that children, even adults, could understand. What is Lala's point, though? I feel like she's talking in code.

"Did you find a helper, Lala?"

"I did. I was down and distraught and discarded. The way Bobby treated me, especially that last time when Alice caught us, made me feel like … like … trash, is what it is. I felt like an old piece of used-up garbage. So, I went and found me a helper."

"Okay, who?" I ask.

"You'll never guess. He went away for a while, but then he got out. We ran into each other at the pub. At first, I was afraid Bobby would find out, but he didn't. I was gradually working my way out of the relationship with Bobby by hooking up with someone else."

"Who, Lala? Who was your helper?"

"Johnston Burr."

I know my face reveals my shock. "The guy who just got out of prison?"

"Yeah. We knew each other from a while back when Bobby introduced me to him. Bobby set him up, you know? Bobby let him take the fall for the bag of dope he was carrying. Johnston was doing drugs and all, but he wasn't dealing like Bobby was."

A tendril of fear made its way up my chest. "But, Lala, Johnston? He doesn't seem like—"

"Like what, Clara?" Lala's voice rose. "Like he'd be interested in a girl like me? Is that what you're saying?"

I shake my head. "No, no. That's not what I mean. Come on. You know me better than that. It doesn't seem like he'd be the kind of guy you'd be interested in."

My voice falls flat. I know Lala would be interested in anyone who showed even a modicum of interest. No, what I really mean is why would Johnston Burr be interested in her? Unless there is some ulterior motive on his part.

"Look, Johnston rescued me, Clara. He came at the right time. He and I are broken people. We understand each other. And we both hated Bobby. That brought us closer together. I love him, Clara. And he loves me."

Lala and I both glance at the clock at the same time. We stand. Lala reaches in for a hug. As she opens the French doors to go outside, she says, "Oh, and I know Johnston will be here to see you later today."

I shake my head. She knows I can't tell her about any of my clients.

"Oh, don't worry, Clara. Johnston tells me everything."

# CHAPTER 33

I need a break after Lala leaves, and, apparently, so does Addie. She yells from the kitchen that she'll bring us tea. I sit down outside and watch the gulls ride the wind. The air smells thick and briny. It's humid today. Addie comes out with two mugs of peppermint tea.

"I put in a teaspoon of butterbean honey," she says.

I take a sip and close my eyes. This is the perfect remedy to restart.

"The session with Lala was really something, wasn't it?" Addie asks.

"Indeed it was."

"So, what do you think? Do you think she killed Bobby? Or do you think she knows who did?"

I don't know how to respond to that. On the one hand, it's very unethical for Addie to ask me that kind of question about a client. She knows better. Then again, who am I to judge? I mean, I actually did ask the question during the session. Should I respond like the experienced therapist that I am? Or should I just get down to it and be truthful? I've been trying to be more upfront and honest, but this whole thing feels like a house of cards that will fall down all around me. I've never been one to be truthful because it's the moral thing to do. No, I am … was the kind of person who would hold the truth if it meant that I would be protected, anonymous, a secret keeper. If pushed, I'd lie outright and without any remorse. I have always been a survivor. Life's knocks made me into one. Still, a liar isn't what I long to be anymore.

"I don't know, but I don't think so. I mean, Lala wasn't saying everything she knew. That, I feel certain of."

"What about Johnston? Were you surprised that she's with him? I mean, geez, that guy scares me just by the looks of him."

"I know what you mean. He's the sort of guy that I could imagine killing someone. And true, he had a beef with Bobby. I mean, he ended up going to prison because of him."

"And he's coming in later today. You know that, right?"

I take a sip of tea. "Yeah, I know. I'm not thrilled about seeing him. I'm never too thrilled about court-ordered clients. They don't want to see me, and they're often not interested in making progress. At least, that's the feeling I get from Johnston."

"Me, too," Addie says. "He definitely doesn't seem like he wants to reflect on his choices and improve his life. If anything, he seems like the opposite."

Wait, what? My scalp tingles.

"What do you mean by 'he seems like the opposite'?"

Addie reflects for a moment. "Well, I knew from the first session that he wasn't interested in coming for therapy. I thought it had to do with being required by the judge. Then, something about how Lala talked about Johnston as being a helper. It was as if there was another purpose to Johnston being here with you. So, I started to wonder how Lala's 'helper' might help her."

I could feel the edges of my brain sizzling. "Addie! I never thought of that. So, what if Johnston had helped Lala? And himself, let's not forget that. What if offing Bobby was the key to getting rid of Bobby for good and wrapping it up as a 'gift' for Lala, who would then adore him and call him her hero?"

"Bingo. That's what I'm thinking, too. So, are you going to see if you can pry information out of Johnston?"

I grin. "Yes. Yes, I think that's exactly what I'll do."

Addie and I finish our tea. She goes off to her cubby and finishes her notes about the session. I sit in my armchair and think about my strategy for questioning Johnston. I have to be careful; he's a dangerous guy, to be sure. He probably learned a few extra tricks while in prison. He'll suspect me if I ask him outright, like I did with Lala. I have to be even more sly than he is. After all, this is for a good cause. Alice is a good woman. She and Brian need someone to be on their side. That someone is going to be me.

An hour later, Johnston knocks at the front door. I open the door and plaster on my best welcoming smile. He does not take the bait. Instead, he stomps into the sitting area and flops onto the couch. He looks around the room, focusing first on the books in my bookcase, then on the framed photographs of my parents and me as a child. We're standing in a group with other neighbors, including Alice, Brian, and Bobby. He stands suddenly and walks toward the corner shelf. He pushes his face close to the picture, then scowls and sits down.

"What's wrong?" I ask.

"That picture," he says and points to the corner. "I recognize those people. Your parents, you, but I didn't expect to see Alice, Bobby, and Brian."

"Yeah, Alice and my mother were friends."

"Wasn't your mother death?"

"You mean 'deaf,'" I correct him. "Yes, but Alice and Mom had a special way of communicating."

Johnston's intense gaze pierces me. "And Bobby? Were your parents friends with Bobby?"

"Johnston, what's your point here?"

He shuts down. "No point. Come on, let's get this over with. What questions do you have for me today?"

I sit silently and regard him. His demeanor tells me he doesn't want to be here. In fact, he looks hostile, like anger is seething inside him, ready to explode. I feel on edge myself, probably because his behavior is so unpredictable. He's a large guy, too. Tattoos cover his muscular arms. He has a tattoo of a viper going up his chest and around the side of his neck. This is definitely not a guy who plays around, which is exactly the type of person who could theoretically have murdered a double-crosser like Bobby. Even if he didn't kill him, he is the perfect profile, someone to take the focus off Alice. I now feel a whole lot better.

"Let's start with why you went to prison in the first place."

Johnston's laugh sounds like a growl. "Uh, I'm pretty sure you know this. You have the court papers." Sarcasm drips from his lips.

"True. You went to prison for dealing drugs."

"Dealing? Uh, try holding."

"Holding?" Sarcasm seeps into my own voice.

Johnston rises to the challenge. "Yes. Holding. I was holding your friend's bag of oxys when the cops came and busted me. You know, Bobby didn't even come out of the Royal Farms to see what the commotion was about. He stepped out of the store just as the cops locked me in the back seat. And you know what he did next? He smiled. The fucker looked me dead in the eye and smiled."

"Come on, Johnston. You're trying to tell me that the bag of drugs you were holding only belonged to Bobby? You had taken possession of a bag of some *aspirin* and didn't think twice about it? I think we both know better than that."

I am aware I'm poking the bear, but I don't realize how much until Johnston sits back on the sofa and stares at me. All of a sudden, I feel like I've walked too deeply into a cave, and now I'm looking straight at a giant grizzly that is going to maul, then eat me. The hairs on the back of my neck stand up. I break eye contact even though I know he will interpret it as weak. One minute stretches to the next, then to the next. Johnston leans forward, an innocent shift that appears suddenly menacing.

"Clara Starr. Oh, excuse me, *Doctor* Clara Starr. The shrink who gets to sit in the chair and tell others how to lead their best life. The person who has the answers for all of the fools who don't. I didn't realize that I was in the presence of such greatness," Johnston says, stretching the last word so he sounds like a snake.

"See, the thing is, *Doctor* Starr. I don't think that you're any better than me. No, not at all."

I straighten my shoulders despite wanting to run out of the room. "I never claim to be better than anyone else. Not even you, Johnston."

His lips part and reveal crooked, nicotine-stained teeth. He looks more animal than human.

"Oh, you don't have to tell me that, Clara. And you know why?"

Suddenly, I feel a faint buzzing inside my head, like I might throw up or pass out. I have miscalculated this man. He knows more than even I want him to know, although I can't explain how I know this. I just need to stop him from talking. He's going to reveal something that I've desperately wanted to keep secret from everyone.

He continues. "Oh, poor Clara, what's the matter? You look like you need a cold rag." He turns to face the wall behind which Addie is sitting. "Maybe we should see if someone can bring you a glass of iced water? Hmm?" He grins.

"No," I whisper. "No."

Johnston reveals his reptilian smile once again. "No. I thought not. You see, Clara, Bobby and I were actually pretty good friends before I got busted. I would even venture to say that I was his best friend. And do you know what best friends do, Clara?"

I shake my head, willing my hands to stop trembling.

"Best friends tell each other their secrets. But that's not even the best part. Do you know what the best part is? No, I don't suppose you do. The best part is when you tell each other everyone else's secrets, especially the dark, soul-crushing ones that shape a person's life. Yeah, those secrets, Clara. Those kinds of secrets bend a person into submission, now, don't they? And Bobby was a master at bending people. He knew exactly what he had to do to get a person to do what he wanted. And we were such best friends, Clara, he taught me how to do it, too."

# CHAPTER 34

When my eyes open, I'm lying on the sofa with a cool washcloth on my forehead. I startle when I turn and see Addie sitting on the floor near my head.

"Hey, hey. It's all right," she coos. "You're okay. Let's just take a few minutes here."

I sit up, and the washcloth, still damp, falls in my lap. Addie removes it and places it on a coaster on the coffee table.

"What happened?"

Addie stares at me.

"What happened, Addie? I'm serious." I look down at my clothes; nothing is out of place. My arms feel okay. I don't hurt.

Addie sits beside me on the sofa. "Nothing really happened. Johnston was talking, then he left abruptly. I guess he didn't like what you said," she says, a grin forming on her lips. "When he left, I finished up my notes and came around to congratulate you on pushing his buttons. You were sitting in the chair, kind of stone-faced. You stood up and then laid on the sofa and closed your eyes. I asked if you felt okay. Geez, your face was so pale. So, when you laid down, I went into the bathroom to get a cool cloth. How are you feeling now?"

"I feel okay. I don't know what happened. One minute Johnston was spewing out his anger on me, and the next minute I wake up here on the sofa."

"It didn't sound like he touched you. I was sitting in my alcove, and I would have heard if he tried to hurt you. I didn't hear anything unusual at all," Addie says, but I can see she's lying.

"I don't know. Maybe I'm tired. I haven't been sleeping well," I say. "Tonight will be an early bed night." I chuckle.

The relief on Addie's face is palpable. She doesn't want to ask a question that she's not prepared to hear the answer to. That makes two of us.

"Come on, let's go to the patio for a glass of wine," I say.

While Addie is filling our glasses, I go back to my bedroom and slide open the drawer of my bedside table. I open the prescription bottle and dump a Xanax into my hand. As I begin to close the cap, I think again and dump out one more pill. I can't let Johnston and his insinuations get inside my head. That's all I need is for someone to open up this Pandora's box and crush me in the process.

When I go out onto the patio, Danny is sitting with Addie, drinking my glass of wine. As I say hello, Addie jumps up to get another glass. I settle across from Danny. Addie returns with a glass full of wine.

"Hey, there. Clara, you don't look so well. Are you okay?" Danny asks.

My eyes shift to Addie. She told him. I know because her face is turning a pastel shade of pink.

"Oh, I'm doing okay. I'm tired, not sleeping. Same ole, same ole. You know."

"I know, Clara, but there isn't anything you can do for Alice except to be her friend. Support her. Support Brian. Just be there for them."

"I know. I'm trying. It's a weight bearing down on me, is all. Too much emotion, too much turmoil, too much mystery."

"Now, when does Clara Elizabeth Starr not love mystery?" Danny smiles.

I return the smile, remembering our childhood adventures exploring old, abandoned houses in the fields on the eastern shore.

"Remember that one old house way out on Tilghman Island? The one in the middle of that farm along the bay?" Danny asks.

I grin. "Remember when we opened that door, the knob came off in my hand?"

"Yeah, and we were afraid we'd fall through the rotting staircase—"

"Into the basement where all of the murdered bodies were buried?"

Danny and I laugh, caught up in our childhood memories. Danny turns to Addie.

"Clara really loved exploring. Not only houses, either. She'd drag me to barns, outhouses, crabbing shacks, hunter stands—just to see what we could find."

Addie smiles. "It sounds like you two were close friends."

"The best," Danny says.

"Always together," I add.

The three of us watch the bay and sip our wine. I feel Danny's eyes on me and turn to him.

"You know, Clara, there is nothing I wouldn't do for you," he murmurs.

"I know, Danny. I know."

"If something's going on, you can always tell me. No matter what."

I pause and look at his expression. His eyes are glossy, like he's about to cry. I know that mine mirror his. Suddenly, everything that is happening feels too overwhelming. The weight of Bobby's murder and how police suspect Alice makes me feel like I'm losing control. I feel like I am falling down a dark hole.

Addie says, "Listen, we're all here for you, Clara. There isn't anything that we can't handle together."

She reaches over and puts her hand on top of mine. Danny stands and puts his hand on top of hers.

"We're all in this together. No one has to bear the brunt of the whole situation alone," he says.

"But, Danny, it's hard not knowing. Can you tell me what's happening with the investigation? Is Alice still a suspect?"

Something in Danny closes. His tone shifts. "Nothing to report on that front. We talked with Woody Winters. Nothing came up there. We even talked to Shaun, though the only thing he's guilty of is taking over Bobby's crabbing territory on the bay. Oh, one more thing. The weird thing is that mysterious bacterial infection in Bobby's tissues that forensics found."

Addie says, "Oh, really? So it wasn't a homicide after all?"

Danny shakes his head and rubs his face. "Well, we can't go that far. Some experts were called in from the CDC because this is an infection that isn't familiar to that special M.E. There's still the problem of no water in his lungs, despite drifting in from the bay."

"Oh, so maybe someone tried to kill him by dumping him in the bay without knowing he already had an infection? Like he would have died on his own, but someone couldn't wait that long?" Addie asks.

Danny smiles. "I see Clara isn't the only one who likes mysteries, eh?"

It's cute how Addie blushes.

"I don't have all the answers yet, Addie. I'm working on finding a motive and determining who had the opportunity to kill him, but, unfortunately, we have a whole community who had reason to see Bobby dead. It's pretty frustrating, really."

My mind is going in a different direction. I need Johnston Burr out of my life before he detonates it all over Mystic Beach.

"Maybe," I begin but then stop.

"Maybe what?" Danny asks.

"Maybe you should call in Johnston Burr for questioning."

"Johnston Burr? Why would he be involved in this?"

I have to be careful. I'm legally obligated to keep my client's sessions confidential. At the same time, I don't like Johnston Burr. I don't like his influence on Lala's life or his hostile nature and veiled threats. I definitely don't like the way he thinks he can bend me into … what? Keeping quiet? Signing his court paperwork so he's free to do as he pleases? No. Johnston Burr is not going to intimidate me and get away with it.

"I can't break confidentiality by telling you anything specific. Take it as a tip from a friend. Johnston Burr is someone who might be of interest."

"Can you give me a little more to go on, Clara? I can't walk into the chief's office and say, 'Hey there, Captain. I'd like to pull in Johnston Burr. He's an interesting sort of character.' See what I mean? Chief won't go for that kind of thing. He doesn't want the community viewing us in a bad light, you know?"

I consider how much I can tell Danny. Even though I don't have anything definitive, there is certain information that I know for sure. For one, Johnston's using Lala for his own purposes. Second, he's a brute who exploits and controls people for his own personal interest, like his *best friend*. Third—and there's no way I'm going to tell Danny this—I think he knows something about me that I don't want him to reveal. It's not that Danny doesn't know my secrets because, God knows, he's aware of the many bad things I've done, especially when I was a teenager. I just don't want them pulled out of the past and hung on the flagpole for everyone to see. I've been so careful to rebuild my life and recreate my reputation as a professional, educated, and kind person. No, I can't say anything about the specific secret Johnston might know.

"Without breaking any laws, let me just say that Johnston holds grudges."

"Are you referring to Bobby's role in getting him locked up?"

"Yes," I whisper.

"Soooo …," Danny fishes, "he hasn't forgotten nor forgiven his old friend's set up at the Royal Farms? Like maybe good ole boy Johnston has a motive for wanting Bobby dead?"

This time, my voice is louder. "Correct."

"All righty then. Thanks for the tip." Danny stands. "I'm going to go home. I can't walk into the station with red wine on my breath. First thing tomorrow morning, I'll ask the chief if we can chat. Thanks, Clara. You really are a sleuth, after all."

# CHAPTER 35

The next morning, I wake up in my bed, but my mind is foggy. I kick off my blankets, which are damp from sweating overnight. I don't remember going to bed. Looking down, I see I'm wearing yesterday's shirt and underwear. Where are my pants? And who undressed me and put me to bed?

My mouth tastes like vomit and feels like someone stuffed it full of cotton balls. I try to think about what happened yesterday, but my head feels fuzzy. I remember seeing some clients. Oh, God, I saw Johnston Burr, the bastard. I move to sit up, but my head is spinning.

I hear noises coming from my kitchen. Who is in the house with me at this time of the morning? Oh, wait. I look at the clock and see that it's nearly eleven. Did I miss my first appointment this morning? I slowly drag my legs to the side of the bed and place my feet on the floor. The spinning isn't so bad if I move like a snail.

The noises from the kitchen continue. I hear drawers open and close, the faucet turning off, then on. Who is here in my house? It has been a long time since I've blacked out like this.

A disturbing image from my past takes shape in my mind. I'm on the floor under a bed. The smell of urine and mold assault my nostrils. Someone bends down and pushes aside a dirty blanket. A hand reaches under the bed to me. No. I am not going to pull back a curtain in my mind to go here. My heart starts pounding and I suddenly don't want this memory to surface. I jump up to prevent my brain from breathing life into this memory. The pounding headache and swirling room forces my memory to retreat. I hear the sound of clanking dishes. I open my bedside drawer and reach for the pepper spray I keep in there.

As I slide my hand to the back of the drawer, my fingers roll over my pill bottle. The lid is off. I grab the amber-colored plastic bottle and extract it. Empty. Did I take the rest of my Xanax last night? Impossible. Those days are long gone, or at least so I thought. Maybe someone took them from the drawer. Xanax is a form of money on the streets. You can exchange pills for just about anything you want, beer, a ride, or someone to plow the snow off your sidewalk. Maybe someone came into my room while I was sleeping and stole them.

Even as I say this, my thoughts ring hollow. They're the thoughts of a drug abuser, someone who's addicted to drugs and needs a fix. I am not that person anymore. Yet I have this sinking feeling that I somehow reverted back to my old habits. I remember going to Narcotics

Anonymous meetings and working the steps. The people there were firm in their belief that once you touch a substance again, even after a long sobriety, it was considered a relapse, and you had to start the steps over again. Well, I don't have to accept their definition of my actions. Even if I took one too many Xanax last night, that's hardly a drug relapse. I mean, I was upset yesterday and needed to calm myself down, to refocus on what to do next in solving Bobby's murder.

I jump as I see the profile of someone walking toward the living room. The person does a double-take and turns toward me. Addie. A whoosh of relief escapes me.

"Geez, Addie. I about had a heart attack. I was getting my pepper spray to take down the intruder."

Addie walks toward me and stops closer to me than I'd like. She looks worried as her eyes take in my puffy face and the stench of my breath. She reaches out like she's about to touch my shoulder, but I pull back. I don't like to be touched spontaneously like that. She drops her arm to her side.

"I was worried about you, Clara," Addie whispers.

Suddenly I feel self-conscious. I push my hair back from my face and take a step back. "What do you mean? Why were you worried?"

"How much do you remember from last evening?"

I attempt a laugh, but it comes off sounding like a cough. "What are you talking about, Addie? Of course, I remember last evening. What's the big deal?"

looks at the floor. It's as if she's debating how much to challenge me on this. When her eyes find mine, she says, "Clara, I don't want you to be defensive about this. I'm not attacking you. If anything, I'm protecting you. Do you remember Danny stopping by last night?"

I try to remember the details. My last appointment was with Johnston. There was something off about him, something dark and sinister. He scared me, and I get offensive when I'm scared. Yes, I remember Danny came by to say there wasn't much going on with the investigation.

"Is it coming back to you?" Addie asks.

"Nothing left me, Addie. How can it come back if nothing left?" I snap, knowing full well I'm being defensive. "Yes, I remember we were drinking wine on the porch last night with Danny. He was talking about the investigation, that Alice was still the main suspect."

Things are a little fuzzy after that, but I don't need to tell Addie that. Probably the Xanax that I took before I went out on the patio starting to take effect. I should have never started drinking wine after taking the pills. Stupid. Familiar, but stupid.

Addie continues, "Right. And you told him that he should

investigate Johnston Burr."

"I did? I told him to investigate him?" I ask, astonished.

"Well, you didn't come right out with it like that. You told him that maybe he'd want to talk with him, you know, after that bad session yesterday."

The memory of the session starts to materialize in my mind. Lala is enchanted with him, but he's using her, I'm sure. Something about Johnston's tone made me think he knew something about me, which can't be true because we never knew each other. It felt like a gut punch when I realized he and Bobby were close. I couldn't trust Bobby one iota; no one could.

"Right," I say. "What happened after that?"

Addie's face reddens. "Well, after Danny left, you filled your glass with the wine and, for some reason, kept going back to the bedroom, saying you had to go to the bathroom. It wasn't even an hour later that you were having trouble walking straight. You were slurring your words and nodding out on the porch."

"And so you put me to bed?"

Addie nods. I am horrified that Addie got a glimpse of the old Clara.

I fumble for my words, but Addie interrupts. "Clara, look. You don't have to worry. No one knows about it. I put you to bed last night and slept on the couch."

"You slept on the couch?" My voice is louder than I intended.

She nods. "I didn't know what to think, Clara. What if something happened to you? What if no one was here? And that Burr character is bad news. I knew it from the moment I first met him."

Addie steps forward again, putting her hand on my shoulder and giving it a little shake. "I've got you, Clara. I will always have your back."

It has been a long time since someone told me they've got my back and actually meant it. At least, I hope she means it. Because I have a feeling in the pit of my stomach that things are about to get a lot worse.

# CHAPTER 36

Addie and I drink a cup of coffee and eat a sandwich on the porch. The sun is blindingly bright, but its warmth feels good on my sickened body. I'm not going to have a repeat of last night. In fact, I'm not even going to get my prescription refilled. Just imagine if, in my intoxicated and drugged state, I'd decided to rip open my soul and tell her all my secrets, even my biggest one. That would have been self-destructive.

Addie tells me she asked Shelby to reschedule his morning appointment and to come in this afternoon instead. Shelby and I have a close relationship, so I knew he would be okay with that. By the time we finish lunch, I am showered and dressed, ready to start the day. At 12:30, I see Shelby crossing my yard, looking chic as always.

"Hello, loves," he says, flinging himself down on the porch chair.

"Hiya," Addie and I say simultaneously.

"The day is just too beautiful," Shelby says. He glances across the bay. "Is that Shaun's boat out there? He took no time at all taking over Bobby's crabbing area, eh?"

I shrug. "I don't think Bobby cares at this point."

Shelby's eyes snap back to me. Addie's shoulders start to shake. I snort. Shelby opens his veneer-filled mouth and belts out raucous laughter. The three of us hold our stomachs, tears dripping from our eyes. Some might call it disrespectful to laugh at the dead, but for us, it's about as much respect as Bobby can get from us now.

I groan as I stand up. "Okay, okay. Come on, Shelby, it's time to get down to business."

Shelby's eyes crinkle as he says, "Addie, get back to your cave, love. There's business to attend to."

When Addie is back in her cubby and Shelby sits down, he sniffs. I notice he's not fidgeting with his clothes. In fact, Shelby looks very comfortable today.

"How are you doing, Shelby?"

A wide grin stretches across his mouth. "Truly, Clara, I'm doing better than I ever have."

"Why's that?" I say, my smile mirroring his.

"With Bobby gone, Marshall and I can feel at peace."

I cock my head. True, but what a strange thing for Shelby to say. "Why does Bobby's death bring you two peace? Because he can no longer blackmail you?"

Shelby pauses. He runs his hands down his thighs and shifts in the chair. "Well, Bobby was like a herpes virus."

"What?" I chuckle.

He grins. "A herpes virus. He would go dormant for a long time, sometimes even years, but then he'd pop out and rage. If he wasn't trying to blackmail me or convince Marshall that I was cheating on him, then it was Bobby just being an ass, following me around town, jeering at me, calling me names."

I know what Shelby is saying is exactly right. "That's true. Bobby clung to people like stink on a skunk," I say.

Before I can ask the question that has been on my mind lately, he says, "But then someone got to him before me and made sure he was put to rest ... for good."

"Have you heard anything more about the Bobby investigation?" I ask.

"Not me. All I care about is that the bastard is gone for good. He won't be walking up on my doorstep anymore. And the whole thing has rekindled my relationship with Marshall. You never know the kind of effect a constant, low-grade stress can have on a person. With Bobby gone, it feels like I've been reborn. And, girl, let me tell you, it feels sublime."

"Shelby, I'm so glad things are going well for you now."

Shelby yells, "Addie, hey Addie, come out here."

Addie appears from around the corner. "Eh?"

"Come out here, girl, and sit with me and Clara."

Addie comes over and sits next to Shelby. He looks happy.

"I don't think I need to come for therapy anymore. Truly. Now that Bobby is gone, I feel like the last remaining thorns have fallen out of my soul. I'm happy and content. Marshall and I are thinking about moving to Barbados. We're going to start fresh somewhere beautiful." Shelby claps his hands in glee.

"Wow, Shelby, are you sure?" I ask, but I can clearly see a fundamental change in his demeanor. I can't help but be happy for Marshall and him.

Addie claps. "I think that's great, Shelby. I hope you're not planning to move too quickly, though. I'd like to have some time to get to know you better. You seem like such a cool guy."

Shelby's face reddens. "Aw, sweetheart, what a lovely thing to say."

Addie jumps up. "I know, let's celebrate with," she glances at me, "some apple cider!"

"Sounds marvelously bougie."

"Yes, apple cider is perfect," I say as Addie heads to the kitchen. "Shelby, when are you thinking about making this move?"

Shelby leans forward and beckons me closer. "Well, after Bobby's investigation is closed," he whispers.

"What do you mean?"

"Your old flame, Officer Danny, told Marshall and me that at this point, everyone's a suspect and to not leave the state. I might have laughed in his face if Danny didn't have those toned, buff biceps. I think he was serious, though. I get the feeling there's more he knows but won't say."

I sit back in my chair, stunned. "No. Why do you think that?"

"Believe it, girl. Danny has some tricks up his sleeve."

Addie interrupts my shock when she comes in with three mugs of hot apple cider.

Shelby says, "I don't know who in the world drinks hot apple cider in the middle of summer, but you know what? I like how you girls roll."

After Shelby leaves, Addie and I return to our normal spots on the porch. I share with her that Danny told him not to leave the area because they're still working on the investigation. Addie is surprised like I was when Shelby told me. We are silent as we watch the white caps form on the bay.

"The breeze is picking up," Addie says.

"It is. It really is."

From around the corner, Brian's car comes to a stop in front of the house. I stand and run to the passenger side.

"Oh, Alice! I'm so happy to see you!"

Brian walks around the car to open the door for his mother. "Hiya, Clara."

He offers an elbow to his mother as she stands on unsteady legs. Alice looks like she's aged twenty years over the past few days.

Her voice is shaky. "Hey, Clara. Can I sit with you a bit?"

"Sure, sure. Addie, can you get Alice a glass of water?"

Brian, Alice, and I make our way to the porch. Alice's legs quiver as Brian lowers her to the chair. I don't ask questions; instead, I offer Alice the opportunity to decide to talk or not talk.

After a few moments, Alice says, "Clara, I'm real sorry about yelling at you the other day." Big tears drip down her cheeks, and her face crumbles.

I stand and go to put my arms around her shoulders. "No, no. Alice, don't you worry about a thing."

Brian produces a tissue from his pants pocket and hands it to his mother.

"I should have never been so rude to you. You were the one who came to get me out of that awful place. You drove me home. You've been nothing but good to me and Brian. I am ashamed and awfully sorry. I was so scared when they put me in the back of the police car.

Did you know you can't get out of the back seat? The officer has to let you out. It feels like you're in a cage."

"Oh, Alice. There's nothing to apologize for. I'm just so upset that all of this is happening. Have you heard anything else about the investigation?"

Brian says, "No, we haven't heard anything, but another officer stopped by yesterday to 'check in' and make sure we're 'okay.'"

"Huh?"

"Yeah, he said he wanted to make sure we're okay, a.k.a., hadn't left town. Then, he says, 'Make sure you don't leave the area in case we need to talk with you again.' You'd think they'd have some respect for a lady of Mom's age."

Addie and I agree. Neither of us can imagine Alice murdering Bobby, even though she had a million reasons to do so. After a few moments, Brian asks me to walk with him to the shoreline. Addie and Alice chat happily. We walk to the wooden steps.

"Hey, Bri, you remember that big, ugly storm we had here a couple of weeks ago?"

"Yeah."

"There was a guy standing here, right on this step, looking out to sea. It was pouring rain, thunder, and lightning, but this guy was just standing there. It was weird."

"So what happened?"

"I went to get my rain slicker and see if he needed help, but when I came back, he was gone. The whole thing was right around the time Bobby was found."

"Huh, strange. No way I'd be standing out in a storm like that," Brian says as if the discussion is concluded, but then he says, "Hey, Clara, you should know something."

Oh, no. "What, Brian?"

"I overheard the cop when he came to the door to talk to Mom. I was eavesdropping, ready to pounce on that dude if he upset my mother again."

"Okay."

"He was asking Mom about Dad's relationship with you."

"What? What does that mean?"

"I'm not sure, but it sounded like the officer wanted to know some details."

"That's ridiculous."

"I know. He seemed to be trying to find out what you and Dad were involved in around the time your husband died."

"George? When he died?" I parroted.

Oh, my God. This is so much worse than I thought. If the police were poking their noses into Bobby's and my sick relationship, then things were about to get ugly. And if anyone saw me rolling the damn fool's body into the bay, I'm really stuck.

"We're better off that he's dead, Clara. And no matter what, I've got your back," Brian whispers.

I try to control my facial expressions as we stare at each other. He takes my hand in his. "Any way you look at it, it is good that Dad is gone. And whatever it takes, I'll protect you."

"From what?" I whisper.

"From whatever comes."

# CHAPTER 37

I can hardly breathe, but somehow Brian and I help Alice walk back to the car and get her situated. She puts her hand on my forearm and looks at me with watery eyes.

"I love you, Clara," Alice says.

"I love you, too, Alice. There isn't anything I wouldn't do for you, you know that, right?"

"That I do. I hope no one ever finds out who killed Bobby," she says.

"Why's that?"

"Well, as far as I'm concerned, that person did me a great service by ridding this earth of a wicked, violent man. No one needs to be convicted for it. In fact, someone should be awarded a Medal of Honor." Her laugh gets caught in a deep cough.

"Come on, Mom. Let's get you home to rest."

Alice lays her hand on her son's thigh. "This here is the best son I could have ever had. My Brian is back now. I have been so lonesome since you left."

Brian's neck turns red. "No need to talk about that now, Mom. I'm here. I'm not going anywhere."

Alice turns to me. "And he's so smart. But you know that, Clara. He's so smart going to work and messing around with those … those … marine …."

Brian laughs. "Microorganisms, Mom. Marine biology."

Alice continues, "Yes, that. He's going to make the bay healthier, so our crabs and oysters are plentiful. That's my boy."

I grin at Brian. "Yeah, he's a real-life superhero. Maybe he should wear a deep blue mask and cape—Captain Chesapeake."

Alice and I laugh. Brian interrupts, "All right, all right, you two looney tunes. We've got to go."

I can't hide my trembling hands when Addie and I return to the porch. Addie jumps up and returns with glasses of iced tea for us. She doesn't stare at me and instead looks out across the bay.

After a few moments, she whispers, "What happens next?"

"I don't know," I murmur. "I really don't know."

Suddenly, we hear a loud crash coming from the other side of the house. Addie and I jump up and run toward the sound. As we round the corner of my house, there's nothing immediately evident to account for the noise. I look up and down the street to see if someone has crashed into a mailbox or something. Addie yells, and I turn. The large bay window at the front of my house has a huge gaping hole in it. Addie and I thrust open the door and step inside the living room.

Glass shards are everywhere. I yell for Addie to be careful as I crunch over the glass to the chair where I normally sit. On the seat lays a large rock. It looks like one of those rocks the Department of Natural Resources uses to erect retaining walls to prevent erosion on the shore.

I walk to the chair, and a shiver races down my spine. Had I been sitting in that chair talking to a client, I would have been knocked out cold, maybe even killed. Had someone intentionally tried to harm me? Was this a message? Wait, there is a note wrapped with twine around the rock.

I pick it up and try to untie the twine. It's tied with a million small knots. I go to Addie's desk and retrieve her scissors. With a little saw action, I am able to cut the twine and unroll it from around the rock. Someone definitely wanted me to get this message.

When I open the folded plain paper, three words are etched heavily in black ink.

*Secrets are dangerous.*

For a moment, it's hard to catch my breath. I stare at the message as the edges of my vision blur. I feel Addie's hand on my shoulder.

"Hey, hey. It's okay. Let me see what you have there." She slips the paper from my hand and crumples it into a ball. "Is this the best he can do?" She sighs and walks back towards the kitchen. "I'm going to get a broom."

I stand rigid with my heart pounding in my chest. The breeze blows through the hole in the glass and causes me to shiver. I rub the sweat from my forehead. Addie returns with a broom and dustpan and sweeps up the glass.

"Clara, why don't you go into the kitchen and get an iced tea? I'll have this cleaned up in a second."

Like a robot, I turn and walk into the kitchen. *Secrets are dangerous*? They sure are, and it feels like someone is getting too close to revealing my secret. I don't want anyone digging into my past. That would derail my whole plan for recreating my life. I simply cannot allow Johnston to bully me into falling into old habits. Taking my tea, I walk to the bedroom door. I open my bedside table and slide my hand inside in search of my bottle. I hear someone behind me.

"Oh, Addie. For a moment, I forgot you were here."

Addie walks to me and gently grabs my arm. "Come on, Clara. You don't need what's in there."

I allow her to lead me back into the living room, where she's cleared all the glass from the floor. I don't see the rock or slip of paper anywhere.

"I called the window company to replace the bay window. Brian is coming over to put plywood across the hole. Do you think we should call Danny to make a report?"

"No!" I shout. I see Addie's shock and continue, "No. I don't think it'll do any good. I'll bet that Johnston Burr got a visit from Danny, which prompted this."

"It makes sense," Addie says. "Still, I don't want him to do something worse."

I take a deep breath and use my confident voice. "Don't worry. I think we've scared Johnston enough that he knows he should not be playing around with me. Anyway, we have no proof it was even him."

Addie looks satisfied with my answer. "Thank goodness there are no more clients today. Should I go ahead and cancel tomorrow's?"

"I think so. I mean, the wood across the window will make this room seem more like a witch's castle than a therapeutic space."

Addie chuckles. "You're right." She hunches over and, in her best witch's voice, says, "Come here, dearie. Come visit with me in my lair."

"Why don't you go on home, Addie."

"Are you sure? I can sleep over again tonight if you want. To keep you company?"

"No, no. I'll be all right. You go ahead."

I need to be alone with my thoughts. Johnston Burr has stepped too far with me. Now I'm convinced he knows about my past. I must do whatever it takes to prevent him from revealing my secret. I don't know what to do at this point, how to stop him. I definitely can't tell Danny. Whatever our connection to each other, this is something he could never understand.

I do the next best thing I can think to do. I decide to go visit my mother. Although not even she knows my secret, she will calm me down. One thing I definitely don't want her to do is to read my cards. Then she'll know the extent of what's happening, and I couldn't bear that. I'll tell her to put away her tarot cards and just hum for me like she did when I was a child. She can make all the bad energy go away. And there's a lot of bad energy.

# CHAPTER 38

I'm on autopilot as I drive to Sunview. Thank goodness I've driven it a hundred times. My muscle memory takes over and gets me there. It's a different story in my head, though. Tendrils of panic creep inside me. The edges of the walls in my mind start to buckle. I thought I had created the perfect life, a rebirth after a long, dark journey. I got clean; rebuilt my career. I mistakenly thought I could put my past to rest. Someone is intent on blowing up my life, but I can't come up with one suspect. Well, that's not true. Johnston Burr has a reason to want revenge. I tossed his name to Danny like a dog bone.

I'm stuck behind a line of traffic. I turn off the radio. Music irritates me when I feel overwhelmed and can't think straight. I glance out the passenger side window and watch the leaves rustle in the wind. The green foliage sways. Since I'm stuck in line, I push the button to open my convertible top. The breeze is warm. Leaves hiss in bursts as the wind blows through the branches. The sound of trees blowing jogs a memory. That memory.

I am under the bed in a dark, rotten house. I see boots and hear someone reaching down to push aside a blanket or sheet. A man. White hair. Blue eyes. Bobby. It was Bobby who bent down. I had taken his hand as he helped me slide out from under the bed. Wait, that doesn't make sense. If I had been hiding from Bobby, I surely would not have reached out to grab his hand. Yet, I did.

"There you are, my sweet," he had whispered.

I remember the feel of the scratchy wooden floor as he slid me out from under the bed. A crack of lightning split the sky and illuminated the dark room for only a second. I remember my body wrenching, trying to expel whatever was inside my stomach. I remember the hard, heavy hand on my back as Bobby tried to steady me. There was someone else in the room, lying on the bed. The odor in the room was strong, like urine and decaying animals.

I had tried to pull my arm free, but Bobby held tight. I remember his fingers digging into my flesh. I was scared and tried to fight him. His grasp tightened.

"Shhhhhh, now shhhhhh," he said. "We've got to get you out of here."

Something about this memory is off. Why would I ever go with Bobby anywhere? No. It couldn't, wouldn't happen.

I fix my mind to bring the memory clearer, but I am interrupted by a series of loud horns. The impatient drivers behind me want me to snap back to reality and get moving. I raise my hand to indicate I heard them. I step on the gas and close the gap between me and the car in front of me.

I pull into the parking lot at Sunview and breathe deeply. I can't go into my mother's room looking like this. Sweat pours down my forehead. My hair stands up from driving the convertible. I reach into my glove box and pull out a brush. I wipe down my face with a leftover takeout napkin.

The lobby of Sunview is eerily empty. As I sign in at the front desk, I ask the receptionist why no one is around. She plasters a smile and explains there is a special event this afternoon, a musical group that plays '50s music. I hear a faint melody somewhere in the building. Good, I know my mother won't be there.

In the elevator, I push the button for the third floor. The hallway is empty. At the end of the hallway, I see Mom's door propped open. When I walk in, she, Emma, and Jane are sitting together, my mother's tarot cards spread out on the coffee table.

My mother holds up a hand, instructing me to wait, and continues to read the cards with her friends. "There will be a man who expresses his desires for you," my mother signs, looking at Jane.

"Oh, really?" Jane responds and wiggles her eyebrows.

My mother smiles. "Yes, but you will feel the pull of someone else. You'll want to focus on someone else, but the man who comes to you first is the one you should choose."

Jane looks disappointed. "But why can't I go with the other guy?"

My mother flips over another card. "Because he is not the person you thought he was."

Then my mother collects the cards and shuffles them. She stacks the deck and puts it on top of her dresser drawers. Emma and Jane snap out of their conversation and realize I'm standing there. They both jump up and shower me with kisses.

"What's up with them?" I ask Mom, taken aback by their affection.

Mom chuckles. "They miss you. We all know this investigation is taking a toll on you. They want you to know they love you. Come, sit down. Do you want anything to drink? Eat?"

I shake my head and lie down on the sofa as Emma and Jane leave the room.

"What's wrong?" Mom asks.

"Nothing," I sign, making two O's with both of my hands.

My mother scans my face. "No, that's not true. Clara, there's something very wrong. I can see it on your face." She reaches over to the drawer and picks up the stack of tarot cards. She raises her eyebrows, asking me if I wanted a reading.

"No!" I sign.

My mother's hand pauses mid-air before she lays the deck on the dresser. Tears flow down my cheeks, and my body shakes with fear. Mom sits beside me and envelops me with her arms. My hand automatically goes to her neck to feel her humming my childhood soothing song. We sit like that for what seems to be a long time.

Mom pulls away and signs, "Tell me."

I raise my hands, unsure of how to begin. Mom, sensing my hesitancy, signs, "Start anywhere. Tell me what's going on."

And I do. I tell her how Alice looked when she came to my house earlier. I describe Johnston Burr's menacing presence. I tell her about Danny's reluctance to share information about the ongoing investigation. I exhaust myself telling her everything. I even tell her about Addie having to stay over because I had taken too many Xanax with wine.

While I pour my soul onto my mother's lap, she keeps her warm hand on my knee, occasionally squeezing. She lets me know that she loves me.

To my surprise, I sign, "And I miss George, Mom. I really miss him."

"I know, sweetheart, I know," she tells me, her fingers softening the signs.

"I can't believe he died and left me all alone to deal with … with …everything. My life, everything."

"Yes, his death was tragic. You two were so happy in your marriage. I know there were problems, but you always seemed to gravitate back toward one another."

I continue, "Then, when we were going through a particularly rough patch, he had to die. He should have known not to go into that dangerous area of Annapolis. He should have known."

"Yes, but, sweetie, sometimes people have to learn their life lessons on their own terms, you know? You can forewarn and threaten and demand, but in the end, we all learn the lessons on our own terms. Maybe that's what's happening now."

I sob. "He left me to pick up the pieces all alone, Mom. He never should have been in that area at night. He never should have been by himself. He should have been at home."

All at once, a thick wave of nausea comes over me. I jump up and run to Mom's bathroom. After I throw up, I walk back to the sofa.

"You're sick?" Mom asks. Though I know she can't hear me puking, I'm sure she could smell my bodily fluids.

"I'm just overwhelmed and upset, Mom."

My mother pauses for a second. "Look, George was a man who fell short of being a good husband. He was a good provider, yes, but he was always sort of self-centered and looked after his own needs first."

Wait, what? How did she know that about him? I thought I'd kept it hidden well. George started out being a wonderful husband. He was a lawyer working many hours, trying to make his bosses see he was worthy of becoming a partner in the firm one day. He was handsome, well-dressed, and made a positive first impression. Those were the qualities that hooked me, anyway. I felt certain my mother did not know about George's habit. To be honest, using cocaine on a regular basis only became an issue when he had won a few cases and was assigned a high-profile case about a man shooting a bunch of people on the waterfront. George was relentless in preparing that case. He got very little sleep; hence, the serious cocaine use. Then, suddenly, he's gone. The police found him near a wooded area near the historic downtown, just inside the tree line.

I feel the nausea rise again. I need to get out of here before my mother pries any more information from me. Maybe I shouldn't have come. Yes, she could always calm me down when I was upset, but I didn't expect her to raise so many memories for me. I didn't expect her to know so much, too much.

I stand and tell her I needed to go home and lie down. "I'm upset and not feeling well, Mom."

My mother stands and embraces me in a tight hug. "I-L-Y," she signs.

"I love you too, Mom."

"Wait, before you leave, pull one card."

I shake my head. "No, Mom."

She pushes the deck towards me. "Just one. It can help. Really, it can help you."

I sign and split the deck. I pull off a card and flip it over. Card XV, The Devil. Great. I turn to leave, but Mom grabs my wrist.

"Wait, Clara, wait. Yes, The Devil can seem like a terrible card to pull. It represents the shadow self, the darker side of humanity. But see?" Mom points to the naked couple that appear to be chained near the Devil's feet. "See?"

"Yes, Mom, I see. They're chained to the Devil because they can never escape their situation. They're bound to the Devil, powerless and hopeless." My signs snap at her.

"But look closely, Clara. The chains are loosely tied around their necks. They can be easily removed."

I take the card and peer closer. She is right.

"Clara, whatever struggle you're going through now can be relieved. The Devil is presenting you with a seemingly impossible situation, a puzzle that needs to be solved. Solve the puzzle. Escape the torment."

I had never considered that interpretation. Maybe my mother is right. Rather than push against the negativity being thrown at me, maybe I need to lean into it. Maybe I have not yet learned my life lesson to the fullest. Like the couple in the card, pulling against the chain will only strangle me. I need to move toward the beast to loosen the noose and, finally, remove it from my life altogether.

# CHAPTER 39

Thank goodness I remembered to put my convertible top up before I went into Sunview. The sky looks ominous with thick, dark clouds covering the sky. The wind has picked up. Trees bend, straining. Was a storm predicted in today's weather forecast? I should have checked, but then again, what does it matter?

I decide to stop at the grocery store to pick up a few items. I bypass the produce section, where I would normally buy ingredients for a salad. Instead, I walk to the frozen food section and grab a pizza. Then I go to the next aisle and grab a box of ice cream. Tonight feels like the perfect time for junk food. I'll worry about eating healthy once I get through this situation.

When I leave the store, small rain drops are hitting the parking lot. I jog to my car, throw in the groceries, and close my door just as the droplets turn into large water balloons. I drive slower on the way home and watch the straining tree branches. That's all I'd need is to have a limb fall on my car while I'm driving.

Up ahead, I see the flashing yellow lights of the electric company. Great, it looks like the electricity may be out. Hopefully, it's restricted to this area and doesn't reach out peninsula. Again, I find myself stuck in a line of traffic while the work truck maneuvers toward the electric pole.

The cars inch past, but traffic doesn't let up after I pass the truck. I remember there are a couple of dips in the road ahead that tend to flood. I don't have anywhere to be, so I can take my time. My ice cream may get a little soft, but I'll put it in the freezer when I get home.

When I pull into the driveway, I see the ugly plywood covering what used to be my beautiful bay window. I walk into the house and realize there is no electricity. Great. I shove the pizza and ice cream into the freezer and hope the electricity comes back on before all my food thaws.

I walk to the French doors and look out at the bay. It's angry with sharp white caps and dangerous swells. The darkened sky makes it look like it's night rather than dinner time.

A crack of thunder vibrates the glass in my door. Rain pelts my windows sideways. Light zigzags across the tumultuous sky. I think about Bobby's blue eyes as he pulled me from under the bed. Although I was frantic to get away from his grasp, it wasn't him I was afraid of. No, something else happened that night.

The full picture doesn't form in my head. I close my eyes to try to remember. It stormed that night. The rain was torrential. George and I had argued. I'd discovered a piece of paper with a phone number in one of his jackets. I had accused him of cheating on me. He vehemently denied it, but I could see he was lying. He had become quite the liar, too. I didn't catch on about his drug habit until it was well past the time for fixing it. One thing a recovering addict should avoid at all costs is getting over-involved with someone else's addiction. I remember crying and yelling, hitting George on the chest. He grabbed my wrists and told me not to worry. He reached into a pocket of his suit jacket and pulled out a small plastic bag with white powder.

Even as I shook my head no, I followed him into our living room, where he swiped papers off the glass coffee table. He dumped some white powder on the table and chopped it with the edge of his credit card. He pulled a small gold straw from his pocket and held it out to me. I shook my head but could feel myself weaken. This is not what we needed to do. I tried to recall what my NA sponsor had instructed me to do if I found myself in this very situation. I could not remember.

George pulled my hand and closed it around the gold cylinder. At that moment, I cracked. All the hopes I had for my life had seeped out of me onto the beautiful oak floors. I leaned over the table with George's hand on my back, easing me down. The rush was incredible. Oh, how I had missed my old friend.

Our argument stopped. A different kind of urge emerged, one that took precedence over everything else. We blew through the small bag of cocaine within ten minutes, and then we wanted more. There was only one place I knew where we could get more immediately. Clay Street. It was dangerous, yes, but that's where all the drugs flowed in abundance. I had told George to go upstairs and change out of his thousand dollar suit, but he felt so desperate to get more drugs, he disregarded my suggestion. I didn't argue with him. There would be no point. Instead, we got into his white Mercedes convertible and turned the corner toward Clay Street.

A crack of thunder rips me from my memories. Flashing lights bounce off the house next door. It's probably another truck speeding down the street to get our electricity going. I hope they fix it soon so I can heat up my pizza. I watch the mesmerizing blink of the yellow lights. The wind is howling as it rushes through the trees. The furniture on my porch vibrates, threatening to blow into the yard. Wind catches my door as I open it. I use my full body to prevent it from slamming. I pull it closed and retrieve the bungee cord I use to keep my furniture in place during bad storms. Wet from the rain, I am on my knees, connecting one hook of the bungee to the other.

Someone taps my shoulder, and I jump. I turn wild-eyed to see who is behind me. With everything going on, the last person I want to see in this kind of storm is Johnston Burr. To my relief, it's Danny.

I stand up and bend over to catch my breath. Danny scared me. I motioned for him to follow me into the dark living room. He holds the door as he and the wind wrestle. Once inside, I close the door and turn the bolt.

"Geez, Danny. You scared me to death. What are you doing out in this weather?"

I notice Danny's face is stony. He's wearing his uniform. He reaches out to touch my hand. "Clara," he begins. "Clara?" His voice is shaky like he's afraid.

"What is it, Danny? Has something happened? Is it Alice?"

He shakes his head and glances over his shoulder to look outside. Who is he looking for?

"Listen, Clara. I stopped by to tell you something."

"Tell me what? What's going on, Danny?"

"I'm trying to tell you." He looks over his shoulder again.

"Why are you looking outside? Is someone stalking you, like that guy Johnston?"

Anger seeps into my body. I am weak when it comes to sadness or grief, but anger? I can do anger quite well. "If it's Johnston, I'll take care of that. Just one letter to the judge that he's not following parole, then wham! He's back in jail."

Danny shakes his head so hard that it looks like it will roll off his shoulders. "No, no. That's not it. Clara, look. They're coming."

"Who? Who's coming, Danny?"

"The police. An officer is coming to your house."

"The police? Why would they come to my house?" The color drains from my face.

"Look, I don't know the full story. The chief came to me and said I was off the investigation. When I asked him why, he told me my involvement was compromised. Effective immediately, I'm on desk patrol."

"But why? Why are you off the case?"

"I just follow orders, but when I saw two officers whispering and casting looks my way, I knew something was off."

"And why is an officer coming to talk to me?"

"No, Clara, no. He's not coming to talk to you. He's coming to question you."

"Question me? Question me for what? What did I do?"

"They think you murdered Bobby."

"What? Why would they think that?"

"I don't know. I only know someone is on his way, and I have to get out of here before he arrives."

# CHAPTER 40

I watch Danny leave. I am trembling and f the edges of my vision blur. Why would they want to talk to me? How could they possibly think I had something to do with this? I place my hand against the walk to prevent myself from falling.

A few minutes later, another police cruiser stops in front of the house. Two officers get out of the car. Before they get to the door, I open it. The officers ask me if I would go with them for questioning about the murder of Bobby Ward. Whew, at least they don't read me my Miranda rights. To show them I am agreeable and cooperative, I go with them without a fuss. One of the officers asks me about the boarded window. Rather than telling him I have a stalker client who gets a kick out of threatening me, I explain that a neighborhood kid accidentally batted a ball through the window. The officer nods because they know the neighborhood is full of children who like to play ball in the street. The streets on the peninsula don't have many thoroughfares for traffic.

I glance at the badge of the officer closest to me. "Officer Bennett? I don't think I know you."

The tall officer glances down, his face like stone. He grunts. His partner seems more congenial.

"That's Officer Mark Bennett, and I'm Officer Robert Engel. Right, we don't normally work out of this precinct."

"Where do you usually work?"

"Out of downtown Annapolis, but we were called in for a special assignment on the case."

"Special assignment?"

"Yeah, we hear that the police and the residents are a little too close over here."

Bennett snickers.

"What do you mean?" I ask as if this is new information to me.

Bennett looks at Engel with a warning glance. Engel signals back to him through their secret eye language before turning back to me.

"The people involved in this case are too personal with the officers investigating it. We were called in as a fresh set of eyes without any previous relationships with anyone in Mystic Beach."

"Too personal with the officers?"

"Exactly what the officer said, Ms. Starr. Now, if you will come with us down to the station and answer a few questions, then you'll be on your way."

I don't like Bennett from the start. For one, he looks like he just got out of high school despite the muscles outlining his tight uniform chest. Second, he seems he has a God complex, like he's the rule-maker, and I need to be the rule-follower. Finally, he has no manners. He doesn't need to be a bull about it. I can tell they're not from around here. Even the worst of neighbors always wave or make small talk. The community is too small, and gossip keeps everyone engaged.

Engel opens the door of the police cruiser, and I slide into the back seat. Alice is right; there's no way to get out. Despite my forced friendly face, I feel sweat trickle down my back. The officers don't say anything to me as we drive the three miles to the Mystic Beach precinct.

Once we arrive, they escort me to an interviewing room. One officer gestures towards a metal chair at a table, then they both sit across from me. I see the blinking red light in the corner of the room, and I'm aware I'm being videotaped. The heavy metal door opens, and the officer who sat at the receptionist's desk when I came to get Alice walks in with a manilla folder. She hands it to Bennett, who barely registers her presence.

I take a breath. "I'm happy to answer any questions you have, officers. I'm confused about why I'm here, is all."

Bennett starts. "Why don't you start by telling us about your relationship with Bobby Ward."

An easy question. "Bobby lives ... I mean, lived in the neighborhood. He knew my parents and me as a child."

"Did you have a romantic relationship with Mr. Ward?"

I snort. "A romantic relationship? You have to be kidding. No. I was not involved with Bobby in that way."

"And what about your former husband?"

Wait. What is happening here?

"George? What about him? He's dead."

Engel interrupts. "We're aware."

Bennett opens the manilla folder and removes three photographs. He slides them across the table over to me. The top one is a police photograph of George's body when they discovered him. George looks grayish blue. His suit is rumpled, his normally crisp white shirt dirtied. He's leaning over on his side like somebody dropped him off like a bag of trash. My heart starts racing, and my hands shake. A buzz fills my ears.

"Ms. Starr? Ms. Starr?" Engel steps out and returns with a plastic cup of water. He slides it over to me.

Bennett leans forward and moves the top photo to the side. He lays the other two beside it. The second photo is a picture of a dilapidated house, a Victorian with a sagging porch and rotten steps. The front door is open. Light shining through the door shows the drug paraphernalia of a crack house. I know this house.

The third photograph appears to be a bedroom in the house. The bare mattress is dirty, with a twisted sheet lying on top. There are a multitude of stains, different shapes and colors, all grotesque. The wood floor is scraped with pieces gouged out. I close my eyes and remember the awful smell. My stomach threatens to spew its contents. I must not let them push me toward this. I feel waves of panic mixed with sadness.

I look up at the officers and wipe a tear from my eye. "Yes, I know these pictures. And?"

I am determined to slam the door on my emotions. They are taunting me, trying to break me, and I won't let it happen.

"Your husband's death. Do you know how he died, Ms. Starr?" Engel asks.

"Of course, I know how he died. He died of an overdose."

"Where did he die, Ms. Starr?"

"Why are you asking me questions to which you already know the answers?" I snap. "And for the record, you can call me *Doctor* Starr."

Bennett sneers. He looks like a reptile ready to pounce on a mouse. I lock eyes with him. I've grown up with men like him my whole life. I am certainly not threatened by sneers and snickers.

"Of course, Dr. Starr. We want this to be as accurate as possible," Bennett says, not bothering to contain his disdain. "Now, tell us the circumstances of your husband's death."

I glance at the camera and pull my shoulders back. I can do this.

"George got involved with drugs when the pressures at work started to grind on him. He needed to work longer and longer hours to keep up the pace for upcoming high-profile cases. I didn't realize he had gotten in so deep until I discovered a bag of cocaine in his pocket."

All true so far. I feel my resolve hardening. Bennett will not break me.

"Apparently, his drug use was more out of control than I realized. When I got the call from the police saying they had found George's body lying along Clay Street, I knew."

"Knew what?" Engel asked.

"I knew he had overdosed. It's always a risk with drug users."

"And how would you know that?" Bennett taunted.

"Because, Officer Bennett, you know as well as I that I have a history of drug use going back to my teenage years."

"And again, I ask, what was your relationship to Bobby Ward beyond being a neighbor?"

"He was my dealer at the time."

"And who was George's?"

I pause. He knows the answer to the question, but all of a sudden, I feel like something is happening behind the scenes. Something I haven't caught onto, like I'm about to be entrapped in a snare.

"Bobby was. Bobby was George's dealer."

"So, Mr. Ward was responsible for George's death, right? I mean, he supplied the drugs to you and George. You both were flush with drugs. Isn't that right, Dr. Starr?"

I drop my head. "Yes, he did," I whisper.

"Did you kill Bobby Ward, Dr. Starr?" Engel asks.

"No. No, I didn't."

"Then what about this?"

Engel slides another photograph from the folder. The picture is grainy, like a still taken from a doorbell camera. At first, I don't catch what they want me to see. I squint and bring the photo closer to my eyes. Oh, no. Oh, no. No, no, no.

In the photo is a dark picture of Bobby Ward and me. Bobby has his hand around my wrist and appears to be pulling me off the porch stairs of the old house. It looks like I'm fighting him, but his strength was never a match for mine. My mouth is open as if I'm screaming. My body is angled, and it looks like I am trying to escape.

"Okay, so? That's me. That's Bobby. I don't know what that has to do with a murder."

"And what about this?" Engel slides over another photo, this one a different quality, more recent.

I am on the beach kneeling beside a large mass. My face shows the strain of pushing the thing. Engel slides over a series of photographs blown up to show the detail. In the pictures, side by side, I am pushing, pulling, and rolling Bobby's body back into the bay. I am standing in the bay waist-high, shoving his bloated body back out beyond the shoals. I am walking back to shore, grabbing my coffee cup. I'm wet and tired looking. It's over. I'm done. I'm sinking into the abyss, and there's nothing I can do about it. All of this is thanks to my neighbor, Barbara. She's the one who took the photos, I'm sure.

"Is this you, Dr. Starr?" Bennett asks.

I look up into his dark eyes. There is no use trying to lie. "Yes, it's me."

A small, evil smile curls on Bennett's lips. "Dr. Clara Starr, you are under arrest for the murder of Bobby Ward."

# CHAPTER 41

The police bring me to a room and ask me to stand against a wall. They tell me to look at the camera. Snap. Turn, snap. Turn again, snap. They bring me to a table and place my fingertips on a digital scanner. I'm exhausted by the time the whole process is finished, but when they put me in a cell, I feel jumpy and nervous. Outside the small window high on the wall, I see daylight breaking.

The stale air and bland coloring of the cell reminds me when my mother asked an officer to show me what being locked up would feel like. I had been suspended from high school when the school officer found me in the bathroom, snorting speed. I was belligerent and rebellious when I was a teenager. I remember sitting in my cell singing as loud as I could just to show the police and my mother that I was unfazed. I was confident in those days. Not anymore.

I hear the faint banging of doors somewhere in the building. The tap-tap-tap of footsteps echoes in the hall. I stand and wrap my fingers around the bar. When I see Danny come into view, my breath wooshes from me.

"Oh, Danny," I say as I reach through the bars, tears dripping down my cheeks.

Danny steps closer, his fingers brushing against mine. He steps back and looks at my face, hair, and clothes. I run my fingers through my hair. I must look a fright.

"Danny, what's happening here? What's going on? They think I did it! Asshole Number One and Asshole Number Two, they think I did it. Where did those guys come from?" I ask, trying, and failing, to sound like a smartass.

Danny looks over his shoulder to make sure no one else is lingering. He glances up towards the camera that we both know is videoing us.

"Look, I can't be long, Clara. The captain told me I had two minutes with you. I know you're probably upset and scared," Danny says.

"You think?" I interrupt. I can't help myself. My world feels like it's closing in on me. I know time is short, so I rush. "Look, I know what this looks like, but it's not what it seems."

"Clara, I know. I know you." The warmth of his fingers on top of my clenched fists helps me loosen my grip on the cell bars. "You haven't told me everything."

It isn't a question. Danny knows me well enough to tell when I'm lying. Shoot, he probably knew something was off all along. Danny doesn't press, though. He was always such an accepting and trusting person, even when we were children, even when he watched me slowly kill myself with drugs in high school. I should have realized earlier that I didn't need to hide from Danny. I could hide from everyone else, but not him.

"I know, Danny. There are things I want to tell you, things that you should know."

Danny cuts me off. "I know, but I only have a minute. Addie is aware that you're here."

"What? How?"

"I called her last night after I left. I told her I suspected you were going to be hauled down to the station for questioning. You know the officer who usually sits at the front desk? She called me last night when Bennett and Engel told her they were arresting you for murder. I called Addie right away because I have to be careful of how much I'm involved, at least as far as the people around here."

"It's okay, I get it. What's next?"

"Officers were called to your house last night after you left. The judge had signed a search warrant. They're going through your things right now as we speak. Addie is going to have an attorney represent you this morning when you see a judge for the arraignment. Hopefully, the judge will grant bail, and then we can figure this thing out."

"Okay. I understand. Will you let my mom know what's going on? I'm sure she's going to figure out something is happening."

"Yeah, I'll go see her in a couple of hours. She probably isn't even awake this early. You hang tight. I'll see you soon."

Danny's hand squeezes my fingers as he turns to leave. When he's almost at the door, I yell, "Danny?"

I hear him pause and take a few steps back so he can see my face pressed against the bars. "Danny? Thank you for everything."

"Don't thank me yet, Clara. Just make sure you tell the truth. Get everything out there on the table. Now is not the time to try to weasel yourself out of a bad situation, like when you were in high school. This is for real this time."

"I know. You're right. I'm not that girl from high school anymore. I will tell them everything when given the chance to speak. I love you, Danny."

"I know, my girl. I love you, too."

The door slams behind him as he leaves. I'm left here to wait for this attorney that Addie is getting for me. I can hardly believe that she's willing to find someone to help me through this mess when she hasn't known me that long. She's a true friend, the kind I've never had before outside of Danny.

I go to the metal cot and lay down on the thin mattress. I watch the day become brighter through the window. There are faint noises, like people coming to work. There's an occasional belt of laughter. A cough. The day is starting, and I'm afraid.

A few hours later, the door down the hall opens again. An officer comes to my cell and unlocks it. "Come on, Dr. Starr. Your attorney is here to see you."

The female officer escorts me through the hall door to another door. Through the window, I see a woman, her back turned toward me. She's wearing a red blazer. Her hair is shoulder-length and brown with subtle highlights. She stands as the officer unlocks the door.

The lawyer has dark brown eyes and a calming face. She looks at my wrists.

"No handcuffs?" she asks.

I wiggle my arms. "I guess not."

"Thank God there is some sense in this place." The lawyer gestures to the officer, who steps outside the room and closes the door.

The attorney holds out her hand. "My name is Laura Marsh."

I shake her hand. Her grip is firm and comforting. "Marsh? Are you related to Addie?" I ask.

"Yes, Addie is my niece."

"Nice. I didn't realize."

Laura sits in the chair and places her briefcase on the floor. "Yeah, she calls me her fairy godmother auntie."

"Oh? Why's that?"

"Because when Addie needs something, she thinks I swoop down like a fairy from a magical kingdom to help her out." Laura laughs. "I don't think of myself as a mythical creature, but I know that I would do anything in my power to help her out."

"It was your ... the accident ... uh ...."

"Yes, it was my brother and his wife that were killed. After that, Addie decided she was going to carry on despite the loss of her parents. I sent her money to help with the bills, but in case you haven't noticed, Addie is strong-willed."

I smile. "It's one of my favorite things about her. She's a bit of a fairy godsister to me, too. She came into my life just when I needed her." I look around the room. "And here I am. Addie must share your magical talents."

Laura reaches down and pulls a folder from her case. "Let's hope my powers still last. Now, let's get down to business so I can prepare for your arraignment this afternoon."

Laura slides me the same photographs the officers showed me last night. I am not so taken aback by them this time. I pull the photo of

George's body to me. This photo doesn't capture how handsome George was, how gregarious. A tear drips from my eye, but I immediately wipe it away.

"Let's talk about George. He wasn't a saint, but as it turns out, he's the one who saved me."

# CHAPTER 42

"George and I met at an N.A. meeting. At first, I ignored him, but, boy, he was gorgeous. Not only that, but he was also nice and open-hearted. He kept asking me out, but I'd decline. Eventually, he wore me down. He ended up saving me."

I smile, remembering his smile, the way he opened the door for me, and how he ordered for me at our first dinner date.

"How did he save you?" Laura asks.

"I was on the verge of a relapse at the time. I hadn't yet taken the step, but for some reason, I was still struggling with my father's death."

"Died?" Laura asks.

"Died by suicide when I was in middle school," I explain. "I just about flunked out of school, but my mother had gotten me tutors. My drug use was at its heaviest then. Looking back, I don't think I was in full-blown addiction. It was more like I was in full-blown grief, and the drugs helped me cope."

"Okay. And George?"

"That first dinner date led to a whirlwind romance. Once at an NA meeting, on my way to the bathroom, I accidentally dropped my purse. A baggie of small white pills fell out. George picked it up.

"I started to explain, but George put his hand on my arm and guided me back into my seat. 'You don't have to explain, Clara. It's okay,' he told me. 'I'm going to support you enough until you work this through. I promise you that.'

"That closed the deal for me. There was no judgment or disdain. I ended up dumping the pills in the toilet."

"And did he deliver on his promise?"

I smile. "In fact, he did. He and I developed a plan. We always went to meetings every day. George made me a better person. Together, we were unstoppable. That is, until," I pause.

"Until?"

"Until he got into a pricey high-profile law firm. Our marriage started to change. He started working late hours. We had a lot of money coming in, more so from his job than mine. I mean, a social worker doesn't really bring in bank, you know? I had just finished my doctoral program by that time. I was clean, functioning well, and dreaming of the future. Looking back, I realize now that it takes a toll when two people are putting in more time at their jobs than in their marriage. We had long before decided that children were not part of our plan. Instead, we dove head-first into our careers. The stress mounted. It didn't end well."

"And then?"

I explained to Laura about finding the drugs in George's suit jacket. The strain of our busy lives, coupled with a marriage that felt like it was faltering, caused a momentary lapse of judgment on my part. When I realized George was using and had probably been for a while, I couldn't take it.

"The pressure to join him in using was enormous. I gave in. Then I tried to justify my behavior by telling myself that it was my turn to save him, just like he had done for me years before. I knew from being into that lifestyle for so long that it would be hard to convince George to get clean when I, myself, was sober. Saying it aloud sounds stupid now, the thought that if I joined George in using, I could also pull us out gently, that he'd trust me like I trusted him, and I'd show him the path toward sobriety."

"And?"

"And it didn't work. Oh, God, how it didn't work." More tears drip from my cheeks onto the table. I sniff and continue. "When we used up all the cocaine that night at the house, George and I went to a place on Clay Street to buy more. This house is known among druggies as a place to buy any kind of drug you can think of, use in private, and basically check out from the world. By the time we arrived that night, George was itching to get more. I saw him on the phone, but when I asked who he was texting, he didn't answer me. Bobby showed up a short time later.

"Bobby was bad news, I knew. When he got there, he and George went off into another room. I tried to follow, but George told me to go upstairs and wait for him there. A few minutes later, George came upstairs and sat on a bed next to me. He immediately dumped out some of the powder on a bedside table and started chopping up the small rocks. He pulled that damn gold straw out of his pocket and snorted two thick lines."

"Did you do it, too?" Laura asks.

"I did. I thought we'd do a small line and then go back home, but George wanted to continue. It was then, in that dark, stinky room, that I realized George was deep into his drug use. His tolerance had built up, and his mind was like a steel trap, closed for good. He wasn't going to listen to me. Still, I sat right there beside him while he snorted the whole bag himself."

"So what did you do?"

"I went downstairs to find Bobby. He was sitting in an old, tattered armchair in the living room. When I saw him, I became enraged. I asked him how could he do that? How long had he and George been doing deals? I demanded to know what was going on."

"And what was Bobby's reaction?"

"He smiled at me. He told me he didn't owe me any explanations, that if George hadn't confided in me, then he wouldn't, either. He said that George's money kept him flush with enough to fix his crab boat and buy a set of new crab pots. Then he laughed."

"He laughed?"

I can feel the old anger rising in my body as I remember all this. "Yes. He laughed at me. He told me that my temper tantrum reminded him of when I was a little girl. He laughed so hard that tears fell from his eyes. I felt infuriated. The thrum of the cocaine in my body kept me wound tight. I pushed Bobby, and he fell, laughing, into the chair. I stomped upstairs to try to get George out of there."

I pause. The weight of my memories is crushing me. I am filled with the long-ago anxiety and distress from that night. It's as if I'm back in that house, hearing Bobby's laughter, like I'm trapped in some sort of morbid house of mirrors. I remember rushing up the steps, tripping on one and sliding down. I don't focus on the pain in my shin and instead climb the stairs again. I burst into the bedroom and see George lying on the bed, drips of blood leaking from his nose.

I scream at George to get up, we're leaving right this moment. I push on his arm and yell for him to get his ass up and go. The mattress bounces as I jostle George to get him up. George isn't responding, though. I jump on the bed and straddle him. I shake his shoulders and command him to get up. It's when I'm on top of him, my hands on his shoulders, when I realize that although his eyes are part-way open, he isn't responding.

I shriek and put my fingers to his neck. There is no pulse. I stand over George, pushing as hard as I can into his chest. I'm trying to remember how many compressions before I give him a breath. I am frantic as I count, one and two and three and four and five. I tilt his head back and breath into his mouth. There is only a slight movement of his chest. I push his head back further and breathe again. His chest rises. I go back to the compressions. One and two and three and four and five and six. Breath. Breath. Nothing.

I can't remember how long I tried to revive him, but eventually, I stopped. George was gone. His fingers and hands were cooling. I saw that the gold straw had fallen on the floor and rolled to the wall next to the bed. I bent down and picked it up.

On the bedside table were two more thick lines. I thought that if he was gone, then I was going to follow. I sniffed in the powder and felt my nostrils prickle. I pinched the bridge of my nose and felt the rush of the drug fill my mind. My body started to involuntarily tremble. I looked at my husband on the bed. Gone. He had left me. He wasn't coming back. I'd sat there and watched George overdose. I didn't do a damn thing to stop him. I might as well have pulled the trigger of a gun myself.

Laura looks mesmerized as I continue. "The next thing I remember was being pulled out from under the bed."

"By whom?" Laura asks.

"Bobby. Bobby Ward held out his hand and told me to come out."

"And then what happened?"

"I took Bobby's hand. The next thing I remember is Bobby telling me to go home. He'd take care of things. He told me I wouldn't want to ruin my life by being found at the house, under the influence, with a dead husband by my side. He said that I had things to do in my life. Nothing was going to bring back George, he told me. I knew he was right."

"What did you do next?"

"I went home. The police found George's body on the ground down the street from the drug house." I tapped the photo from the police.

"But how did his body get there if he died on the bed at the house?"

"I don't know. When I left, George was still on the bed."

"And how did you get home?"

"I don't remember," I lied.

# CHAPTER 43

Laura must be good at what she does because she convinces the judge to let me out on bail. She tells the judge how I'm a long-time upstanding citizen in Mystic Beach and points out my professional accomplishments and community awards. She reminds the judge that even he had known both of my parents once upon a time. Her argument works, and shortly thereafter, Laura and I bail out of the police station into the bright, warm sunshine.

As we step out, Addie rushes up to me and folds me into a tight embrace. I am so happy to see her. She hugs her aunt and says, "Thanks, Laura. You're the best fairy godmother anyone could ask for."

Laura hugs Addie back and laughs. She walks back to her car. Addie takes my arm into hers.

"I'm glad you're out of that nasty place," Addie says. "Did anyone mistreat you in there? Did Big Bubba try to make his move?" she jokes.

I laugh. "Nah, I didn't get to see Big Bubba this visit. Better luck next time."

As we walk towards Addie's car, I see someone sitting in the front seat. The car door opens, and my mother gets out.

"Mom!" I yell and sign as I run into her arms.

She signs to me, "You all right?"

I nod and hug her again. She reaches down, grabs my fingers, and brings them to her throat. I have never felt so happy feeling her song on my hands than I do right now.

Mom pulls back and signs, "I wanted to make sure you got out and were okay."

I sign, "I am okay, Mom. You don't need to worry about me."

"Oh, I know that already. I pulled the Strength card from the major arcana before Addie picked me up. You're going to be fine."

We three get into the car and go to Sunview to drop off my mother. I escort her upstairs, where Emma, Jane, and Edward are waiting for her. I leave them to their discussions, not wanting to go through my ordeal detail by detail. My mother has always been good about giving me space and privacy.

When I get into the car, I ask Addie, "What's next?"

"Just you wait and see," she says.

When we pull into the driveway, she turns to me and says, "The house was a wreck after the police left. I take it they didn't find anything because I watched them closely. They took your computer and some of the file notes, but that's about it. I tidied up so it doesn't upset you too much."

I open the front door and see that things look pretty much like I had left them. Relief washes over me. Addie points me to the shower and tells me she'll put on the coffee.

I scrub my body with my favorite peppermint Castile soap and let the hot water rinse off the suds. Stepping out of the shower, I pull a fresh, thick towel off the rack. Addie really thought of everything. I change into shorts and a T-shirt. When I walk to the living room, I see that Addie is already outside on the porch, the French doors open for me. I join her on the patio.

We sit quietly, taking sips of coffee. The breeze feels cool against my wet hair. A group of seagulls fly at different altitudes over the bay. In the distance, I see Shaun's boat still running parallel to the shore.

"He's crabbing late, isn't he?" I ask Addie.

"Yeah. Maybe he's got a lot on his mind."

Despite everything that's happened, I feel a calming sensation growing in my chest. I don't know how things will shake out, but I know I can't control this process anymore. In fact, there are so many things that I wanted to control, but now I know that I can't. The only thing I have for certain is this moment, right now. The police are going to do what they need to do. Whatever happens, I can accept this. I don't have to hold on to all those secrets. Spilling my story to Laura felt horrible at first, but the more I kept talking, the easier the words flowed. I feel relieved that someone knows the story of George's death. I hadn't realized how that particular secret bore down upon my soul.

A car pulls up and parks. Brian jumps out and opens the door for his mother. When Alice sees me, her smile is gigantic. Brian holds her arm as they make their way over to the porch. When Alice steps towards me, I stand and embrace her.

"Oh, baby girl. I'm glad that you're home. I was so worried about you," Alice says.

"Geez, news travels fast," I say, and grin at Brian.

"Always has, always will," Brian says.

"Hey, what happened to your front window? We drove by here earlier today and saw it boarded up." Alice asks.

"Someone miscalculated a throw and a rock sailed through the window." I don't need to tell them about the note. I don't want Alice to be even more upset than she already is.

"Not to worry," Addie says. "The repair company should be here soon to replace the glass. Hey, do you want some coffee or some iced tea?"

"No, thanks. I've got to get Mom home," Brian says.

"That's right. Brian took a few days off from his lab to help me with the gardening. That and bringing over a few guests," Alice says, her lips grinning. She looks up at her son, her deep love for him evident on her face.

"Guests?" Addie asks.

"Puffers. Brian brought home some pet pufferfish."

"Great. I can't think of a better pet to have," Addie jokes.

"How's the bacteria business?" I ask Brian, a grin twitching my lips.

"Why did the bacteria cross the microscope?" Brian asks. After a moment, he answers, "To get to the other slide. Badum-bum."

Addie and I groan. Brian laughs and says, "Come on, Mom. Let's go home."

After they leave, the quiet soothes me. Addie and I watch the sunshine dance on the water. Down the road, I see Barbara walking her dog. My chest fills with disappointment. I am angry at her for snapping those pictures and giving them to the police. I also feel that she only did what she thought was best. It might have gotten me arrested, but I suspect my secrets were on the cusp of being found out anyway.

When Barbara is within earshot, I can't help myself. "Barbara, thanks for giving those pictures to the police."

Barbara's face twists. She waits for a moment while her dog sniffs the grass and crouches to pee. Then she walks over to the patio.

"Oh, Clara. I heard what happened. I can't believe that they think you killed Bobby."

"And the pictures you took of me didn't help, now did they?" I snap.

"Pictures? Clara, what are you talking about?"

"The pictures of me you sent to the police. They showed me each and every one. Thanks a lot for the support." My words drip with sarcasm.

"Clara, honey, I don't know what you're talking about. I didn't take any pictures. What were they of?"

Wait. What?

"You didn't take the pictures?" I ask.

Either Barbara is the world's best liar, which she isn't, or she's telling the truth.

"No, silly. I didn't take any pictures of you. I mean, you're pretty and all that, but what do I need a picture of you for?"

"So … you didn't take any photos of me recently?"

"No, honey. I don't have any recent *or* old photos of you. The last pictures I took were at the community carnival, what, two years ago. Anyway, I've got to run. Someone from a dating app I'm using is supposed to text me soon."

Addie and I say goodbye to Barbara. When she's rounded the

corner, Addie asks, "What were you talking about? Did someone give the police pictures?"

"Someone sure did." I inhale a deep breath. "Addie, look, I feel like I can trust you. Let me tell you about those pictures."

And I do. Addie listens without interruption. I explain that memories flooded my mind when I saw Bobby's body on the shore a few days ago. Memories of George cooling on the bed, his eyes looking vacantly at my face. Bobby's shrill laughter. The buzz of the cocaine. Awaking in my bed the next morning, the other side empty. The profound grief consuming me afterward. The secrecy of George's death and the pain I felt holding it in. All of it had come back to me as I looked upon Bobby's lifeless body. He disgusted me both in life and in death. I had no place in my life for the likes of that man. So, I wanted him gone. I pushed him out to the bay and hoped that the current would take him to the Atlantic, where sharks would feast upon him. Except that didn't happen. Instead, someone took photographs of me pushing him out and gave them to the police.

# CHAPTER 44

After Addie leaves, I change into my pajamas and bury myself under the quilt my mother made for me many years ago. I feel like I've been drained of all my energy by some alien creature. I grab my Kindle from my bedside table but have trouble concentrating. For a moment, my mind imagines a prescription bottle full of pills in my dresser, but, thankfully, my resolve to create permanent sobriety is stronger. I lay on my pillow, thinking about the day's events when I hear a tap on the French glass door. I freeze, panic rising in my chest. I hear faint tapping again.

I slide out from under my covers, grab my cellphone, and walk into the living room. I have the 9-1-1 numbers put in and my finger hovers over the green dial button. If this is Johnston or some other intruder, I'll tap the button, then fight for my life.

When I reach the darkened living room, I see someone's face pushed up against the glass. The person has a hand above their eyebrows to better see inside. I take a step closer, hiding in the darkness of the living room. I approach from the side so I can get a better look. My breath becomes shallow as I take another small step to the door.

I jump in front of the glass. The intruder yelps and jumps back away from the door. I put a hand on my chest and push out a deep breath. I twist the doorknob and yank open the door.

"Danny! You scared me half to death. What are you doing out there?"

Danny is still wearing his uniform. He looks over his shoulder to make sure no one is watching. It can't be safe for Danny being here during an investigation. I understand the risk he's taking just by coming here. I reach out the door and grab his wrist.

"Get in here. Hurry."

I pull Danny's arm and lead him away from the windows where anyone could see him. We go into my bedroom. I flop on the bed.

"What's up, Danny? Bored to death?" I joke.

"More like worried. Clara, how are you? I heard you made bail. I can't tell you how difficult it was for me to act like everything was normal all day. I wanted to get out of there and come over here, but I had to wait until it was clear. Chief won't like it one bit if he finds out I'm here. I'd probably lose my job."

"Well, I won't tell on you."

Danny smiles. "I know you won't." He comes over and sits beside me. I lean into his arms. "How are you?" he whispers into my hair.

"I don't know. They think I killed Bobby. They've got these pictures of me." I hiccup as I start to cry.

"Shhhh, shhhh. It's okay."

"No, but, Danny, no, it's not okay. They have these pictures of me—"

"Pushing Bobby back into the bay," he finishes. "But, look, whatever happened out there on the beach, I know more than anyone what you had to suffer because of Bobby. He was a horrible human being."

"He was, I agree. But still, someone sent those pictures. Who?"

"All I can tell you is that the day before, the officer at the front desk received a large envelope. Inside were the pictures. That's when the chief removed me from the case. I knew something was up. I had to warn you about what was coming."

My hand reaches for Danny's. "I know. Thank you for that."

He squeezes my hands. "I know you didn't kill him, Clara. I know you couldn't do something like that, no matter how terrible someone was to you."

"Thank you for saying that. You have no idea how much that means to me."

I feel safe and protected with Danny. No matter how bad things get, he'll always be here to help me figure things out. I lean forward to look closely at Danny's face. Traces of the boy are still there, but there is more of the man he has become. I watch his eyes scan my face. I look at the whiskers on his jaw. I stare at his lips, then back at his eyes. Maybe Danny has always been the right one for me.

I place my lips lightly on his. When I pull back, I see desire and heat in his eyes. I lean forward again, this time to kiss him harder. His hand reaches around the back of my neck and pulls me forward. He kisses me deeply, and I respond in kind.

"Oh, Clara, I love you so much," he whispers into my hair.

I respond by laying on my back and pulling him down to me. The heat we create causes sweat to form on his neck and back. I reach up and unbutton his uniform shirt. After a moment, we both move at once, undressing each other. The love I feel for this man bursts from my chest. He has always been the one for me. It took me this long to see it. I realize I must have spoken aloud.

Danny responds, "You've always been the one, Clara. Always."

Afterward, cuddled together in bed, Danny's arms encircle me. He shifts so he's looking directly at my face.

"Clara, I'm going to help figure this out with you."

"Wait, Danny. You can't put your job on the line for me. It will get figured out, but it doesn't need to include you. Addie will help me. I know she will."

"Yes, Addie will help, but I'm in it, too. For one, I have access to information that no one else has. I can find out what evidence there is and why it points to you."

"No, Danny, no."

"Just hear me out. Jacob is still working with the medical examiner's office. They sent some tissue samples to the pathologist assigned to work this case. I'll find out where all that stands. I can find out what else besides the photographs they have. I have loyal friends at the station who've known me for a long time. I've helped them out many times. This time it's their turn to return the favor."

"Are you sure?"

His face is determined. "I've never been surer of anything in my life."

"I love you, Danny. You know that, right?"

Danny grins. "Clara, I've known you loved me since we were kids. I knew it all along, only you didn't. I'm glad that you're 'woke.'"

I laugh. "So, what's the plan tomorrow?"

"Tomorrow morning, when Addie comes, we're going to figure out a strategy. We'll identify our resources, tally our assets, and design a plan for getting to the bottom of this. You'll see. Your team is strong and dedicated. With all of us together, we'll find a way to get to the truth."

"The truth?"

"The truth. But, Clara? You need to be fully honest. No more secrets, okay? We can't help you if you have any secrets."

"And the same goes for you," I say.

Danny looks surprised. "What do you mean? I don't have any secrets."

I place my hand on his shoulder. "It was you who rescued me from the drug house all those years ago, wasn't it? You were the one who took me home."

Danny hesitates, but only for a second. "Yes, it was me. Bobby called me that night and told me what happened. He knew how much I cared for you. He knew I would do anything to help you. And he didn't want to get busted for giving George the drugs that killed him. So, he used my feelings for you to get me to save you while, at the same time, he actually wanted to save himself. It was okay, though. Saving you was worth letting Bobby get away. I knew it was only a matter of time until Bobby would mess up again. He'd get what was owed."

"And he did," Danny and I say simultaneously.

"And relocating George's body to the woods?" I ask.

"I guess Bobby took care of that. I didn't stick around to see, and I certainly didn't want to ask. I wanted to get you home. You took a couple of Xanax when we arrived and drifted off to sleep. You never spoke of it to me again."

"How many times in one night can I possibly thank you?" I ask.

"Hmmmm, let's see. I can think of a few more times at least," he says, and reaches for me.

# CHAPTER 45

When I wake up, I realize I haven't slept this well for a long time. Exhaustion took over yesterday, but today is a new day. I reach over to the other side of the bed and feel the indentation of where Danny had slept. He probably left early this morning to go home and get ready for his shift. I swing my feet over the side of the bed and grab my robe. I pad to the kitchen for a cup of coffee.

As I get my mug ready and the Keurig started, I hear murmuring. I walk to the French doors and look out on the patio. Danny and Addie are sitting in the colored sunrise, talking about something, most likely me. I knock on the window and, with satisfaction, startle them. I raise my finger to let them know I'll be outside in a minute.

I take my steaming coffee outside to join them. The morning is cool; the sunrise bursting with color. As I walk past Danny, he puts his hand on my waist and lets it trail off as I move toward a chair opposite him. Addie smiles and dips her head for another sip of coffee.

"Well rested?" Addie asks.

Danny and I smile.

"Oh, yes," I answer.

Addie looks back and forth at us. "Good, I'm glad you two finally found yourselves again. We need a solid team if we're going to figure out this mystery."

My mood drops. I may be outside enjoying coffee at sunrise now, but if I'm blamed for this murder, then all of this will come to a halt for the rest of my life. There's a lot on the line.

I add information about George to the story I started telling yesterday on the ride home from jail. I am not proud of myself for how I've lived, but it is what it is. The only way for me is forward. I've been clean for a long time, except for recent slips taking Xanax. I won't be refilling that prescription, anyway. Too much harm has come to me because of numbing my feelings and keeping secrets. There's a lot I need to work on, I realize. Now that Addie and Danny know everything, I feel embarrassed but not judged.

"I've got to get to the station this morning, Clara. I need to go home and shower first. I'll text you later to see how you're doing," Danny says and stands.

He walks over to me and kisses me gently on the lips. My face reddens, and Addie grins. Addie and I watch Danny start up his car and take off.

Addie snaps me back to attention. "Okay, I've been thinking about this all night."

"Thinking about what?"

"Our plan. Our strategy. How we're going to go about finding out who the real killer is."

"The police have a lot of damaging evidence against me."

"Perhaps, but it's all circumstantial," Addie says. "They don't have you in possession of a murder weapon."

"It was poisoning," I tell her.

"Okay, poison then. They don't know the who or why of the murder. They don't even know what poisoned him, if it happened that way at all. Let's start by reviewing what we know. Who would have motive to kill Bobby?"

"Everyone," we say simultaneously.

"Let's start with Alice," Addie says.

I feel my shoulders tense. Addie is right. I love Alice like a second mother, but I don't want to take the blame for a murder that I didn't commit.

"Okay, let's talk about Alice."

"We know Alice has spent a lot of years living with Bobby's violence and drunken fits. He's done her wrong in so many ways. He was a homophobic asshole who liked to drink, fornicate, and beat people. That means there could be hundreds of potential murderers, or rather, good Samaritans," Addie says.

"We know shortly before Bobby died, Alice caught him with Lala. Alice was probably happy that he was meeting his needs with other people. I think she had long ago given up any hope for a loving relationship with her husband.

"But she could have access to a poison. She didn't need to be big and brawny to beat him up and throw him in the bay. She could have put a little poison in his food or whiskey over a period of time. Then, poof, he falls off his boat one day and dies," I say.

I think back to when Alice told me that whatever Bobby had on me was now a non-issue with Bobby dead. I know Alice had the notion that Bobby was holding something over my head. Still, I don't see Alice being the one who actually took matters into her own hands.

"True, true. But Alice wouldn't want to leave Brian alone, right? She'd weigh the risk of getting arrested and put away for the rest of her life. What happens to Brian then?"

"That's true. I think, for the same reasons, Brian is not likely to be the murderer, either. He wouldn't want to leave his mother alone to fend for herself while he stayed locked away."

"Okay, let's talk about the number one asshole these days," Addie says. "Mr. Rock-thrower extraordinaire. Mr. Whiney-Man, I've had a hard life in prison, and now you're trying to judge me."

"Johnston," I say.

"Yep, the one and only."

"I think he's a good candidate. His hostility toward me is palpable. He was probably furious when Danny went to interview him."

Addie's eyes narrow. "What do you think he meant by his message, 'secrets are dangerous'?"

"Hard to say, but I'd guess Bobby told him something about me, about that night at Clay Street. I don't think Bobby would ever reveal so much that he'd incriminate himself, though. If Bobby told him he was the drug supplier that George overdosed on, then Johnston would have the leverage to make Bobby do anything he wanted."

"Yeah. Bobby and Johnston are both cut from the same cloth. They're vile, despicable scumbags."

"So, I bet on Johnston as a valid suspect," I say.

"Me, too. Do you think it could be any of your other clients?"

My eyes snap toward Addie. "My clients? Impossible. I think I'd know it if something was wrong there."

"I know you're protective of them, Clara, but I mean, look at Lala. She's with Johnston now. Maybe she knows more than she's revealing."

I contemplate Addie's implication. "Lala may be sleeping with Johnston, but she's not vindictive or conniving. He may be using her, but I don't think she'd willingly go along with killing Bobby. Remember? She was in love with Bobby. She thought he would leave Alice."

"True. She didn't have a hard time replacing him, hopping from Bobby to Woody to Johnston. Nah, she didn't look like she grieved too hard for Bobby. What about Shelby?"

"Shelby?" I ask, surprised.

"Yeah, well, didn't Bobby blackmail him about making those porn videos shortly before he went missing?"

I hadn't thought about that. When I last met with Shelby, he seemed elated that Bobby was out of the picture so he and Marshall could move out of the country. I can't picture Shelby doing something to Bobby.

"Shelby had good reason to kill him, that's for sure. I just don't see it, Addie. He paid off Bobby. Why wouldn't he just move away like he's planning now?"

"I don't know. Maybe Shelby felt like Bobby would always follow him because he saw him as an endless well of money," Addie says.

"Anyway, I think if anything were to happen, like Shelby killing him, it would likely have happened when he was a hot-headed teenager and Bobby beat the crap out of him and Brian out on the pier."

"Oh, that's right. I remember Shelby saying that. Yeah, I would imagine that one of them would have done him in right then and there. So, let's rank our possible suspects," Addie says.

"Okay, Detective Marsh. Let's do it. Who's first?"

"Definitely Johnston Burr. There's something there, some deep rage about Bobby that could definitely be a motive for murder."

"Agreed," I say. "Next?"

Addie looks into the distance. "Lala would be my next choice."

"Really? Lala? Why?"

"I know she's important to you, Clara. But Lala is a scorned lover. She admitted she was in love with Bobby. She wanted them to have a life together. Then he's gone, and who does she end up with? Johnston Burr. Being with Johnston is kind of the same as being with Bobby. Both are violent, angry, drug-dealing, manipulative men. Going from Bobby to Johnston was like being with the same man, except not."

"True. Lala was always easily manipulated by men. I guess under duress, she'd do anything, even something illegal, if she could win a man's love and devotion."

"Next would be Shelby. I mean, he had a reason for wanting Bobby to go away."

"True," I say. "I don't see it, though. Shelby doesn't have a rage that burns from the inside out. He's happy with Marshall. He'd stand to lose everything."

"I agree. Shelby is an unlikely suspect. That leaves Alice and Brian, and we both agree that neither of them would risk being sent to prison for the rest of their life and leave the other alone to fend for themselves."

"I'm with you. I don't think it could be either one of them."

"What about Shaun or Woody?"

"The watermen? Why do you think that?"

"Well, Shaun moved in to grab Bobby's fishing spot fast. And Woody, well, he's a thieving brute." Addie puffs out her chest and sticks her tongue in her cheek to mimic a big brute.

I laugh. "Maybe, but I don't get the feeling that either of them cared whether Bobby lived or died. They had their own lives going on. They had their buddies at the Pub. No, I see them as benefitting from his death, just like many people here in Mystic Beach."

"Okay then. We're in agreement that Johnston is our number one, right?"

"Agreed."

"Now, let's figure out a plan to reveal him as the murderous, drug-addicted, drooling convict that he is." She holds out her hand.

I reach for her hand and laugh. "Let's do it.

# CHAPTER 46

Addie cancels all my appointments for today and tomorrow. My clients are understanding because, as usual, they've already heard of my arrest and posting bail. Addie assures me they were supportive. She wasn't able to reach Johnston, which was a primary concern because if we were able to reach him, we could find out his location and watch him. He didn't respond to her call or her text. I doubt he could legally leave town because of his parole status, but I'm sure he certainly isn't anxious to get back in touch with me.

"Why don't we go see your mother this morning?" Addie says.

"You think? I feel embarrassed by everything going on."

"I know your mom is a source of comfort for you. She's on your side. Plus, she has those mystical powers of hers. Maybe she can help us track down Johnston."

I laugh. "Well, maybe so. It can't hurt, anyway. I'm sure Mom is worried about me."

We drive to Sunview in Addie's car. We hold the elevator for Edward, who wheels up at the last minute.

"So sorry, ladies. It's these wheels that slow me down. If only you had seen me in my youth. Boundless energy, I had." He laughs.

"I'm sure. I can see your inner light shining right through you," Addie tells him.

"My dear, you surely know how to make an old man's heart pitter-patter."

The elevator opens on the second floor. He raises his hand and says, "Ta ta," as he wheels out. We continue up to the third floor.

Mom's door is open as usual. She's put a tarot spread on the coffee table in front of her. This one looks complex. When we walk in, she looks up and smiles. She reaches to hug me first, then Addie.

"I knew you'd be coming today, my daughter. How are you feeling?" she signs.

Palm down, I wiggle my hand, telling her, "So-so."

"I know, I know." She turns to Addie and signs, "Hello."

Addie raises her hand to wave. Mom turns to me and signs, "Is Addie being a good friend?"

Addie interrupts and signs "Of course, I'm being a good friend." She looks delighted..

Mom and I open our eyes wide. "You've been practicing. Your signs are much better."

Addie lifts her hand tentatively, palm down, and wiggles it, "So-so."

We laugh. Mom gestures for us to sit around the coffee table. She tells us she wants to explain the spread. She thinks it will help us.

My mother signs and uses her voice so Addie can understand. "This tarot card spread is called the Celtic Cross." She points to the position of the cards. "In the center is card one; it represents the situation now. You see the Eight of Swords? It means someone—you, Clara—feels trapped, powerless, in crisis."

My mother looks at me. Yeah, that pretty much describes my current situation.

"Card two is on top of card one, crossing it. The Fool. It means that a new beginning is needed. Something needs to change, a new path taken. Card three is above cards one and two and represents the conscious awareness. The Ace of Wands indicates that the person knows a new beginning is needed and will bring growth."

Again, my mother looks in my direction. "Card four is below cards one and two and represents unconscious energies, things not known. The Two of Pentacles indicates though the person may not know it, they are flexible, having dealt with ups and downs. The person knows how to maintain balance and be resourceful, though she feels trapped and restricted now."

"Oh, wow, Clara. Your mother has this exactly right. I had no idea she was this good," says Addie.

I glance at the floor, then look at my mother to continue the reading. "Card six is what is ahead. The Eight of Wands represents that there is action and movement. Someone will rush into a series of actions, working hard to determine a solution."

The next four cards, seven, eight, nine, and ten, are lined up vertically to the right of card six. Card seven is at the bottom of the line.

"Card seven represents someone's attitude."

I interrupt. "It's okay, Mom. I know you're doing the reading about me. Go ahead and read it for me."

"Okay, Clara, card seven is a major arcana card, the Hierophant. This is a powerful figure representing traditional values, convention, and tradition. The Hierophant represents spiritual guidance, education, and learning."

Addie looks at me wide-eyed and signs, "Yes, that's pretty much Clara."

"Card eight represents the people around you, Clara. The Eight of Cups reveals that those who you thought were with you, in support of you, are now gone. People have walked away from your life, which might be why you're feeling so trapped and despondent," my mother signs as she taps the first card.

"Card nine is your hopes and fears," my mother signs.

I sign and speak, "The Six of Wands. I want victory, success, and achievement. That's absolutely true. I want to emerge from this nightmare in one piece."

Mom taps the final card at the top, card ten. "Ten of Swords. Clara, all is not what it seems. There's betrayal and enemies. You'll need to gather your strength for this one. You probably won't see the betrayal coming."

Mom leans back on the sofa. Her face clouds and her eyes darken. The spread is a warning for me. I will be okay. I just need to figure out how to proceed. One thing is certain, though. I need to take action and not wait for something or someone to come look for me. I feel a new resolve, a firm confidence forming inside my chest. I can do this. I really can. Despite everything happening, this is just a complicated puzzle that needs some figuring. Not every tarot spread is perfect. Maybe this one is testing me.

Addie's face reveals that she's thinking the same thing. "We can do this, Clara. We're a good team and good people. We'll figure out who killed Bobby Ward."

"And it wasn't you," Mom signs and points to me.

I put my two fists on top of each other and extend the index finger on both. I tap my fists together and sign, "Right."

Addie and I give Mom a hug and tell her we'll be in touch. I have the energy to overcome my feelings of doom. I need to wait for Danny to see if he has more information about the toxicology report. Somehow, I feel like that might be a key, but I can't sit around and wait.

When Addie and I are back in her car, Addie asks, "Where to, boss?"

"I think we need to go see Alice and Brian, see how they're getting along. Maybe we can figure everything out."

Addie pauses. "Are you sure, Clara? What if Alice and Brian are somehow involved?"

I laugh. "No, impossible. Alice has known me my whole life. They will be assets in figuring this out. I just know it."

Addie puts the car in drive. "You're right. Okay, let's go talk to the other members of our team."

# CHAPTER 47

Addie and I rap on Alice's screen door. I can hear Alice and Brian talking somewhere in the back of the house, maybe in the kitchen. As I knock again, their talking stops. I hear Brian's footsteps.

"Hey, there, ladies! Good to see you," Brian says as he opens the screen door for us.

I walk into the house and notice immediately that the furniture is different. "What's this? A facelift?"

Brian smiles and turns as his mother shuffles into the room. "Oh, Clara, darling. I'm so happy to see you."

"Clara was just asking about the new set up here at the house," Brian says.

"Oh, yes, Brian moved all of his things back into the house. Doesn't it look wonderful? Mother and son are back together again." Alice's joy lights up her face.

I notice a huge aquarium. It's so large, it takes up almost the entire back wall. "Oh, Brian. This is cool. What's this?"

Brian walks to the glass saltwater aquarium. "My pets, of course. I've always had a special love for marine life. I mean, I'm a marine biologist, after all."

When Addie and I walk closer, I see that it's not one large aquarium. There are several separated cubes of glass that look like a mosaic. We push our faces close to one of the glass cubes. Inside is a medium-sized fish with grayish-brown coloring on the top half and a white underbelly.

"Why do you have these fish in their own cubicles?" I ask Brian. "It's like they have their own large condo but no friends to play with."

Brian laughs. "These are Tetraodontidae."

Addie says, "Uh, come again?"

"Tetraodontidae is the scientific name, most commonly known as pufferfish."

"Are they the kind that blow up like a balloon when they're threatened?"

"Yes, the very same. They're not the fastest fish in the bunch, but they have an elastic belly that fills with water and makes them an unappetizing ball. It's a pretty good superpower, if you ask me."

"What do they eat?" I ask.

"These eat mostly invertebrates and algae. Larger pufferfish can crack open clams and mussels, but these are smaller. Here look." Brian puts on a thick waterproof glove and removes the lid from one of the cubes. He sticks his hand in the tank and gently touches the back of the fish. It immediately begins to inflate. Brian removes his hand and puts the top back on the cube. The fish stays inflated.

"Will it deflate?" Addie asks.

"It'll take a few hours. It takes a longer time to deflate than to inflate."

"Why are they in their own tanks?" I ask.

"Oh, they don't get along well playing in the same sandbox. They can be very territorial and sometimes fight to the death."

"So why do you have all these puffers? Do you eat them?"

Brian laughs. "If I did, I'd be sorry. But you know, the Japanese eat them as a delicacy called Fugu. Their chefs are specially trained to filet and cook them, so they don't make their customers sick."

Alice says, "Come on, everyone. It's time to stop the shop talk. Here, come on in the kitchen."

We follow Alice into the kitchen. A small television is sitting on the counter. It looks like she's watching a soap opera.

"I haven't watched General Hospital in years," I say. "I can't believe it's still running."

Alice chuckles. "Oh, my, I don't know how I'd survive without it. Here, come sit. Would you like a glass of lemonade?"

Yes, please," Addie responds.

Brian excuses himself to the back yard, where he continues to work on the vegetable garden. I watch him bend and run his fingers along the soil to pull weeds. A breaking news announcement interrupts General Hospital. Suddenly, a picture of me is flashed on the screen. I get a sick feeling in my stomach.

"Breaking news from NBC4 out of Washington. Police announced the arrest of Dr. Clara Starr, a native of Edgewater, Maryland. Dr. Starr was arrested early yesterday morning for the murder of Robert Ward, another Edgewater native. She was released on bail and is expected to—"

Alice turns off the television. "Oh, darling, I'm so sorry this is happening to you. If only they knew what a terrible man Bobby was." Alice shuffles over to wrap her arms around my shoulders.

I am frozen in place, unable to say a word. Addie comes to the rescue. "Alice, that's why we're here, actually." When Alice looks puzzled, Addie continues, "See, we don't think that Clara killed Bobby."

"Even if she did, I wouldn't blame her," Alice starts.

"Alice, she didn't kill him," says.

"Of course not, dear. What I was saying is that it doesn't matter who killed him. He needed to be gone from this earth." She shakes her head. "He's hurt so many people, some more than others." Alice rubs my arm.

"So, what we want to know, given that Clara didn't kill him, who do you think did?"

Alice thinks for a moment. "What about that man? That big one who recently got out of prison."

"Yes, Johnston Burr? That's what we were thinking, too," Addie says.

"That one is trouble, I'll tell you. Before he went to prison, he and Bobby had some kind of business relationship. And by business, you know what I mean?" Alice looks at me, and I nod.

"Do you know anything specific about Johnston?" Addie asks Alice.

"Not really, just that he's someone I wouldn't want to come across."

I lean across the table and place my hand on Alice's. "Alice, I don't want to upset you, but I need to ask you about something else."

"Yes? Go ahead, dear. You know I have no secrets from you."

"It's about Lala, Lala Chance. You know her?"

Alice frowns. "Yes, I know the girl. And before you say anything else, let me tell you I know about her affair with Bobby."

I raise my eyebrows.

"Yes," she continues, "I knew about it for quite some time. And I didn't care one hoot about their affair. As far as I was concerned, Lala was doing me a favor. As long as she satisfied his needs, he didn't come bothering me. In fact, I should have paid her for her services."

"So you weren't upset? Even though Bobby told her he was planning on leaving you?" Addie asks.

Alice laughs until it wheezes into a cough. "Oh, dear ones. Do you think Lala was his only affair? There have been countless women over the years. I've never begrudged a single one of them. In fact, I almost pitied them because if I knew anything about Bobby, I knew this. He was a liar, a womanizer, and a bastard. I knew it from the get-go. We grew up together, remember? But in those days, the world was different. If our families wanted us to marry, then we married. Divorce wasn't an option. I understood Bobby, and he understood me, for better or worse. So, I knew he would never leave me, even though I would have loved him to go. He'd leave his house? Risk me filing for divorce and getting not only half of his crabbing business, but the possibility of getting alimony, too? No. He wasn't going anywhere. In fact, Lala and I had lunch one day about it. I told her she was welcome to him. She seemed relieved I wasn't mad and happy that I wouldn't interfere in their relationship."

My thoughts reorganize themselves. So, Lala had an understanding with Alice and Bobby. There was no reason for her to hold a grudge because Bobby was going to continue to be with Lala even though he was married. Maybe Lala didn't tell me everything because she wanted to protect Alice and Bobby.

"What about Shelby Cross?" I ask.

"Shelby Cross. I haven't thought of that boy for years and years. What does he have to do with this?"

"I don't know. Do you think he had a reason to kill Bobby?" I don't want to give too much away.

"Well, now, I don't know him quite as well. I remember Bobby had a fit when he found out Brian and Shelby had a little something-something going on. That was a long time ago when they were youngsters. Bobby was never one to sit with what he called 'going against God.' Me? I thought Bobby was just stupid. If God made him the way he was, then surely God made Shelby and Brian the way they were. Why do you think Shelby could have been involved?"

"Because Bobby was blackmailing Shelby with pornographic pictures," Addie says.

"Oh? I don't know anything about that. But Brian might, because he knows Shelby better than I do. Want me to call in Brian so you can ask him yourself?"

"I'll talk with Brian later. You're right. The idea of Shelby being a killer doesn't sit well with me, either. It just doesn't feel right," I say.

"Shelby doesn't seem like the type to murder someone. I mean, he's got that rich guy who takes care of him. Marshall, I think his name is. Shelby was always such a soft-spoken boy, a gentle soul. I'd be really surprised if he killed Bobby. Honestly, I think your best bet is that Johnston fellow. He was bad news before, and I'll bet he's still bad news," Alice says.

She has a point there. Everyone had a reason to kill Bobby. That is no secret. Not everyone has the gumption to do it. It wasn't like someone shot Bobby in the head; the medical examiner would have found that. I think the killer had to feel comfortable being up close and personal. It takes a certain kind of person to kill someone. If it was poisoning, then it was a planned out process, well thought out. Johnston surely had a lot of time to plan and plot while he sat in the jail cell. He had a motive: revenge. I just need to collect evidence to show that he had the both motive and opportunity to have murdered him.

# CHAPTER 48

Addie and I stop by the pub on the way home. It's a little too early, but I know the pub will fill soon enough once the watermen finish the day's work. We pull open the heavy wooden door and walk into the dim light. Once known as the William Brown House and the Londontowne Public House, the pub has roots tied to the mid-1700s. It's on the main road that connected Williamsburg, Virginia, and Philadelphia, Pennsylvania. The South River runs alongside the tavern; it once brought passengers by ferry. From 1828 to the mid-1960s, the Public House served as an almshouse, providing respite for people who could no longer support themselves. Nowadays, it's a tavern where locals gather and spend their money on cheap liquor and fried food. It's dim inside, with a thick smell of old grease.

Diane Meadows sits at the bar tapping on her phone. I lay my hand on her shoulder.

"Hey, Diane. Long time no see, huh?"

Diane's reaction time is a little slow, a sign that she's already had a few, despite the time. "Well, hey, there. It *has* been a long time. How the hellya been?"

"I'm good, good. Hey, I'm wondering, have you seen a guy named Johnston Burr around?"

"Johnston? Not today. He comes in often enough, but he's not here, not yet. What are you looking for him for? He's kind of handsome if you like the rugged look." Diane laughs.

"Uh … not in this lifetime, Diane," I say.

Diane looks Addie up and down. "Who's this with you?"

"My name is Addie Marsh. Nice to meet you." She holds out her hand for a handshake.

Diane looks like she's trying to solve a riddle. For a few moments, she just looks at Addie's face, then suddenly snaps her fingers.

"Your parents, they died a while back. Bad car crash, right?"

"That's right."

"Wasn't your father drinking or something?"

Addie's face closes. "No, he wasn't. Excuse me, I need to use the restroom."

Diane turns to me. "I didn't mean anything by it. Lori, can you make me another Old Fashioned?"

The bartender walks to the middle of the bar and reaches for cheap whiskey. Diane watches her but says to me, "I saw on the news that they're trying to pin Bobby's murder on you."

I open my mouth, but Diane cuts me off. "You don't have to say anything, Clara. Whoever took care of that piece of shit is all right by me. Quite a few people around here had Bobby in their crosshairs."

I take the seat next to Diane and lean in. "Have you heard anything? I didn't kill him, but the cops have a different story."

"Is that why you're looking for Johnston? You think he might have had something to do with it?"

I don't answer.

Diane suddenly yells, "Lori! Hey Lori! You see Johnston around lately?"

Lori shrugs. Diane swings her barstool around and yells to two others sitting at the opposite end of the bar. "Hey, Mark, Terry, you seen Johnston?"

Both the men shake their heads and resume their conversation and drinks. When Addie comes back from the bathroom, I bid Diane goodbye and we walk out.

"So, did Diane know where Johnston is?"

"No, she didn't. She asked Lori, Mark, and Terry, too, which means word will travel around soon enough that I'm looking for him. I get the feeling Johnston isn't going to like that."

"I think you're probably right," Addie says. "Come on, let's go back to your place."

Addie and I wait for Danny to stop by after his shift. Although he didn't tell me he was coming, I know he will. Soon enough, we hear his car pull up and the engine shut off. When Danny gets close to the porch where we're sitting, I can see something is wrong. Addie asks Danny if he wants a glass of wine. I tell her I'd prefer an iced tea. Danny says he'll have a tea, too.

"So, what's up, Danny? You look disturbed."

"Well, my day didn't go as planned."

"Oh?"

"Yeah, Chief called me into his office and asked me straight out if I was still hanging out with you now that you're the main suspect."

My stomach drops. "And what did you say?"

"I looked him straight in the eye and told him that now that I'm off the case, what I do with my own time is my own business."

"He didn't much like that, did he?"

"No, but he understands. I mean, he was born and raised here, too. Everyone we've ever stopped for a DUI or other sort of shenanigans is someone we know. Everyone knows everyone from generations back here in Mystic Beach."

"And then what did the Chief say?"

"He told me to watch my back. For all he knows, you're a cold-blooded murderer, and keeping my distance would be better for my health."

Danny can't meet my eyes when he tells me this. It's just as well, because I feel like the color has drained from my face.

"And there's more. I ran into Jacob early this afternoon," Danny says.

"Did he have more to say about the toxicology report?"

"He did."

"What? Don't leave me hanging," I say as Addie walks onto the porch.

"Jacob told me that the toxicologist isolated and examined the cell structure of the bacteria but hasn't finished all the tests. So far, they say the bacteria is not common in this area but is associated with some kind of marine life."

"Marine life? What does that mean?"

"The way Jacob explained it, the bacteria appear to be associated with some type of marine animals. They're bringing in experts to compare the bacteria structure with blue crabs, oysters, clams, and animals found in the Chesapeake Bay."

"That makes sense, but Bobby was a waterman. Do they still think someone poisoned him?"

Danny sips his iced tea. "Maybe, but maybe it wasn't an intentional poisoning. Whatever the bacteria is, it shut down his organs. Jacob contacted someone at the Chesapeake Environmental Lab and asked if there were any unusual bacterial blooms in the bay this summer. They said there's nothing unusual this year compared to last year."

"I'm not sure if that's good news or bad news," I say.

"What about you two?" Danny asks.

"Addie and I went to the pub today looking for Johnston. Danny, I feel like he's the one."

Danny shakes his head.

"Wait, wait. Before you rule him out, listen," Addie says. "Johnston has all the hallmarks of a very bad man. First, he tried to bulldoze Clara during one of his sessions. Then he smashed her window with that rock and left her a threatening message."

"Wait, what message?" Danny asks.

I stand and go to my bedroom. Extracting the note from my bedside table, I return and hand Danny the message.

"'Secrets are dangerous.' What the hell is that supposed to mean? And how do you know it was Johnston and not some rowdy teenagers?"

"Hear me out for a minute, Danny," I say. "I think it was Johnston's doing because he and Bobby were pretty close before he was locked up."

"Yeah, so?"

"So, I think Bobby told Johnston about George's death so they could have something over me," I whisper.

"Why would Bobby do that?"

Anger rises in my chest. "Because … because Bobby was a piece of shit. Because he didn't want me to tell the cops that he sold George those bad drugs. To keep me quiet. He knew that if I told the police about the drugs, I would also be implicated in his death because I was with him and then left the house that night. I just walked out like nothing was wrong."

Addie puts her hand on my back, but it doesn't calm me. "I know it has to be Johnston. It's the only thing that fits. He's as mean as Bobby was, if not meaner. I'll bet he wants to take over Bobby's drug business, you know, make money just like Bobby did."

"And he's having sex with Lala, Bobby's old fling," Addie adds. "The pieces all fit, Danny. Johnston wants Clara out of his business, but as long as he's Clara's client, he can keep tabs on her and knows she can't tell anyone because of confidentiality laws."

"No," Danny says.

"No, what?" I ask.

"It's not Johnston," Danny says.

"But how do you know? You don't know him!"

"You're right, I don't know him. But one thing I do know is it's not Johnston."

"How do you know that?" Addie asks.

"Because Johnston is a confidential informant for the police."

"What? What are you saying, Danny?"

"Johnston was freed early from jail because he agreed to be a confidential informant. He made a deal with the State Attorney. He'd provide information about the drug network Bobby masterminded in exchange for his early freedom."

"But he still could have killed him," I say. I feel the veins in my neck popping out and my heart pounding.

Danny sits beside me on the couch. "No, he couldn't have. He's working with the police, and they're tracking him with an ankle monitor."

Addie asserts, "No, it can't be. It has to be Johnston. You don't know how scary that man is."

"Addie, I know he's working with the police. In fact, he's working with Engel and Bennett. That's why they were so eager to arrest you, Clara. Johnston Burr must have told them you were part of the drug network with Bobby. So now they think they've found Bobby's killer. You."

# CHAPTER 49

After Danny leaves, Addie says she's spending the night at my house. I tell her she doesn't have to, but she insists. She wants me to know that someone is in my corner even though the clock is ticking. Soon, my trial will be scheduled, and then what? Spend the rest of my life in prison. None of this makes sense to me. Johnston working for the police? He put up a good front, that's for sure. I feel like we're back to square one. And who took those pictures of me and gave them to the police? Was that Johnston, too?

I can't sleep. I run through my sessions with Lala, Shelby, and Johnston. Shelby and Lala seem so unlikely to be murderers. I've known them for a very long time. Is there something I've overlooked? Is there a clue that I've missed? I toss and turn until I finally fall asleep sometime in the early hours of the morning. A loud banging wakes me up. I hop from the bed, not bothering with my robe. Addie and I meet near the French doors. There is something on the glass. I flip on the outside lights, and both Addie and I scream.

The glass is smeared with something deep red. I open the doors and run into the yard, sure that I'm going to find Johnston running away. I don't see anyone, though. My feet are wet from the dew on the grass. Everyone's lights are out. I walk back to the porch and stop before I get to the door. What sick person would do this?

Addie sees my expression and starts to come outside. I hold up my palm.

"Stop! Stop! Don't come out, Addie."

Her eyes follow my gaze to the cement pad of the porch, right near the door. She gasps.

"Who would do something like that?"

I shake my head. "I don't know, but whoever did this is demented. Go get me a plastic garbage bag."

Addie comes back with rubber gloves, a trash bag, Windex, and paper towels. I put my hand in the trash bag and grab the gutted fish. I feel sure this was meant as a message for me. Someone doesn't like that I'm meddling in the investigation even though it's my life on the line. No, this will not deter me. I can clean up fish guts without batting an eye. I've had lots of experience.

"Gross," Addie says. "Someone's afraid you're getting too close."

"I agree. That means we're on the right track. I'm not giving up."

"Me either."

Addie and I finish cleaning up the guts, make our coffees, and sit on the porch. The sunrise across the bay glows pale oranges, blues, and purples. Birds chirp in the distance.

After a few moments of watching seagulls coast over the glassy water, Addie asks, "So, what's the game plan today?"

"I think we should go talk to Lala first. I'm curious if she knows Johnston is a C.I. What do you think?"

"Yes, I think that's a good start. Who knows, maybe Johnston is getting close to her because he thinks she's the murderer."

"I didn't think of that, but you could be right. I can't imagine Lala being behind all of this, but you never know. Maybe Bobby broke her last straw, and she wanted him gone."

"I'll text Lala now," Addie says. "That way she's knows we're on our way."

When Addie and I are dressed and ready, we hop into my VW bug, and drive to Lala's house, about a mile away. We pull into the driveway. Lala bounds out, smiling and clapping her hands.

"What a treat! You both are here for a visit. I have some tasty rolls you today."

We walk into her small bungalow, one of the original cottages in Mystic Beach. Lala has her living room painted a Pepto Bismol-colored pink. Small glass lamps filled with seashells sit on small tables. Lala picks up her fluffy pink bathrobe off the chair and asks us to make ourselves comfortable. I can smell brown sugar and yeast flowing through the house. From the kitchen, she asks if we want coffee. Both Addie and I say yes.

Lala enters the living room carrying a mermaid tray with three cups of coffee and a stack of steaming sticky cinnamon rolls. She passes them out.

Addie takes a bite of the cinnamon roll and groans. "Lala, these are marvelous. I taste something unusual in the icing. What is it?"

Lala giggles. "You can taste it? Perfect. I put some orange zest in the batch of icing. I thought the flavors would meld together well. You like?"

I close my eyes with delight. "These are so yummy, Lala. I don't know how you do it."

Lala smiles and sips her coffee. "Why did y'all want to stop by?"

I swallow the piece of roll. "I want to talk to you about Johnston."

"Johnston? Why him?"

"It just seemed sudden for the two of you to get together. First, it was Bobby, then he died, and then Johnston popped up to take his place. How did it all come together?"

Lala leans back in her chair. "It might seem strange and all, but

Bobby was actually the one who connected me with Johnston."

"How'd that happen?" asks Addie.

"Listen, I know all about the screw up at the Royal Farm. Johnston ended up going to jail for the drugs that actually belonged to Bobby."

"Wasn't Johnston angry at Bobby?" I ask.

"At first, sure. Johnston was really pissed off, but then Bobby told him all would be made whole. I don't know what all they talked about, but it calmed Johnston down. He just needed to bide his time."

"And then what happened?" Addie asks.

"Then Johnston got set loose early," Lala says.

"What are you not telling me, Lala?" I ask.

"Well, there's not much to tell," Lala says, but her face says something different.

"There's more," Addie says. "Are you and Johnston somehow involved with Bobby's murder? Revenge for him because of the drug set up, revenge for you because he didn't leave Alice?"

Addie is being strategic. She knows Johnston is an informant, but she wants to stir Lala into a reaction. It works.

"What? Johnston and me? Killing Bobby? No way. Clara, do you think this way, too?"

I smile but cannot hold her steady gaze. I never thought she was involved. We had to ask, but I can tell from the tone of her voice that she's hurt, hurt we would think that of her.

Lala lowers her voice. "Oh, come on, Clara. I know you don't suspect me, and the person you're really after is Johnston. You don't know him. He got himself turned around." She pauses. "Okay, look. The police approached Johnston and told him if he informed them about Bobby's network of drug deals, they'd give him early release. He would continue to provide tips for the full five-year sentence but only serve two years in a cell. He took the deal. And what's more, he told me all about it."

"Why tell you?" Addie asks Lala. "I mean, what did he benefit by telling you?"

"He didn't have anything to gain except my loyalty and trust. You see, Bobby had introduced us long before all that went down. Sure, I was in love and spent time with him, but only to bide my time. I knew deep down he would never leave Alice, especially after Alice saw us in the shed. She and I had lunch. Did you know that?"

"She told us."

"Okay, so you know. She didn't care at all that Bobby was with me. I knew then that Bobby would never leave her. So, I turned my sights to Johnston. Let me tell you, Johnston may look mean and tough, but he's nowhere near the psychopath that Bobby was. Johnston is smart, ambitious, and loyal. He was just another mark for Bobby. Johnston was a tough kid getting into a lot of trouble. His folks weren't any better than the rest of ours," she says, circling her arms around her chest. "Bobby thought Johnston would follow his every command, but he underestimated him. Johnston was a kid who knew how to play tough but could outsmart anyone. He just needed to get it set up."

I get it. I really do. Bobby played Johnston, apparently just like he played me. He lured people in with nothing to lose and turned them into little soldiers for his business.

"Johnston saw me, Clara. Not just who I am on the outside. He saw who I really am. And you and I both know there aren't many people who can do that in my life."

I know what she means. I feel the same way about Danny. When you come from a particular type of background and made some mistakes that give others the opportunity to judge you, it's hard to find people who can see beneath the crusty layer into the potential of who you could be.

"I get it, Lala. I do. Thank you for being upfront with me."

Lala stands and holds open her arms to me. I step into them, and she squeezes tight. She reaches out an arm to grab Addie into the fold. The three of us hang on like we never want to let go.

Lala pulls back and whispers, "Clara, whatever is happening now, and for what it's worth, I know you didn't kill the scumbag, either."

I give her a quick hug and turn to leave before she can see the tears rolling down my face.

# CHAPTER 50

We leave Lala's house with a bag full of still-warm cinnamon rolls. I sit in the car and hesitate before turning on the key. Addie reaches over and lays her hand on my arm.

"Don't worry, Clara. We'll figure this out."

"It's just that I was convinced it had to be Johnston. I mean, when someone broke my window just after Danny interviewed him, I knew I had it right. At least, I thought I did, which now I realize I never did."

"There's still Shelby, right? And we can talk to Alice again. Maybe Brian will have some ideas? My point is, Clara, there are still people around here who believe in you."

"Maybe spending my life in jail for a crime I didn't commit would be penance for the bad things I've done in my past."

I'm feeling sorry for myself, but everything feels futile. I'm no closer to discovering the murderer than I was before I started.

"What would make you feel better, Clara? Want to visit your mom? Visit Alice?"

I consider her question. Poor Alice. I haven't thought about how she's dealing with all this. She knew my parents and me from the moment I was born. She was my second mother. Right now, I need comfort, someone to tell me it's okay.

"Yes, let's go visit Alice."

A moment later, we're pulling into Alice's driveway. The screen is closed, but the front door is open. I tap on the screen door and walk through to the kitchen in the back. The soap opera is on the television. In the back, I see Alice and Brian hunched over in their vegetable garden.

"I see you've planted some flowers here, too," I say to Alice and Brian. They both turn around and smile.

Alice takes a moment to straighten her back. She reaches her thin, papery arms to me. I step into them and give her a light hug.

"We thought maybe a short visit would raise Clara's spirits," Addie says.

"It's that investigation stuff, isn't it, my sweet?" Alice says.

I bend down to pull a weed that threatens to take over a tomato plant. Brian elbows me and knocks me off balance onto my butt. I laugh.

"Hey, girl, hey. Don't let it all get you down."

"Easy for you to say," I tell him.

"Look, it's circumstantial at best. They don't have any photos of you with your hands around his neck. Oh, wait, they do have photos, but nothing that connects you to the murder," he chides.

I elbow Brian back, and he falls on his butt, too. "Those photos are bad, Brian."

"I know how it seems, but without a direct connection, you'll get off. They have to prove beyond a reasonable doubt that it's you who did him in. Anyway, I get the feeling their heart isn't into solving the murder anyway."

"Why do you think that?" I ask.

"Look, every person around here knows my father was a bastard. He was violent, mean, conniving, and a drug dealer. He preyed on everyone, including you, me, and anyone else he could get his hands on. I mean, as far as the residents of Mystic Beach are concerned, you or someone else did the neighborhood a favor by scourging the devil from our lives."

"Yeah, well, it doesn't feel like they're not investigating it. I'm out on bail, but a trial will come. A reckoning will take place whether anyone believes me or not. They let me out on bail because I am a long-time resident. They know I have nowhere else to go."

"See? Things are already shifting on your side. Hey, now, don't cry. It will all be all right. You'll see. By next summer, we'll be back to cracking the shells of blue crabs out on the picnic table."

I stand and walk over to Alice and Addie. Alice asks me if I want lemonade, but I know she's tired. Her concern lines her face. I don't want to add to her worry by showing up here a wreck. I decline the tea. Alice insists on walking us out.

As we walk through the living room, I look at the illuminated tanks. "That Brian," I say, "He has always been one smart cookie."

Alice laughs. "I know, seeing who his parents are, it's a wonder he has any brain cells at all."

"Now, now, Alice. I know Brian is more you than his father. His father had no conscience about how he treated you both," I say.

"You speak the truth, Clara. Now that I think back, I was so naive and willing to settle for Bobby. I could have become anything, but my family convinced me I was nothing. You're special, too, Clara. You always have been," Alice says and wipes her eyes.

Addie and I hop into the bug and start back to my house. I feel tempted to stop at Lou's Grocery and Liquors on the way home, but I resist. I remind myself about how far I've come. Now is not the time to be blurry-eyed and fuzzy-brained. Maybe Danny will have more information this evening.

When we arrive home, Addie grabs us glasses of iced tea. We watch the rhythmic rise and fall of the small waves. A breeze has picked up, but the sunshine is bright and warm.

"I love summer," I say.

"Me, too. This summer has been extraordinary, that's for sure," Addie says.

I look at Addie and smile. "You think?"

"How can it be that we can lose so much ... your father, my parents? We can scrape and claw and bully our way through life. There always feels so much pushing back against us. Life can be a burden; just trying to survive it is an ordeal."

"I know. I wonder how long I'll continue to struggle. Sometimes I look at other people and imagine their lives, carefree and without deep scars of pain. How far we could have all come had everyone started off in the same place in life."

"Sometimes I miss my parents so much that the ache feels hard, like a bone spur in my chest. I often wonder what they would think about me now if they were alive," Addie whispers.

I put my arm around her shoulders. "They'd be so proud of you, Addie. Look at all you've accomplished. You have your college degree and a job. You pay your bills. You are a genuine heart, Addie. As genuine as they come," I say.

Addie lays her head on my shoulder for a brief moment. "You've taught me a lot, Dr. Starr. You've not only been a mentor but also a friend. If it weren't for you and Danny being a steady guide, I think I could have easily lost my way."

"Speaking of the devil," I say as Danny's personal car stops in front of the house.

Danny's wearing a navy T-shirt and worn blue jeans. I feel the urge to rake my fingers through his hair. He steps onto the porch and says, "I'll get myself an iced tea. Be right back."

Addie and I grin at each other. When Danny steps out, he bends down and kisses me loudly on the lips. I blush, hearing the smack, and Addie laughs.

"You're in a good mood, Danny. You got something?"

Danny smiles and reaches into his front pocket. He retrieves a piece of white paper and flaps it in the air.

"What's that?" I ask.

"That," he says, "is the toxicology report for one Mr. Robert Ward."

Addie and I lean forward on our chairs. "Oh?" I ask.

I don't know if he's trying to make me pass out by opening the paper so slowly, but I want him to hurry. He grins and flattens the paper out on his lap.

"Well, was he definitely poisoned?"

"Oh, yes," Danny says. "The bacteria infection was the primary cause of death."

"What was it?" Addie asks.

"Tetrodotoxin," Danny says.

"Tetro-what?" Addie asks.

"Tetrodotoxin, a bacteria called Vibrio."

I yank the paper out of Danny's hands. "That tells me nothing. Let me see for myself."

# CHAPTER 51

**PATIENT: ROBERT MARTIN WARD**
**AGE: 72**
**RACE: CAUCASIAN**
**MEDICAL EXAMINER: MAGNUS TORRY, MD**

**SUMMARY**

The patient is a 72-year-old Caucasian male recovered on Mystic Beach which borders the west coast of the Chesapeake Bay. Body was discovered lying on the back on the sand at approximately 6:30 p.m. by EMS. Upon EMS arrival, technician confirmed that patient was deceased.

EXTERNAL EXAMINATION: The body is that of a 72-year-old well-developed, well-nourished male. There is significant peripheral edema of the extremities. Hind- mid- and fore-foot of right leg is missing. Phalanges of left foot missing. Left hand is missing at the radiocarpal joint. There is significant abdominal bloating with waxy appearance on exposed skin. There is skin slippage around the neck area and lower chin. Skin appears shriveled around the right hand. Lacerations and abrasions noted on the front and back sides of exposed torso. Uncertain whether lacerations and abrasions are antemortem trauma or postmortem trauma, such as scraping along rough surfaces in the water. Dark purple discoloration noted over the body.

INTERNAL EXAMINATION (BODY CAVITIES): The airway has evidence of bloody froth; swab indicates blood in mouth. Water is not present in the stomach or lungs. Cerebral edema is noted. Internal organs significantly decomposed, indicating death occurred between 2 to 4 days prior to the discovery of the body. Unable to perform further testing due to the significant decomposition of internal organs.

TOXICOLOGY:
Blood alcohol level:.22*
Drugs: no drugs detected.
Bacterial presence: tetrodotoxin caused by bacterial Vibrio.

*Blood alcohol levels are generally valid up to 48 hours after death but may yield a false positive due to postmortem fermentation during putrefaction.

INTERPRETATION RECOMMENDATION:
The patient's death is determined to be the result of a bacterial Vibrio infection and the presence of tetrodotoxin. Vibrio is a bacteria found in the Chesapeake Bay and can cause tissue paralysis, explaining the lack of water inside the lungs. Therefore, the manner of death is changed from homicide to accident.

# CHAPTER 52

I read the report several times before Addie reaches over and takes it from my hands.

"I don't get it. What? He died from a bacterial infection?" I ask.

Danny's head bounces up and down. "Yes! Vibrio is a bacteria that can be found in the Chesapeake Bay."

I shake my head. "But I don't understand. Why is this good news? Why would an infection help prove it wasn't me?"

Danny jumps out of his chair. "Don't you see? I did some research on the web. Tetrodotoxin is a powerful neurotoxin that can be found in marine life. It can cause all manner of wounds and infections, even paralysis. It's found in brackish waters near the Chesapeake Bay. So, chances are Bobby ate some type of seafood that had the bacteria. See? You're in the clear. He died fittingly for a waterman who was the scum of the earth."

My heart is banging in my chest. Addie and Danny are pounding me on the back, congratulating me. I want to believe this is really happening, but at the same time, I need to temper my excitement. Sometimes things aren't what they seem.

Addie picks up her phone and asks, "Clara, can I take a picture of this and send it to Aunt Laura?"

"Yes," Danny says. "Do it! She'll get your case dismissed for sure now."

Addie waits for my answer. When I indicate my assent, Addie snaps the picture and sends it as a text to her aunt. About ten minutes later, Addie's and my phone buzz at the same time. It's a text from Laura.

```
Congrats, Clara. Your case will be dismissed. Left a message for the State's prosecutor. Will be back in touch.
```

I can't believe it. In the flash of a second, one piece of paper, one test, one result, one specialist can clear up a story and write a happy ending. I want to call Alice to tell her the good news, but Addie cautions me. I don't want to jump too fast. Let the prosecutor and Laura discuss the case. Let the process of the law move in the right direction, one gear at a time.

Addie, Danny, and I sit with smiles plastered on our faces. We all know things can go wrong at the last minute, but this time, it seems the case will be closed. I can finally put all of this behind me and continue to focus on my practice and getting my life back to normal. It's as if a veil was lifted, and I can see my clients without wondering if one of them killed Bobby. I can't forget that Bobby's absence from this planet is a good thing, too.

Danny asks Addie and me if we want to go out for dinner.

"Come on, let's celebrate," he says.

"The case isn't officially closed yet," I say.

"It will be. Come on, Clara, trust this," Addie says.

We decide to go to the Edgewater Restaurant, a local family-owned business just outside of the neighborhood. We each order the lump crab cakes, the very best sampling of Maryland's blue crabs. When the dishes are delivered, Danny raises his water glass and prompts Addie and me to do the same.

"Congratulations to Clara, whom Bobby tried to pinch one last time from beyond the grave."

I start to take a sip, but Danny stops me.

"I'm not finished. To Bobby, we eat these crustaceans who, thankfully, have been washed and cooked to a temperature that would kill all potentially deadly bacteria."

He emphasizes the word bacteria and makes Addie and I laugh.

"It's too bad you didn't cook your seafood before you ate it," he concludes.

We all take a big bite of the delicious crab cake as a toast. "To Bobby," we cheer.

***

On Monday morning, Laura texts me and asks to stop by the house. When she arrives, I invite her to sit on the porch overlooking the bay.

"Holy cow, Clara, I didn't realize you have such a beautiful view. Addie told me you lived in Mystic Beach but didn't say your house looks out directly onto the bay. It's stunning."

"It is. I left here once before, but never again."

We're silent for a few minutes, watching the seabirds coasting on wind drifts. We see a young mother and her toddler walking toward the stairs that lead down to the beach. The toddler swings a red sand bucket with a handle attached. The mother holds her child's hand.

Barbara walks by and waves. Her dog sniffs the edge of the lawn, but she pulls the leash.

"I don't have time to stop and chat," Barbara calls to me. "I have a date with someone new," she says and wiggles her eyebrows.

"Good for you, Barbara," I say.

Laura turns to me and says, "Well, it's official. The charges against you have been dropped."

"Thank you. I can't even begin to tell you how much I appreciate you coming to my rescue at one of the darkest moments of my life."

She squeezes my shoulder. "I understand a thing or two about dark moments. I'm glad I could be there for you."

"Just one thing. Did you ever find out who sent those pictures to the police? Or find out who broke the window? I never even reported to the police about the fish guts smeared on my window."

"Fish guts on your window?" Laura asks and points to the French doors.

"Yeah. It was truly disgusting."

Laura shakes her head. "No, we didn't get into anything more except their statement that they've dropped all charges against you. I expect the chief will issue a press release, probably not hold a press conference. All those reporters will want to know how he could get things so wrong. It doesn't matter to you, though. You're free and cleared. Now you can go on with your life."

"I am so relieved to have this behind me. Thank you again for everything. I'm especially thankful for Addie."

Laura smiles. "Yeah, that niece of mine knows how to hold down the fort when things get rough."

Laura excuses herself because she has a court case right after lunch. I bid her farewell but stay in my seat to watch the bay. Danny will come by today after his shift for a private celebration. I gave Addie the day off. She deserves it. I didn't know I had the capacity to open myself to friendship. I have been burned so many times before that I thought I had forgotten how to trust. Addie changed that. She slipped in the crowbar before I closed the door on humanity for good.

While I wait for Danny, I go into the living room and open my new laptop. I still haven't gotten my things back from the police. I needed a new computer, anyway. The new bay window is gleaming. I had them install a bench seat so I could set some plants on it.

Something still doesn't feel right. What if I was set up? What if the whole thing with the pictures, broken window, and dead fish were part of an elaborate plan to frame me? I can't help but wonder what it is that I'm missing.

# CHAPTER 53

My fingers hover on the keys in the search bar. I have an inkling that maybe I should let things be. I am cleared. That's all that's important. The how of Bobby's murder shouldn't still be on my mind, but it is. When I try to imagine how Bobby died, I can't quite figure out how he got infected. Had he eaten a bad batch of oysters or clams?

I type into the search bar "tetrodotoxin." The first thing that pops up is an article by the Centers for Disease Control. The article says it's an extremely potent poison found mainly in the liver and sex organs of some marine life. Ingesting tetrodotoxin or TTX through the water is extremely rare. It's the same with indoor and outdoor air. Typically, the neurotoxin is ingested through food exposure, improperly prepared food, or contamination of other food products.

I do another search about what a death from TTX is like. It's gruesome. According to the National Institute of Health, symptoms of tetrodotoxin include tingling of the tongue and lips, headache, vomiting, muscle weakness, and heart failure. Symptoms usually occur within fifteen minutes after eating the contaminated food but can appear up to twenty hours later. People affected by TTX poisoning have motor weakness and speech difficulties. Gradually, they find it harder and harder to breathe. Eventually, the muscles surrounding the lungs become paralyzed, then the deep tendons follow suit.

Bobby's death was befitting of the way he lived. I can't say I'm sad that he died the way he did. The only thing more karmic would have been a drug overdose, the way he killed George. I can't be choosy, though. This death works just as well. I can't think of a single person, including Lala, who is sad he's gone. Bobby hurt too many people. He was selfish, dangerous, and ruthless. I'm glad I'll never have to look over my shoulders again.

I think about Alice and Brian and their beautiful vegetable and flower garden. Brian moved back home to care for his mother. They both must feel relieved Bobby is no longer around to terrorize them. If I feel any relief, theirs must be ten times stronger. They had to deal with him day in and day out.

Still, I am bothered by those photographs, the broken window, and the fish. There are too many unanswered questions. Clearly, someone wanted the police to look at me. Who would want to do that? Were they instances of small-town shenanigans, people jumping to conclusions because they want to?

Danny knocks once on the French doors and walks in. He kisses me on the forehead and looks at the laptop.

"What are you searching?"

"I wanted more details on how Bobby died. It didn't look like a good one."

"He deserved it, didn't he?" Danny asks.

"Indeed, he did. But something doesn't feel right."

Danny rubs my shoulders. "You worry too much."

"But what about the broken window? The photos? The fish?"

Danny shrugs. "I don't know. Maybe it was someone trying to stir the pot. This neighborhood can be that kind of place, you know."

"Oh, I know."

I click on another article about tetrodotoxin poisoning. This one is from the Center for Food Safety. It reports about the death of a twenty-eight-year-old man who developed dizziness and heart palpitations shortly after eating at a Japanese restaurant. On the way home, he developed numbness in his lips and mouth. His extremities started tingling, and his speech slurred. His wife called an ambulance from the side of the road while the man was vomiting. The man lived but stayed in the ICU for a week.

Investigators went to the restaurant to get details about what the man ate. His wife had a simple vegetarian stir-fry dish. She had no symptoms. The man had eaten fish, a pufferfish. The report went on to say that pufferfish are known to have high levels of TTX naturally in their flesh. Apparently, something had been overlooked by the chef, and the fish was contaminated. The man was lucky to be alive.

"Wait. What?" I say.

Danny sat on the sofa, reading on his phone. "Did you say something about pufferfish? Some guy died after eating it? Yeah, so what?"

"Do you know what has a very potent source of TTX? So potent that there are several reports of deaths?"

"What?" Danny asks.

"Pufferfish."

"So?"

"So, guess who has an extensive pufferfish collection?" I say as I stand from my desk.

# CHAPTER 54

The chief had given Danny a heads-up before they went to Alice's house to arrest Brian so we could be there for Alice. Danny and I were sitting with Alice, drinking iced tea at the kitchen table when the police knocked at the door.

When I hear the knock, I yell for Brian to answer the door. It is too painful to watch Alice stand up and shuffle. She has no idea what was about to happen. Brian comes in from the garden and goes to answer the door. Bennett and Engel ask if he is Brian Ward.

Alice stands up when she heard the voices. "Brian, who's that? Who's at the door?" Her voice quivers. "Clara, help me out there. I need to see what's going on."

Danny takes one arm while I take the other. The officers are reading Brian his Miranda rights and asking him to turn around to be handcuffed.

"What's going on?" Alice asks. "Brian? What's happening?"

Brian looks at his mother. "Don't worry, Ma. It's okay. I promise it'll be okay."

A group of officers and technicians enter the home and remove, one by one, the cubicles containing the pufferfish in the living room. I hear some of the technicians whispering to one another as they heft the heavy aquariums to a waiting van. Other officers go upstairs to search the bedrooms.

Alice's legs weaken, and Danny and I help her to the chair. We ask her if she'd like to go back into the kitchen, but she refuses. Her hands shake. She tries to ask the officers questions, but they ignore her in their haste to remove all of the fish and search her home.

Danny approaches the supervising officer to get more information.

He comes back and whispers to me, "Well, the question of who snapped those pictures of you on the beach has been cleared up."

"What do you mean?" I ask.

"The supervising officer told me they traced the pictures to a particular phone. That phone is registered to Brian Ward. Brian took those pictures."

Shock shows on my face. Alice waves us over to her.

"Alice, they think Brian is responsible for murdering his dad," Danny explains.

"Why would they think that?"

"When the toxicology report came back and they cleared Clara, they decided to run one more check on Brian and his work at the marine biology lab. They found … well …."

"Well, what?" Alice snaps.

"They found out he had been working with pufferfish, trying to make a concentrated dose of the highest possible type of tetrodotoxin. His boss reprimanded him; they had even threatened to fire him. Then, over the next weekend, all of the pufferfish disappeared from the lab. Brian told them he sent them to his contacts overseas who were also studying tetrodotoxin concentrations. Apparently, he never sent them."

"My Brian would never do that. Officers? Officers! You leave my boy alone," Alice yells.

One of the officers barks, "Ma'am, you need to stay calm and sit down, or else we'll have to ask your friends to take you to the kitchen."

Alice stops talking, but fear and indignation are evident on her face, just like the time when I picked her up at the station. I can understand; it's hard to think her son would do something so terrible.

Alice is the most genuine, gentle person I know. She couldn't care less about Bobby's death, but that's understandable because he was violent and abusive. Brian, on the other hand, is a different story. He suffered greatly at the hands of bullies as a child. Mystic Beach may be many wonderful things, but it's not welcoming to people of different races or sexual identities. Being a gay male had been hard on Brian, but the community reaction was nothing compared to his own father's brutality.

Alice looks defeated, like she's aged twenty years in the past two hours. We ask her if she wants to go to my house to get away from this chaos. It doesn't take long for her to say she does. Danny checks with the officers.

"Engel says we can take you back with us. The crime scene technicians will still be here for a while."

I text Addie and tell her we're bringing Alice back to my house. Addie says she'll meet us there. When we arrive, Addie has snacks and iced tea on the patio. We help Alice settle into a chair. For several moments, no one speaks. Alice looks as if her life energy has drained away. She looks pitiful and defeated. I'm sure she's worried about what will become of Brian—and even herself.

"The thing is," Alice begins, "I can't blame Brian for it. His father was mean and hurt him in all manner of ways." She shakes her head. "Shoot, if I could have done it myself, I would have."

"You're right, Alice. He was a cruel person who was probably most vicious to you and Brian. I'm sorry it all came to this."

"The officers will most likely want to question you once they collect the evidence they need," Danny says.

"Don't worry, Alice. We're here to support you in whatever way we can," Addie adds.

"I don't know what I'd do without you," Alice whispers.

"Alice, I want to ask you about something that is a little awkward for me," I say. "Someone broke my front window with a rock and left me a threatening note. Then recently, someone smeared my French doors with fish guts. Do you think Brian would have done that?"

Alice looks at me with her watery blue eyes. I sense the emotion behind her gaze. When she speaks so softly, I'm struck with a sense that all is not what it seems.

"Why, Clara, my girl. Why would you think he would do something like that to you?"

I feel chastised. I've known this woman my whole life.

"You're right. I'm letting the situation get the best of me."

"You have to admit, the pufferfish poison was a creative way to do him in, wouldn't you say?" Alice asks suddenly. "I mean, I wonder how the police found out it was tetrodotoxin in the fish that caused his death?"

There is a sudden tightening in my chest. Does Alice know I was the one who tipped Danny off and got the ball rolling to launch the investigation? Or is there something else going on?

"What do you mean?" Danny asks.

Alice's voice gains strength, and tendrils of anger rise in her body. She sits up straight.

"Danny, this is what I mean. How did the police find out about the pufferfish? Clara, did you say anything?" Her eyes bore into me.

Behind her head, I see Danny's head subtly move from side to side. Panic rises in my chest. I am sure my face is flushed.

"I didn't say anything, Alice," I lie. "I guess they checked into Brian's background at work. Maybe they were checking all angles."

"It seems very strange to me," Alice says.

"Why?" Addie asks.

"How all of a sudden you're off scot-free," Alice points her finger at me.

"I didn't kill him, Alice. Somehow, they must've gotten another lead."

Tension lingers in the air. Alice's eyes are fiery as if she already knows I was the one who tipped the police off. I will not back down, though, because a new realization is dawning in my own mind. I shift my shoulders back and stare back.

Danny and Addie look back and forth at us, uncertain about what is happening between Alice and me. The moment continues to unwind. Eventually, Alice is the one who backs down first. She knows that I know. Brian would never do something to his father without his mother knowing, maybe being a part of it. The Alice sitting in front of me, looking frail and defeated, is not the woman I saw in my car a while ago.

"It's all right, Clara, my girl. I know you would never do anything to harm Brian or me intentionally. If you ever did, I'd find out. I have my ways. We'll just have to get a good lawyer, now, won't we? Addie, your aunt is the one who represented Clara, right?"

Addie draws out her answer. "Ye-es."

"And she can keep a good secret, I'll bet." Alice winks.

# PREVIEW

# TIDES OF DECEPTION: BETRAYALS AND BLOODLINES

## Prologue

People assume they have control over their lives, like it's a simple matter of doing the right thing, making the right choice. I don't know about that. I think control is an illusion. If you ask my husband, he might say something different. His motto was, in a tough situation, *choose the next right thing.* To some extent, I see his point. But what if the next right thing is something that many would call abhorrent? What if choosing the *next right thing* is actually a decision between two horrible circumstances?

Case in point. In 2020, Robert Morris was an emergency room physician when the pandemic brought hundreds of patients to the hospital. The administration mandated medical personnel to work long hours and back-to-back shifts to care for the hordes of sick people. One afternoon, the emergency department, along with others across a hundred-mile radius, reached critical mass. There simply weren't enough ventilators for patients. The hospital morgue was full. Nurses and physicians were overwhelmed, overworked, and emotionally bankrupt. Late one night, when there was no other place to go, an ambulance brought a teenage boy to the hospital in severe respiratory distress. The boy would die within the hour. Dr. Morris had to decide whether to let the boy die or save him by taking a ventilator from someone else. The hospital had protocols, sanitary measures, and standards of care, but late at night, without the support of his colleagues, he was forced to decide the next right thing. And so, he did. He removed the ventilator from a middled-aged, obese woman and inserted it into the boy. The woman died within minutes of being taken from the ventilator. The boy died from a bacterial infection three days later.

I think that good and bad, virtuous and evil, are relative. Sometimes, the only choice we have is between a bad one and another bad one. I was in that position not too long ago. Without going into the sordid details, I found myself having to make a decision that would change the course of my life and those closest to me. I had looked into the eyes of one child, then the other, and, like Dr. Morris, I had to decide which one to save. Maybe I did it for selfish reasons. To suspect so would not be wrong. Perhaps it will be thought that I deserved what ended up coming for me. That, too, is correct.

I wonder if by sharing this I can absolve myself from my gravest sins. Perhaps. But what's important to understand is that sometimes good people do bad things for reasons that are unclear to those who have never been forced to decide. What it boils down to is that t I did the best I could when faced with a terrible, terrible choice. In the end, I know I will be called to atone for my mistakes. I am prepared to accept whatever judgment is cast.

# About the Author

Dr. Teresa Crowe is a seasoned academic, clinical social worker, and researcher specializing in social work for deaf and hard-of-hearing populations. She currently serves as a Professor in the Social Work Department at Gallaudet University, teaching a wide array of courses and teaching graduate students to become social workers with expertise in deaf and hard-of-hearing populations. Dr. Crowe earned her MFA from Goucher College, MSW from Gallaudet University, and PhD from the University of Maryland at Baltimore. Her research is marked by a deep commitment to better understanding and addressing the unique experiences and mental health needs of deaf and hard-of-hearing individuals.

As a Clinical Social Worker and Telemental Health Program Coordinator at Arundel Lodge, Inc., a community behavioral health agency, she brings her expertise to the front lines of mental health care. Her research has addressed a range of critical issues, from the impact of COVID-19 on deaf college students to the impact of negative life experiences on deaf and hard-of-hearing adults. These efforts have led to numerous peer-reviewed publications, conference presentations, and research grants.

In addition to her academic and clinical roles, Dr. Crowe is an esteemed author, publishing a true crime book, *Death Space: The True Story of A Deaf Serial Killer at Gallaudet University*, and four companion creative non-fiction books as part of the *Humans In Progress Series*. Her expansive career, marked by a deep dedication to her field, showcases her understanding of the complexities of human behavior and its significant impact on the lives of deaf and hard-of-hearing individuals.

Visit her website at www.teresacrowebooks.com

www.ingramcontent.com/pod-product-compliance
Lightning Source LLC
LaVergne TN
LVHW050541160826
845677LV00011B/2131

* 9 7 9 8 9 8 9 4 5 1 3 1 9 *